Crazy Horse
Susan Everett

route

Susan Everett

Born in 1965 Susan spent her early years in St Albans, Hertfordshire before heading up north. As a youngster she wrote disturbing poems about her experiences in the First World War until people made her stop and write about flowers. She helped her friend to run a riding school for several years until a horse fell on her, kicked her in the head and put her in a coma. For a while she thought she could fly but now she's recovered. She bought her own horse in 1983 and called him Dave. Dave likes head-butting things and chasing pensioners up trees. Miraculously, he is still alive today.

In 1993 her story *Dust* won the *This Morning/Lynda La Plante* 'Humour' prize. She also won the *Carl Foreman Screenwriting Award* (in association with BAFTA) and went to film school in America for 18 months where she directed her first short *White Rabbits*.

Susan now writes for film and television and teaches scriptwriting in Leeds.

First Published in 2000 by Route
School Lane, Glasshoughton, West Yorks, WF10 4QH
e-mail: books@route-online.com

ISBN: 1 901927 06 7

Editor: Mark Illis
Cover Design: Andy Campbell and Dean Smith

Thanks to
Ian Daley, Mark Illis and the editing posse, Lisa Eveleigh, Shirley Warke,
Simon Lacy, my dad and Dave the horse.

Support:: Kath Murphy, Mo Burrows, Olive Fowler

Printed by Cox and Wyman, Reading

A catalogue for this book is available from the British Library

Full details of the Route programme of books
and live events can be found on our website
www.route-online.com

Route is the fiction imprint of YAC, a registered charity No 1007443

YAC is supported by
Yorkshire Ars, Wakefield MDC, West Yorkshire Grants

In memory of my mother,
and the class of '87

Salvation

The moon hung above the stables as bats took off like flying leaves, scattered by the shriek of approaching sirens. Loose horses trotted on the concrete, scraping their metal horseshoes, shaking heads and showing teeth.

A brown car was wheezing by the muck pile, engine flooded, shadows of a female shape inside. An ambulance pulled up at the top gate. Paramedics clambered out, distracted, not sure where they should go. They tapped on the window of the car.

'Where is he?'

The woman pointed at an open doorway further along the stable block, turned her ignition key again, her actions growing more frantic as a panda car arrived.

The paramedics followed a bumbling grey horse as it trotted into the feed room, meeting up with two compatriots, banging bins in search of food. The victim lay bleeding on a makeshift bed of rugs, visible through the scoffing horses' legs. They nudged the animals out of the way and crouched beside him.

'Okay, hold on mate. Hang in there. We're going to sort you out.'

There was an awful lot of blood.

Two policemen approached the stalling car. The elder, PC Dunderdale, sucked in his stomach as he spoke.

'Miss? Was it you that rung this in? Jenny Barker?'

She leapt from the driver's seat in panic, pushing past them. Raced through an open gate into the grazing field. The officers were puzzled.

'What the hell is going on here? Go on, Lacy. Get her.'

The young policeman set off sprinting across the grass, running towards the darkness of a wood. He flicked on his searchlight, its beam illuminating the bright eyes of startled rabbits.

'He's over here! We've got him.' A paramedic shouted from the feed room, emerging with a trolley stretcher, wheels rattling along. A pitchfork stuck out of the patient's stomach like a boastful conquest flag.

Dunderdale hurried towards them. 'Jesus Christ! What happened?' He glanced at the first medic. 'Is he going to live?'

'Hope so. Weak pulse, but we've slowed the bleeding. If he's not damaged vital organs....'

The bloodied man reached out his hand. 'Jen...' He tried to speak. 'Jenny....'

'Alright, son. Hold on now.' A loose horse bumped into Dunderdale, knocking him flat onto the ground. The stretcher trundled onwards.

'Just what the hell is going on!'

He scrambled up, grabbed the animal's headcollar and led it towards the open gateway of the pasture. The horse snorted and started trotting, pulled away from the man's thick arm as it bounded off, bucking and farting, glad to be home in its field.

Dunderdale bent over and took a hasty breath, then looked up and saw three horses abandoning the yard. Headed right towards him. He jumped out of the way as they cantered across the concrete, hoof beats softening when they reached the grass. He closed the gate, relaxing as he watched his colleague walking back.

'Did you lose her then? Not quick enough?'

'Sod off!' PC Lacy had fresh muck plastered on his trousers. 'Bloody horse shit. Look at me. Look at the state of me! Shit!'

'You want to scrape it off, mate. Put it on your rhubarb.' Dunderdale watched the departing ambulance, the blue flash of spinning lights. 'Come on, let's get going.' He scanned the quiet yard. Horses' heads hung out of stables, wondering what the commotion was about.

'Where now? The hospital?'

A strange sound started. Shrill, high pitched.

'Ssssh! What's that?' Dunderdale concentrated.

Lacy reached into a pocket for his mobile. The noise was not from there.

'Where is it? Listen.'

They stared out across the field. Pushed through the gate and walked towards the trilling mobile phone.

'I think it's coming from over here.'

'Ssssh, Lacy. Quiet.'

The noise abruptly stopped.

They looked along the landscape, Lacy lighting sections with his torch. An illuminated circle doubled back over the ground.

'What's that then?'

There was a recent mound of mud, too large to be a molehill. They sprinted towards it, coming across a shovel as they ran.

'Bring that with you, lad! Come on!' Dunderdale thundered onwards, his mate bringing the spade. 'Dig. Quickly!'

The shovel plunged into the earth, then slowed, indecisive, as it reached a softer form. Dunderdale dug at soil with his hot hands, scratching away until his fingernails reached a tight waxy material, something solid, thick. More digging, faster, urgent, and stripes of a deep green coat appeared, two arms tied tight behind it, fingers popping through the earth like little sprouting shoots.

'Come on, come on!'

Dunderdale strained to raise the body upwards, pulling from the earthy womb. He twisted it around, revealing a young woman's face in an afterbirth of soil. Lacy shone his torch close to her eyes. Pupils wide, dilating.

'Is she alive? Is she breathing?'

Her eyes were dazzled by the brightness, muscles tensed. Then a jerk, a splutter, as she coughed up soil and started gasping, sucking in quick gulps of air.

'It's alright, love.' Dunderdale pulled the girl towards him, rubbing soft mud from her long hair. 'You're going to be alright. You're safe now. It's over.'

A distant cockerel started crowing as the sun began to rise.

Six Months Earlier....Flirtation

That night she dreamt of Bridlington. The hot baked beach and soft slow wash of waves against the shore. The decreasing cry of seagulls as hot sand engulfed her face, mouth filling with suffocating salty grains, grinding against clenched teeth. Her body sucked under the beach, air filtering away. Coughing, choking, drowned in yellow sand. When she woke up she screamed.

Jenny lay prostrate in her bed, watching as a small spider shadow crept its way across the ceiling. If it dropped off into her mouth she'd eat it. Strong thoughts for a vegetarian. Her eyes stung as she stared through the gloom towards her calendar.

The tenth of May. A year since she had lost her horse.

Every detail of that last day was etched deep into her brain. Each moment running round her head a hundred times. Returning from a show, victorious, red rosettes sprouting like roses on the dashboard of her purring, rusting car. Mister Majestyk tapping black hooves in the trailer, metal clangs as they pulled into the yard. Rubbing his hot, proud neck with straw to ease the sweat, dark skin glowing through his wet white coat to turn him grey. Pink snorts up Mister's nose, drips of frothy water from his trough. Cooling in his string vest sweat rug, looking smart. A kiss. A hug. Goodbye.

Next morning, before college, the usual routine of mucking out and feeding. Of trying to keep horsemuck off her shoes before she caught the bus. Approaching Mister's stable, the last in a long line of breeze block buildings. His door ajar three inches, a sparrow squatting by an escaped sliver of hay. And Mister was nowhere. His golden straw bed empty except for three piles of manure. Jenny didn't realise at first, tried not to, tried to shrug off the sickened feeling in her stomach that screamed something was wrong. Tried to tell herself one of the girls had taken him for a walk, or to the field. That a misunderstanding had occurred. That Mister had not gone.

A year ago today since she had seen her horse.

Each time she thought of him the pain would stab her bones, crushing from the outside in, making her a walking human car wreck. Ten years of history in her photographs; him as a foal, the moment she bought him when he was nine months old, right up to the day he vanished, with their victory held fast in black and white in that week's Horse and Hound. Winners of the Grade C qualifying round fo Yorkshire, North. Showjumpers on the up. The newsprint was slightly fading, like her hopes. She'd allowed herself a year to find him, thinking that was plenty. Three hundred and sixty five days later, and all she had was rage.

The police tried to help, but their leads led to nothing. One of their sightings ended up being a stray pet goat in Leicester. She'd given them lots of photographs, but all the policemen saw was a big grey horse, white to those who lacked the terminology. An invisible, snow-like blur on the horizon, his features fading as the hours melted by. Jenny had lost track of the number of times she'd driven miles across the Dales, only to find some other horse that was unfortunately not hers. She'd called into the station every week, until it got them mad and then they phoned the parents, said to keep Jenny away as there was nothing they could do.

She flicked strands of hair out of her face, glowered at the bedside clock and willed herself asleep. That same thought kept sticking in her mind. What comes around, goes around. If you do a bad deed, bad deeds are done to you. So, she'd killed the milkman when she was six. She hadn't meant to. It wasn't her fault. Her bad luck, her... everything. Was this a punishment for that?

Ghostly images of opalescent horses glowed from the dull walls, faint shapes galloping through the newsprint, attached to wood chip wallpaper with pale blue sticky tack. Rows of articles and news reports of equine thefts, attacks and deaths. The dark name of the Savager loomed in permanent printer's ink.

Jenny parked her mother's battered car next to a posh pine horsebox with frilly curtains and varnished wood. A man with a pipe peered out from the side window, gaze indicating that she wasn't smart enough to be there. Jenny locked the driver's door and strode towards the showground. A belly full of deja-vu, crunching mud towards the ring as she steered herself in the direction of the jumps. Heart leaping with every horse that flew above the red, white and blue poles, remembering the sensation of Mister's flight, how invincible they were.

A thought. Wit had told her, teasingly, that if she rode a horse too much, too fast, or bounced around unduly, then she could no longer class herself as a true virgin. Something inside was broken. Some thing. She'd have to look it up. Losing her virginity on a technicality would be a bit upsetting. She wanted that moment to be in glorious Technicolor with stereophonic sound. Not like a half-remembered nosebleed.

Jenny's eyes trailed across the field, skipped past dark horses, chestnuts, bays, searching out each flash of grey. She'd lost track of how many shows she had turned up to, how many times she'd gone back home with just a petrol bill and a headache for her efforts. Mister wasn't here.

'Jenny? Jenny Barker?'

She turned and saw a young man on a tall black horse. Sun making him squint, a smile of recognition.

'I thought it was you.' Roger slid down from the hot saddle, catching horse sweat on his stiff scarlet jacket. First place rosette protruding from his pocket. On a high from winning. 'We've missed you, in the ring. Jump offs aren't as exciting. I miss having a laugh. It's brilliant to see you, Jenny.'

He pulled his hat off, rubbing the velvet in his palms, soft as a black cat on the outside, hard fibreglass beneath.

'You never found him then? Your horse?'

'No.'

'I'm sorry about that. It must be awful, not knowing where he is.'

He walked beside her, elbows bent as he led his mount along, weaving through the oncoming traffic of children with ice creams. The horse wedged in between them, nuzzling foam on Jenny's shirt. She looked across the muscled neck, above damp plaits of mane that looked like plump blackberries, and glanced at her inquirer. Roger Mandrake, late twenties, lean and long, dark mocha coffee hair and slate grey eyes. Firm legs that poured into his jodhpurs like a manufacturer's mould, illustrating perfect contours. The most handsome horse rider that she, or indeed he, had ever seen. He reminded Jenny of the man she was in love with.

A giggle of girls behind them. Roger turned, gave them a little wink. He was used to these admirers. They came in rather handy when he needed his stable mucking out. There was always some teenager with a shovel.

Roger deftly undid his girth, flipped the saddle onto his arm, leaving a sweaty circle shape on the horse's back.

'Can you help me load him in the box?' Roger balanced his crop between clean teeth and passed his horse's reins to Jenny, not giving her a moment to decline before he swung from the rear of his horsebox, straining on the metal lever, pulling the creaking ramp towards the ground. It hovered seven inches from the floor. The horse looked quite suspicious. No way would he put a hoof on the flying wooden carpet, even if it had been sprinkled with straw to make it look more homely.

Roger raised his boot and pushed down on the ramp then sprinted up to undo the tail gates. He disappeared into the recess of the longbox, emerging moments later with a bucket laced with feed. He tapped the side to gain the horse's attention, poked rolled oats under the snorting nose and stepped backwards out of reach.

'If you put your own foot on the ramp to push it down, that's when he'll put his hoof on.' Roger showed the feed again.

The black mouth licked. Jenny led the animal up, holding tight onto his reins as the gelding bucked with every creak. Roger laughed, jumping off the back, leaving Jenny inside with the hyper horse while he strained to push the ramp up. Cutting out daylight, leaving the girl in darkness with grass stained licks along her arms.

The side door opened and Roger bounded in, took the horse from Jenny, and with an expert's ease slid off the bridle, replacing it with a leather headcollar before the horse reversed.

Jenny stepped into the empty stall, wondering if she should leave now, or stay and make some polite conversation. Before she had an answer Roger was close beside her, hands wiping wet froth off her sleeves with an old rag.

A smile. 'I should have warned you that he dribbles.' Roger's breath close to her face.

'What's his name?' she whispered.

'Unique the Fourth.'

'Not so unique then?'

'Sorry?' The space between them shrinking.

'I mean...'

His firm lips stole her words. Moistness hit as she stood, goldfish-mouthed, his arms around her back, her bottom wedged against the horsebox wall. Nostrils swelled and she could smell his aftershave. *Obsession*, Calvin Klein. It made her want to sneeze. She shut her chocolate eyes, arms stiff against her side, feeling tight breeches brush against her as he moved. She shivered. Kissed him back. Felt guilty.

His tongue ran lizard-like inside her mouth. She wondered what to do with hers, if she swallowed hard would her tongue slip down her throat, suffocate her on the spot? This was different to how her uncles kissed her. They blew smile-shaped air on the side of her face and made popping noises with their tongues.

Roger seemed to taste of hot-dogs. Jenny opened her eyes, seeing him so close, he looked extremely weird and blurry. Eyes joined together like a one eyed Greek God monster.

Electric shocks hit Jenny's nerves, making her wonder if that elusive quality which women's magazines call sexual chemistry was in fact a basic instinct, and not just something rationed out to women called Carmen who live in Shepherd's Bush.

Dear Agony Aunt,

I am a twenty two year old female, quite pretty, but up to now I've not had sex. Is it because I'm scared of close physical contact, or could it be because I'm in love with this guy at college, and though I don't dare speak to him, I'm sure that he's the one? How can I even think of giving myself to someone else when this man's on my horizon?

Jenny B from Leeds.

Dear Jenny,

The guy at college doesn't even know that you exist. Grow up. Stop being such a child and get your kit off. Your breasts are very nice.

Roger's flushed face near her shoulder.

'I really like you, Jenny. I think you're great.'

His hot hand crept under her shirt, feeling its way up shivering flesh to a size 34B bra from Marks and Spencers which she hadn't actually wanted to show to anyone, especially not him. As he struggled with the easy clip back (the packaging lied) she felt her nipples harden against the satin cups.

The side door opened and a ray of light burst in, cutting a laser strip across the writhing couple. Jenny caught a glimpse of the glaring woman's face, red hair to match her anger. Instant hate.

Roger felt his wife's presence burning through his back. He stepped away from Jenny, who quickly pulled her shirt close to her and ran out of the box. Pushing past the crimson woman at the door, sprinting away across the showground, heart beating fast. Followed by floating words that were either apologies or insults. At that speed she couldn't tell.

Attraction

The three biggest regrets in Jenny Barker's life:

1. Not losing her virginity to Roger Mandrake.
2. Mister being stolen.
3. Killing the milkman.

The second of these hurt the most, but if she'd done the first she could then call herself a woman, and not feel like the eternal twelve year old she knew herself to be.

The parents sat downstairs in silence, pretending they were on their own when Jenny went to join them. They always stopped talking when she walked into a room. It was a long established custom.

'Morning mum, dad.' The scrape of a chair, a rustling box of cornflakes.

'Saddam Hussein again.' Her father, Ray, shuffled behind the paper, thick glasses helping him to read the print. His wife threw him a look, not sure if the comment was aimed at her or just thrown into the ether. She didn't care much either way. More important tasks were on her mind. The ironing needed doing.

Jenny kept her head down, staring at the table, wondering when somebody was going to wash the cloth as the cat had moulted terribly all over it. She didn't hold the animal totally responsible, it was a nice enough pet if you liked ginger felines that sat and stared and didn't do much else, but she found the situation a little unhealthy. She wondered if other households let their cat sit at the table at meal times and eat off the plates and knock the milk jug over without causing any fuss, when she only had to spill a grain of sugar and the tutting would start and there'd be another argument. Her dad would go into the garden for a sulk while mum held serious conversations with the cat about the toils of running a family and how nobody understood what she put up with.

Jenny often wracked her brain to find some reason why their

family tensions were so splintered on the surface. She was sure that things were different when she was younger. Rose-tinted memories of happy days and piggybacks, a laughing five year old girl clutched tight round her daddy's neck. Tucked up at night with teddies and a quilt, mum reading the scary story of the troll under the bridge, waiting with rasping breath to eat gruff goats up for his tea.

Perhaps Jenny should have left home by now. She would have if she could afford it, but not as a struggling student. Anyway, the outside world was rather more daunting than a three up three down with pebble-dashed front and an extension on the back.

She went into town on the bus, and sat there thinking about Mister and wondering where he was and wondering how he was and wondering if he missed her like she missed him. She went way past her stop and ended up near a park in Headingley where people were playing cricket. She stood for a while, wondering who invented cricket whites.

'Do you believe in justice in today's society?'

'What?' Jenny was snapped back to reality by a bald headed guy in a dress who was carrying a clipboard.

'Do you believe everyone has the right to the things they need?' He stared at her, deadly serious. 'That people should pay back debts when it's within their means? That what they get, they pay for.' He ticked something off his sheet. 'That we are responsible for our own actions?'

'Yes, well, probably...' Jenny tried to think. The man smiled at her, pen poised ready to strike, sunlight and pollution bouncing off his pink head.

'Would you be interested in having one of our new Shop-At-Home catalogues sent to you?'

Jenny legged it down the road towards the safety of the towering college building, glass windows staring down like a wall of insect eyes. The bald man hadn't followed her. They normally did. Her father said Jenny attracted strange people because she was a bad seed. Weird things had started happening from the age of three and a half, when a large Jamaican woman took her hostage in the local Woolworth's. Jenny couldn't remember, though it made the papers, which were full of pictures of her eating Pick and Mix. Seems this woman had lost her daughter in an accident, and needed a replacement. Jenny wondered why she didn't choose one of the same colour. Some newspaper articles had suggested that Mrs Tapper was not a criminal but a good Samaritan, after all, where were Jenny's parents? Reports had them sighted in a DIY shop miles away. Abandonment, kidnapping, or simply a forgetful mum and dad? Jenny had her suspicions. Their house was full of secrets, of things they wouldn't tell her. One day she'd work it out.

She fell in love in the lift again. This was a regular occurrence. Every day she would crouch near the college dustbins, spot him walking up, then jog off to the lift and keep it there until he arrived, making it look like some coincidence that she was always waiting, ready to get in when he was. They'd locked eye contact several times, but sometimes he looked away. He always made her blush.

Simon. He was two years below her, but four years older. Twenty-six. He'd spent a couple of years roaming round America and Italy in an attempt to find himself, got lost, then come to Leeds. Myth had it that he'd wanted to go to a college in Warwickshire, but couldn't spell the county properly on the application form, so was refused an interview. Sharon had found that out, Sharon had a knack of knowing everything. Jenny thanked the Lord for his gift of dyslexia. If Simon Marles could spell, then she never would have met him.

The lift stopped on every other floor. Jenny wished she'd pressed all the buttons so it dragged out even more. Each time the machinery ground to a juddered halt the passengers groaned, as if they were keen to get to class and not be stuck on 3rd with Interior Design. Simon never made a sound. Maybe this thing with Simon wasn't healthy. Nina kept trying to put her off him, kept telling Jenny to forget him, pointing out that she'd only got so fixated over the recent months. A substitute, Nina called him. A transference of affections now that her horse was gone.

Maybe Jenny wasn't good looking enough to be in the league of Simon Marles. She wasn't bad looking, and whenever she said she was people would groan and call her beautiful. She didn't believe them though. Her mum had told her she looked just like her father, but she knew what his face was like and it wasn't very pretty. She couldn't see any similarities herself, but guessed she was too close to hold a true opinion.

She stared at Simon, cunningly pretending to read graffiti on the lift wall behind his head. You could tell by how he moved that Simon knew he was attractive. There was a lingering exaggeration in his actions, a deliberate placing of one hand in the back pocket of his jeans, the other over his shoulder clutching a leather jacket. He walked in long straight lines. Jenny watched as Simon ran slim fingers through his short dark hair, spiking up the front. He looked a lot like Roger Mandrake, but didn't smile as often. He was much more Marlon Brando, before the fat arrived. She didn't understand why Nina was so cold towards him. On the few occasions that she had seen the pair together their conversations were really quite abrupt.

Simon got off at the eighth floor and Jenny started breathing. Walked down the skinny corridor on the top level of the building to reach the cluttered room where she spent so many fruitless hours. A handful of students were already there, gossiping or sitting half asleep. Hopeful sunshine filtered through the windows, the glasshouse side of the room that was always too hot in the summer and thick with frost at winter's end. Centuries of chewing gum were ground into dull grey floor tiles. Dirty mugs grew in the sink. The annoying buzz of an angry Walkman played distorted songs too loud, clamped on the head of the most mature student, face to the wall, with his back to them. He never turned around or talked.

'Hey, Jen! Did you have a good weekend?' William, Wit for short, was busy at his table, a pile of sketches hanging off the edge. 'You'll have to take me to a horse sale again,' he chimed. 'I could bring you luck.'

'Sure, Wit.' She placed her plastic toolbox on her wooden desk, pulled up a swivel chair.

'It'll have to be somewhere where they've got soup and chips,' Wit grinned. 'Don't want to starve to death like last time. Got you a surprise.'

Jenny pulled up her desk lid, found a chocolate bar inside.

'Thanks Wit, you're the greatest.'

He did that every week. Varied flavours, sometimes cakes, because she'd mentioned once that she really hated Mondays. Jenny felt relaxed with Wit, her favourite male friend. He looked quite spiky on the outside, with his nose ring and metal piercing in his brow, but she knew it was just show and he was really sugar disguised as spice. He had this radar that could sense when she was down, and he'd do anything to make her laugh, even if it meant putting rubber bands around his face and jumping out of cupboards. Jenny wished she could talk to Simon like she could to Wit. Sure, they never got into really deep personal conversations, and she could never tell him about her little problems or about Bridlington or about being in love, but they had actual conversations and that was more than she could say for Simon.

Wit was the best student in their class. Well, Jenny thought so. There were fifteen of them in Illustration, panicking behind their desks, propping pictures against mucky walls, slapping oil paints on giant canvases or scratching away at tiny ink blot studies. Each student exploring their own style. Six weeks to their degree show, and Jenny still hadn't found hers yet. Maybe this was not her forte. She had picked illustration because she was crap at design. Several of the lads had chosen it because they'd been told they'd go on a week's painting trip to Amsterdam. After they'd signed up for the course it turned out they'd be going off to draw sheep in the Dales instead. In December.

Jenny used to get on all right. She'd made good progress, then got stuck. Her heart just wasn't in it. When she pulled fresh paper out onto her desk all she saw was a blank page.

Heavy footsteps warned that tutor Tex was on his way, the halls reverberating with his presence. He had the biggest boots in Christendom. A tall, muscular man, nudging six foot two, with stubble on his chin and on his arms, an unending supply of clothing from the States and a baseball cap suggesting that, today at least, he supports the New York Yankees.

Jenny kept her head low behind her desk.

'Where's Sharon?' Tex boomed. 'Is she coming in today?'

He rolled his tongue against a thick fat cheek and left it there, like a gobstopper in his mouth. He didn't look at anyone in particular. Didn't have to.

Marcus, nervous but helpful, peered across, yellow paint around his lips from chewing on his brushes. He never washed his shirts. 'I think she went to the canteen.'

'Well, tell her I want her in my office. Right away. We need a little talk.'

These 'little talks' were infamous. Tex was always acting as though he'd kick them off the course, like they were failures. When they were in the first year they used to stand on desks and hear moans and cries coming from his office upstairs. No one actually said what went on in there, but they could guess.

Jenny avoided these kind of tutor interrogations by hiding in the toilets. So far it seemed to work. The last time she'd had an official tutorial with Tex he'd insulted every painting in her portfolio. The only thing he liked was a gigantic oil pastel picture of an orange goldfish, and that was only because it reminded him of a fishing trip he'd had in Filey when he caught an eel, the memory of which sent him on a rambling passage about electric eels in the Amazon, death by electrocution, as well as a brief but poignant reference to bare chested women in the jungles and how their breasts sagged without bras.

'What's the significance of fish?' he'd asked her, as all art tutors do when trying to figure out the symbolism and deep meaning of thought-provoking work.

'Fish are nice.' That's what she said. If she'd been a little more trusting of his interests she might have told him more. About the smell of fish beside the sea. The salt stink sticking to your nose. How she was buried underneath the sand and it had stopped her growing up.

A shadow darkened Jenny's desk. Tex's nicotine fingers tapped bitten nails onto the wood. A fake tan smile across his face.

'I think we should look at your work, Horsey. See what you've been getting up to. Either me or Marvin. Take your pick.'

Tex put Jenny's chocolate bar into his bulging blue plaid pocket and promptly walked away.

The Good Cop, Bad Cop scenario played strongly within college politics. Marvin was the good cop, while Tex was known as bad. Jenny remembered how glad she'd been when Marvin arrived at the start of last spring term. He'd sprayed Mr Sheen on his glasses to make them shine, and told everyone to call him Marvin. His real name was actually Martin but he was training to be a magician in his spare time and thought Marvin the Magician had a better ring to it. He'd shown them lots of card tricks before they trailed over to the pub where he changed the landlord's ten pound note into a twenty and bought a round of drinks. On Fridays he'd come to college dressed in a gold lamé suit and would show them what he'd learnt at his Nearly Magic Circle class.

Jenny found him in the darkroom. She had to knock on the door several times before he let her in. There was a rabbit by the enlarger. It had knocked a glass jar over and its fur stank strongly of fixative. Marvin was wearing fluorescent pink rubber gloves, clashing badly with his unruly amber hair. He stood out very brightly despite the half-tone light. Eyes set in concentration as he watched photos appear in the developer.

'Watch this, Jenny. Look.'

A portrait of his rabbit, stuck in a black top hat, was darkening in the tank.

'Now watch it disappear.'

Marvin rocked the developing tray back and forth, chemicals splashing over the paper. It smelt of vinegar and piss. The white shape clouded, stayed a moment at drab grey, before Jenny's face shone back from the reflected darkness of the blackened print. Marvin whipped the photographic paper out, and with the ease of a fish shop fryer serving chips, gave it a dunk into the fixative.

'Do you always do that?' she wondered, not needing an answer as she spied photos drying in the corner. Variations of the same rabbit pose, going from bright light to greys to pitchest black. The blackest was the last one in the series.

'It's called Constant Stages Of Disappearance.' Marvin seemed quite pleased. The rabbit tried to drink some chemicals, so Marvin scooped him up.

'Tex and I are very worried,' he confessed, trying his best to look like Blofeld the Bond villain, but failing miserably as his rabbit looked nothing like a white Persian cat. 'Your artwork, well, it's a little... basic. I don't know what we're going to do about it. I'm not sure which way to push you. And there's so little time left, it's frightening.'

Heat rose up Jenny's cheeks. Marvin tried to calm her.

'I know you try hard with your animal pictures... but there's no theme. It's very hard to place it in a context.'

'The theme is animals, that's the context.'

'No, Jenny. You're not listening to me.' He stroked the rabbit more aggressively as his patience began to wane. Worry lines around his eyes, increasing every month as he crept closer to being forty. 'Your work has got to say something, not just be something.'

'But what if I don't know what to say?'

'You've lots to say!' A pained smile on his face, like a cut across the flesh. 'You're clever, though you try to hide it. If you want to paint realistic, naturalistic animals, then that's okay, if there's a thought behind it, a connection.' Marvin balanced his rabbit on one shoulder and wrestled with Jenny's folder, zip straining as he pulled it around the edge. He flipped it open. Took a look. Lifted up a picture of a cow made out of paper plates. 'This isn't the direction we thought you were headed in. It's not what we talked about. It's just... weird.'

Jenny hummed. 'Can weirdness be my theme?'

'Only six weeks till your degree show,' Marvin sighed. 'I don't know what to suggest, I wish... I wish I'd noticed earlier, that you'd slipped so far behind. I might have been able to help. Have you got troubles at home, or here? What's been going on?'

He sat in silence while she told him.

So, she'd committed a few crimes. Nothing extraordinary. It's not like she'd been caught or done anything but look. Invasion of property was only a crime when you were seen. Sure, there was that close shave in Exeter, but she'd hidden in the straw and the horse was enough like Mister to have been worth the risk.

'There's lists of missing animals, but it's hard to get a match. We chase up everything, just to check.' Her horse was out there somewhere. 'It's mostly surveillance work we do. Looking in fields, seeing who's hanging around. Writing down number plates from cars. Watching out for new ponies turning up. It's more than sneaking into yards.'

'And you do this quite a lot?'

'Yeah.'

Maybe she was a little bit obsessed. The search for Mister took up too much time as far as college progress was concerned, but it had taught her things about herself. How she had a handy knack for espionage, going to dealers' stables on the pretence of buying a horse, making sure she inspected every stall. Anything grey that moved, she saw it. She had been round most of the dealers in Yorkshire and Lancashire, covered the Mersey too. She'd check adverts in the papers to look at horses on offer, drive miles to sales to see if Mister was there. Every sighting needed a follow through. For ones further south she'd enlist helpers to go into fields at night and take photos of suspect horses.

'Photographs?' Marvin's ears pricked up.

'I've been all over, taken loads. Horse sales, gypsy fairs. Inside a slaughterhouse.' That one had made her sick. 'Not exactly picture postcards.'

'Can I see them? Will you bring them in?'

'Uuummm....'

'And you run this like a proper detective set-up?' Marvin was enthused. 'All over the country?' He rubbed the white rabbit's fur so hard the friction fizzed his hand.

'I don't know anyone in Devon.' Jenny had met people from most other places. The Horsewatch network had grown drastically in the last twelve months, more branches reaching out across county lines as rustling incidents increased. Owners pulled together in support, bands of people whose horses had disappeared, the figures escalating for no cohesive reason. Too many mornings where young kids would go down to the field to see their faithful pony, only to find a piece of string and a cut lock by the gate. Indented tyre tracks of horseboxes on mud the only evidence left behind.

It was more serious now. More than a fear of your pet being sold across the continent, its final resting place being on a plate in Belgium. The encyclopaedia of horse crime had spawned another chapter. Mutilation. The Savager attacking animals across the country, incidents dotted around the map on Jenny's bedroom wall. Red pins for the deaths, blue for injuries and yellow for false leads. There were a couple of blue drawing pins in Kent, but mostly they clustered inside Yorkshire. Another Ripper in their midst, but in the fields this time, not on the streets. There were no lead stories on the television news anymore, just accounts in free papers, reports wedged between missing cats and sofabeds for sale.

Smoke filtered through the bar, rising from ashtrays and catching people's breath as it suffocated air. Empty pint pots rattled on the juke box. The scrunching of discarded crisp packets mixed with a bumping backbeat as lines of males trod the littered carpet to the gents.

Jenny watched as Wit balanced assorted drinks on the way back from the bar. Dark roots were shooting through the base of his cap of bleached blond hair. He'd invented the style himself, some sketch he'd scribbled in his notebook then transferred onto his head. Jenny had trimmed the sides with dog clippers, shearing it down to millimetres of brown growth. His fringe stood upwards, glued with gel, waving like a yellow Van Gogh cornfield.

Wit deposited the drinks on the table, to a polite response of thanks. He felt the back of his scalp, massaging that small lump he'd got at the Duck and Drake last year. Some fucker with a bottle had called him Skunk, so he got the fists out. Wit didn't take shit from anyone, apart from his brother Walter who'd done a bout of boxing.

Nina took a sip of margarita and expounded on her theory.

'It's completely true, it's obvious. You have to fish in your own circles. If you date a person more attractive than yourself, it's bound to fail.'

'Not really...' Jenny hoped.

'Think about it.' Today Nina's cropped hair was black. A few weeks before she'd dyed it red vermilion. 'If your partner's gorgeous and you're a dog, you'll be dead insecure. You have to match your attractiveness levels, or you haven't got a balance.'

Nina's pretty pixie face topped a supermodel body. If she went by her own ruling, she could pick anyone she wanted. But here she was, still single. Jenny had her own suspicions. Nina wouldn't admit it, but Jenny thought her friend was secretly seeing someone on Monday afternoons. Every Monday, without fail, she would disappear for almost four hours back to her flat and turn the answerphone on, to pretend she wasn't there. Perhaps she had a secret boyfriend who wasn't up to her own standards?

'That's very shallow isn't it?' said Wit. 'To judge so much on looks.' He glanced across at Jenny, pale face framed by a long curtain of auburn hair. Her nose turned up like a perfect porcelain doll.

'It even works in friendships,' Nina continued. 'No one wants their best mate to be ugly, do they? It would make them feel embarrassed.'

'Good job that I'm not bothered,' Jenny teased.

'I tell you, it's true.'

Nina was a Gemini, the split personality of the zodiac. At times it felt like Jenny had two different best friends. They went way back to infants school, right from that first day when Anthony Hopgood shit his pants and hid in the girlie loos until teacher coaxed him out with sweets. Nina and Jenny had sat together by the door, where the smell was not as bad. Squealing Nina wanted to go home, she'd needed peeling off her mother when she arrived, but once everyone got a miniature bottle of milk and a vitamin biscuit as well as a pack of crayons to eat, she decided that school was a hip place to be. At home-time crayola bright-toothed Nina planted herself under a table and refused to come out until her irritated mother promised four fish fingers, chips and peas for tea. And she wanted Jenny there as well. So they were pretty well established as best friends from that day onwards. They shared everything, did everything the same. They both kissed David Bosco in the coal shed. Puckered lips, no tongue.

You had to wonder about Geminis though. They had a darker side. A secret side. Especially on Monday afternoons.

Jenny's attention was drawn towards the bar. To the back of

Simon Marles' head. Those dark tufts of hair, cut close into his nape. His wide shoulders, slender hips. Her face flushed as she walked over, on the pretext of buying a packet of cheese and onion crisps. Jenny's sleeve rubbed against his jacket, but she didn't look at him. He picked up two pints of Guinness and moved across to join his friends. When Jenny turned around Nina was staring.

'I wish you'd fucking stop that,' Nina moaned. 'You're getting embarrassing. Can't you just grow up? What d'you think, Wit?'

'She can do what she likes.' He looked away across the room, not wanting to be dragged into the conversation, discussing Jenny's desired man. He spotted Sharon coming over, leapt up and offered to buy her a drink. She said she needed one. Tough day.

'How was Tex?' Jenny enquired, feeling worried for herself. 'I hope you weren't in any trouble.'

'I don't want to talk about it. He's a bastard.' Sharon pushed Jenny's bag onto the floor and took a seat. She took up a lot less room than when they had first met. In the first year Sharon had had a big moon face and a swelling of flabby bosom, but now she was the same dress size as them. A trio of size tens. Maybe Nina's theory was right, perhaps Sharon had melted away her fat so that she could still be their friend. Shame Jenny didn't really like her.

'Hey!' Nina remembered. 'I saw Chumbawamba, earlier, at the back of HMV.'

'The hairy thing from Star Wars?' Sharon was not impressed.

'No! You silly southerner. The group! They come from Leeds.'

They ran out of conversation so filled in the gaps with drinks. Sharon accepted what was offered, but left when it was time for her to buy a round. Nina wandered off later and didn't return. Jenny stared at the bottom of her glass and considered dropping out of college before Tex had a chance to kick her out himself. What would she do, if she failed? Years wasted, all those hopes. Maybe her dad was right when he said she'd never amount to much, that she was jinxed. Maybe it was true.

Jenny was on the verge of being drunk when her mobile phone started ringing. It was Wit who dealt with it, Jenny couldn't work the buttons. He retrieved the call from voicemail. Roger Mandrake had left a message. He said he thought he'd seen her horse.

Repossession

Ferrybridge Power Station glowed grimly in the distance, thick smoke from the water chimneys pushing black clouds into an even blacker sky. Darkness swathed the farmyard as they stood and looked and checked everyone was sleeping. No lights in the farmhouse, all in bed at 1 am. A lone cockerel perched on a railing, waiting for dawn to break. His yellow eye blinked at them, beak twitching a moment, but the moon kept him from shouting out his cry.

'Can't you just call the police?' Wit's palms were still sweating from driving Jenny there, her weathered trailer bouncing behind his groaning Ford. He'd given her a lift home after she panicked at the phone call, he'd sat up with her and tried to calm her down. She'd called Roger back, wanting to know how he had got her number, and where he'd seen her horse. Several vodkas later, Jenny decided she was going to go over there to bring him back. Wit wouldn't let her drive.

'Why can't we do this in the morning?' worried Wit. 'Do it properly. Check the place out and call the cops. Get your horse back legally.'

'He's my horse. I want him home. No fucker's going to stop me.'

Jenny made Wit park near the entrance for a quick escape, rolling the car the last few yards so it would make less noise. She'd thought of everything, even down to sackcloth pads she'd brought for Mister's hooves.

The horse was in one of the back buildings, that's what Roger had said when Jenny pumped him for information. He'd tried to apologise for the kissing incident, but Jenny cut him off.

Wit opened the first door of the long, shadow-painted building. Nothing but hay and straw, a couple of thoroughbreds dozing in their stalls, and a dribbling Shetland pony. Jenny cringed as the entrance to the other building juddered open, the door vibrating against the concrete floor, hinges drooping with years of gathered rust. A ray of speckled moonlight cut through the wedge of dark so she could see him. That innocent oyster coat glowing softly, a mirage on the horizon, a long lost ghost returned.

'Is that him?' Wit peered around the box. The answer was on Jenny's face as she hugged the animal's neck. The horse was dreaming on his feet, thinking of meadows and summer and clover in green fields. He snorted himself awake, too relaxed to recognise the grinning girl as she crouched down in the straw, tying pads onto his hooves to muffle unwanted sounds. Tears spilling from her eyes.

'Are you okay?' Wit watched her, anxious.

'I'm happy, Wit! I'm happy!'

She had forgotten how it felt. She bounded over to her friend and gave him a huge hug. Kissed him with her lips, her heart. He smiled.

They crossed the yard slowly, stars spying like white eyes peeping through the black sheet of the night. The trailer ramp was down and waiting, so as soon as they got near enough Jenny ran towards it, beast trotting at her arm, not even looking back to check if anyone had seen them as she tied him up inside. She jumped with Wit into his car and they sped off.

Elated and talking ridiculously fast, Jenny directed Wit towards her horse's rightful home. A happy ending, unbelievable! Perhaps things would start changing for her now. Perhaps things would be all right. She wouldn't fail her degree. Simon would fall in love with her.

'Blue Hotel, on a lonely highway!'

She sang along with Wit, Chris Isaak on the tape player.

'Blue Hotel, life don't work out my way!'

But it did now. Everything was going to work out now.

'Blue Hotel! Blue Hotel-hell!'

Jenny smiled at the thought of when Wit had taken her to see Chris Isaak at the Town and Country Club. She'd stood, transfixed until her woeful idol hit the stage, glittering in a suit so bright it could be made from electricity. An Elvis lookalike sort of crooner, singing about love and loss and loving people who never love you back. They'd walked along in the dark as Wit escorted her to Nina's house, and laid down on a grass verge, staring at the sky, naming stars things like Chris Baby and Twin Peaky. Guessing what their movie hero David Lynch had worn at art school, and if he'd really worn a tie as some journalist suggested.

'Don't you think Chris Isaak looks like Simon?' Jenny had asked. Wit hadn't known which Simon she was picturing, until she said his surname.

'Let's make Chris Isaak happy!' They had yelled, oblivious to the people walking by who gave them troubled looks.

'Let's make Chris Isaak happy!' They'd agreed as they promised to think about each other every time they said it, and remember what a special evening it had been. How when you had a friendship as close as theirs you could lie on your back tossing names at stars and know that whichever one you pick out to be the brightest and the best, the next star alongside would always belong to the other. Planets permanently aligned.

Deacon's yard was dark enough to almost scare her, if she wasn't as happy or as pleased or as optimistic as right now. Jenny led the big grey horse into his shrine of a stable, and stood watching as he guzzled water down.

She started to cry. Her head was throbbing. Vodka brains.

'I love you Mister. I missed you so much.'

Wit held Jenny tight in his arms, feeling warmth radiate from her body.

'I love you too, Jenny Barker.'

Wit said this in his head. It was all that he could manage.

Wit stayed on the floor in Jenny's room, wanting to sleep as his head felt heavy enough to drop, but his hyperactive mind buzzed with annoying regularity. He knelt beside the bed and watched her dream, bewitched by the way soft air sang down her nose, playing through a harpsichord of nostrils. At one point he was sure that she was singing, as the notes were too precise to be mere respiratory functions. He leant over and kissed her forehead, then lay back on the floor, smiling at the fact that he'd spent the night with her at last, even if only in a literal, cramped-against-the-carpet context.

The parents' mouths dropped open when Jenny brought Wit down to breakfast. They stared at the silver ring piercing his left eyebrow, ran their looks down his baggy combat trousers, and decided he was male.

'This is Wit. My friend from college.'

Her mother shook his hand, holding onto Wit's fingers for longer than seemed normal. She gestured that he should take a seat and poured him out a cup of tea. Her husband looked over the top of his glasses and made a snorting sound with his long nose.

'About time our Jenny got herself a boyfriend, don't you think, Ray?'

'Hmmmph.' The spoon clicked against the senior Barker's teeth when he placed rice crispies in his mouth. Milk trickled down his chin.

'We always wondered, didn't we, Ray, if Jenny was... you know... If she preferred the girls.'

'Mum! Don't.' Jenny reddened.

Ray was leaning closer towards Wit. 'I suppose you used protection?'

Wit spluttered into his tea cup. 'No, we didn't, I mean...'

'If she gets pregnant,' pondered Ray, 'the council might give her a flat. We can't be taking care of you forever, Jenny. We've got our own lives to lead.'

'I'm not having a baby!' Jenny choked. 'And Wit is just my friend.'

'Whatever you say, love.' Her mother gave a little smile.

Poured Wit another cup of tea without asking if it was needed. He couldn't look the woman in the eye, so stared at the ginger cat instead, wondering why it was sitting on a place mat and not on the floor like normal pets. He felt a rubbing against his trousers, and glanced across at Jenny to see if it was anything to do with her. Both her hands were clinging to a piece of blackened toast. Wit lifted the dangling table cloth, and saw a shaggy miniature collie intently humping his leg. He tried to shake it off, but it was glued.

'We thought, didn't we Mary, that Jenny wasn't normal?' Ray looked pointedly at his wife. 'That maybe she was brain-damaged or something. With all those times she's fell off horses.'

'Thanks Dad!' Jenny jumped up out of her chair, pulled her mobile phone from her pocket and dialled Nina's number.

'You want to watch it with those phones,' remarked her mother. 'They microwave your brains. Give you cancer tumours the size of marbles.'

'Or Alzheimer's, like your mad grandad,' mumbled Ray. 'You're bound to inherit his genetics. Crazy bugger.'

'Don't you insult my father!' Mary snapped.

'I'm just saying, she'll get that from you, love, not from me. She'll not get nowt from me.' Ray stared at his wife. 'I fancy a pot of yoghurt.'

Mary stormed out to the kitchen and rattled some forks. Jenny threw a timid smile in Wit's direction, hoping that his parents were no less strange than hers. They were so embarrassing.

Nina eventually answered Jenny's phone call, and was instructed to meet them at the stables for a surprise. Mary loaded Wit up with home-made pies from her freezer, and told him to come again.

Nina stood in the straw and stared. She looked back at Jenny, at Wit, then at the horse again.

'What have you guys done?' Nina ran her hand over the horse's legs and lifted his front hooves up. 'Since when did Mister have pink feet, Jen?'

His off-fore had a salmon stripe, clean against the black. That tell-tale half warped hoof was missing.

'This isn't Mister, Jenny. Shit, what have you done?'

Wit sucked in a breath. Jenny remained calm, convincing.

'His hoof grew back differently, the blacksmith said it might. He's been gone a long time. It got different.'

'Jenny?' Wit was getting worried. 'Isn't this your horse?'

'You love me, don't you, Mister?' The horse breathed down her nose, glad of the attention. Thicker hairs formed a moustache on his snout, tinged a shade of yellow by years of eating barley and rolled oats. 'See! He knows who I am! He's my baby, aren't you, boy?'

Nina sank beside the feed trough, frightened that her friend wouldn't acknowledge the deviations. The hooves were wrong, the legs too white, not flecked with grey like Mister's, and he didn't have that small scar on his knee. Even his face was too long to be the same. They were more like distant cousins, not blood brothers.

'That's not Mister, Jen. You know it isn't.' Nina watched, concerned, as her friend ran eager fingers through his mane, sucking up his presence. Happy to be surrounded by the smell of hay and horses. 'He's not your horse, Jen. Mister's gone. I don't think he's coming back.'

The spell was broken.

Jenny deflated down into the straw, banging her head against the stable wall. A slice of skin ripped from her temple.

'Jenny! Don't!'

Nina leapt across, grabbing hold of Jenny's shoulders. Wit watched, stunned. Jenny shivered like a fish, mouth gaping, blowing bubbles of invisible words. Rocking from one side to another, with Nina clinging on, trying to keep her still, to keep her head from banging.

Jenny could see everything again. His empty stable, those three piles of manure. Fresh blades of straw blowing across the path. That bird outside his door.

The story had made the papers. Sad, they said it was, a prize-winning horse disappearing like that. If someone had been hurt or died they would have called it tragic. Jenny blamed herself, of course, for being doomed at birth. For killing that stupid milkman and being cursed with a whole lifetime of bad luck. She could hear his milk float in her head. Purring. Whirring. That battery operated plaything of a vehicle, bottles clinking, chinking glass.

'Jenny! Stop it! Stop!' Nina pulled Jenny away from the wall and blocked it with her body. Her confused friend started sobbing, dry, painful chokes of air as she struggled hard to breathe. Wit couldn't bear to see this. Disturbed, he went outside, sat down on a mildewed water butt and rolled a much needed joint.

Nina held tight onto Jenny. 'It's alright. I'll take care of you. I promise.'

They could take care of each other, that was true. They'd always managed that. Been there. Done that. Everything the same.

'Sssh, Jen. I'll make things better for you.'

They'd got too involved with horses in the first place. Another phase, that's what their parents called it when they begged and sulked and cried out for a pony. How they schemed and saved to try to buy their own, pulling buckets of peas in summer and polishing people's shoes. They collected empty bottles out of bins and took them to the shops for the deposits. When Jenny eventually saved up enough for Mister, aided by paper rounds, Saturday jobs and several years of birthday money, she had let Nina ride him too.

They shared everything, pleasure, pain. As Jenny knelt quivering in the straw, she felt again the fear they'd held as children, when the smallest problems scared them, and they imagined that they'd grow wiser later on. That when they turned into adults all the riddles would be solved.

Nina lay Jenny on the back seat of her car, underneath a hairy dog blanket. Wit watched in silence, feeling like a third wheel on a bike.

'Can I do anything, Nina?'

'Just keep an eye on her. Don't let her bang her head.'

'Maybe I could buy the horse for her,' Wit offered, nervous. 'If she likes this one so much.'

'Sure, she likes it,' Nina gave him an anxious look. 'But it's not her horse. It isn't Mister, and we can't let her pretend. Where would you get the money from, anyway?'

Wit shrugged, dejected. 'My family?'

Nina gave him a mocking look, smiling at his clothes. How could somebody who only seemed to possess two pairs of jeans afford to buy a horse?

'Just keep your eye on her, Wit. Okay?'

Nina loaded the grey horse into the box, glad that no one else was in the yard. This would be rather difficult to explain. People expected Jenny to do occasional bizarre things, she'd always been a little crazy, but horsenapping was a serious departure.

Wit and Nina drove back to Ferrybridge, a pair of panda cars on the farm driveway a sure sign that the crime had been discovered. They panicked, driving past.

'Shit.'

Nina couldn't think what to do next.

'Shit, shit!'

'What are we going to do?' Wit lit another smoke.

'We're going to let the horse loose on the main road, Wit, so it can get splattered on the motorway. What d'you think?'

'Why don't we just put it in that field?'

Wit pulled the car off the main road, and parked up by the gate. There was a field full of sheep on the left, so they unboxed the squinting horse and set it free inside. It stood watching them for a moment before galloping off across the grass.

The police came round to visit Jenny the following afternoon. They pretended to be on a social call, but she knew they weren't really. A horse had been taken from its stable, they said, but it must have broken free and galloped off. They just mentioned this in passing, as if they weren't trying to trick her and get her to confess and while she was at it she might as well confess to a couple of other things too, as crime was mounting up and unsolved cases were so bad for morale.

The owner thought the horse might have got out on its own, though how it could have done that was a mystery to them as it had been well enough secured, and they wondered if it could have any connection with her own missing horse? They had the details on their file, along with lists of Jenny's frequent visits.

'May 10th, last year. That's when he disappeared.' Jenny counted off the days.

'This horse looked a lot like your own animal, that's what we thought.' The policeman had a photograph. Mister in the paddock, with that leather headcollar she had bought him for his birthday. 'It was a jumper too. Won lots of money, apparently.'

The police didn't arrest her. They suggested helpfully that the thieves may have been disturbed this time, that they were getting sloppy. Once they had a lead as to who the culprits were, they might find clues about Jenny's horse.

'It could be a false hope,' the officer growled. 'We could be barking up the wrong tree completely.'

'Woof, woof,' thought Jenny.

'Or it could have been, unfortunately, an attempt at something else.'

The Savager. Jenny didn't need to hear them say it. She could read their minds. Don't worry the poor kid, don't tell her scary things. She doesn't look strong enough to take it anyway.

'How did you get that injury, Miss?'

'Oh, I did it after I stole the horse I thought was mine and even though he wasn't I wanted him to be, because Mister can't be dead, he mustn't be dead, if he is my luck will never change, Simon will never love me, and I may as well be dead too as nothing will ever be good in the whole, entire, fucking world.'

She didn't say it. They didn't even ask. They probably thought she had fallen off a horse. People can't see what's right in front of them sometimes.

Jenny started itching as soon as she learnt that the horse had been kept in isolation at the back because it was suffering from a contagious bout of ringworm. Perhaps it was the fact that this horse was kept so separate that had intrigued the rustlers, who must have thought the animal was worth more than the rest.

Apparently they found the horse in a rival farmer's field and now nobody could catch it. It seemed to have got particularly attached to one of the sheep, and they couldn't catch that either.

After the officers left, Jenny sat alone, skin cold, clammed up with worry. They had her on their files, they'd said. On their files, official. In their little black book of victims, the unfortunate bereaved. If they had her in their wanted book she could at least feel a bit less guilty.

Could policemen spot a criminal at once, or would they have to guess? If you killed a person, maybe, in an accident, would a trained eye be able to tell or would they never know?

Infatuation

Dear Agony Aunt,

Simon still hasn't noticed that I exist. How can I make him fall for me if we don't have a conversation? What if he finds somebody else before he knows I'm here? It's so unfair that I can love him as much as this and he doesn't know about it.

Jenny B from Leeds

Dear Jenny,

It's a good thing he doesn't know it, psycho! How would you like to be pursued by somebody with such a strong obsession? Have you ever heard of transference? This man is not your horse. Calm down. Concentrate on your artwork or you will fail your degree. Try to take your mind off Simon. Why not accept that kind offer from your friend, and have an evening out? Who knows, you might even enjoy yourself.

Wit had invited her to a party at someone's house in Kirkstall. Jenny liked the sound of that. Kirkstall. It reminded her of that day when everyone at college had dressed up like characters from *Star Trek*. They played at beaming people up and down in the department's lifts. Simon had been Captain Kirk, of course, and he had looked the best.

'I wouldn't bother with that party, Jenny,' Nina had advised. 'It'll be full of wanky designers and really boring.'

'But you're a wanky designer.'

'Yep, and I'm not going.' Nina was stern. 'Why don't you and Wit go to a movie? Make it a proper date.'

'It isn't a date.'

It was just two people going to the same place at the same time. Jenny mentioned to Wit about Nina's objections, that maybe they shouldn't go to this party, that maybe it would be dull. Wit told her that she didn't have to do everything Nina suggested.

'But I said I wouldn't go,' wheezed Jenny.

'And if she's not there, how will she know? Come on Jen. For me. It really might be fun.' Wit put on a face like a garden gnome and made Jenny start to laugh. She prodded his shoulder with her finger. She wished Wit was her brother. She'd always wanted her own brother.

Jenny skipped over cracks in the pavement in a misguided attempt to fend off more bad luck. Jenny was born with bad luck, that was obvious, and the same for James Dean too, with whom she shared her February birthday. She'd read a quote by Nicholas Ray, director of *Rebel Without A Cause*.

'The intensity of his desires and his fears could make the search at times arrogant, egocentric, but behind it was such a desperate vulnerability that one was moved, even frightened.'

There was something a little mad, rather possessed about James Dean. He used to have a lot of nosebleeds, apparently, and liked to sleep in coffins.

Jenny followed Wit along the road. They stopped at an off-licence on the Burley Road and picked up some wine and beers. Jenny carried hers very carefully in case she tripped and smashed them before getting smashed herself. It had just begun to rain and the roads were shining as the filtered spray seeped down.

As she walked along with the cheap bottle of Leibfraumilch Jenny thought about her childhood milkman. They called him Ernie Bernie after this old Benny Hill song he used to whistle. Ernie, the fastest milkman in the West. She could see his face quite clearly. Smiling. Always smiling. He'd come to her house for tea and biscuits and a ciggie, and used to give her marshmallows and pretty penny sweets, and would make her mother laugh. He never stayed for long, and sometimes didn't come for weeks, although he still delivered milk.

He'd left them wine with their milk at Christmas. Then on his way to someone else he fell onto a blue crate of cold bottles. A piece of glass pierced straight through his warm heart. As he died there on the front porch some half blind old biddy stood and moaned at him that his milk looked as pink as a strawberry shake and she'd take her custom elsewhere if he didn't buck up his ideas. She took a couple of pints from his crate and had milkman's blood on her cornflakes.

It was Jenny's fault. She'd killed him. She shouldn't have gone snowsliding in front of the next door neighbour's house, especially with a milkman in her path. She'd never forget the sight of his happy smiling face as she glided towards him, then knocked him down. She could never stomach the thought of milk again. The noise of clanking milk floats always filled her with regret.

It was a secret, that. She didn't tell it. Not even to Nina, and they told each other everything. Jenny often wondered if her parents saw it or had guessed. They never spoke of him, their milkman. But she had seen her mother cry, and she'd always felt that they held something against her.

'Wit?' Jenny began to shiver. She moved closer as they walked. 'Can I tell you something private?' She saw his gentle eyes, they sparkled. 'There's this guy at college who I've liked for quite some time, but I've never been able to tell him. I don't want to mess things up.'

Wit brushed a spot of rain from Jenny's cheek. 'Maybe he already knows. Perhaps he's been waiting for you to talk to him about, say what he wants to hear. I bet he'd really love you.'

Jenny hugged onto him, squeezing so tight she felt blood rushing through her arms. 'You don't know how good that makes me feel. I was sure you'd laugh at me.'

Wit smiled, giddy with enthusiasm.

'Could you find out if he likes me? I can't ask him myself as it looks dumb. But you're a guy, you can. Blokes in the toilet kind of stuff.'

Wit pulled back, hurt. Jenny didn't notice.

'Oh, Wit! I love Simon Marles so much. Don't you think he's gorgeous? Isn't he the bestlooking man you've ever seen? Do you really think I've got a chance? With our attractiveness levels,

I mean, because I'm not up there with him.'

Wit stood, the wet air cutting through him.

'Look, Jen, the party's at that house up there....' He pointed further up the hill, to an open door, glowing with artificial voltages. 'I've got to get some matches.'

He ran off down the street where they'd just come, fading out into the dark. Jenny felt an enormous weight lifted from her. She was glad that she had told him about this thing with Simon. It would be good to glean a touch of male advice. Jenny increased her pace towards the house, footsteps marching with the music.

Her and Simon, this would happen. She would talk to him tonight. She had heard he would be there.

She didn't know the people at the door, not by name anyway, though she had seen them hanging around on the eighth floor. A clique of ultra trendy designers were discussing the influence of the Swiss Bauhaus on the structure of today's letter headings and the layout of the *Independent*. They dragged their syllables and swigged back home made sangria by the glass.

Jenny Barker and Simon Marles. Have a drink and talk to him.

She pushed through static bodies into the front lounge, where people huddled around a low table of snacks, dropping nachos and Twiglets as they reached into each dish. Lukewarm onion bhajis became animated footballs as fingers flicked and flustered, dipping the greasy balls into a mint green sauce. The deep red throat of carpet quickly swallowed fallen food. The room smelt of warm beer.

There was no one Jenny knew. No sign of Simon either. She fumbled with the nearest bottle opener to give herself something to do. Hot faces shouted round her as the music rose again, the gangling youth behind the turntable revving up the noise in the hope someone would dance. Headphones clamped onto his shoulder, hearing the sounds pump through his skin. Legs swaying to the rhythm, satisfied, while all around him yelled into their neighbours' ears. Three girls ran in, laughing, flinging up their arms, shouting about Ibiza, ready to dance the night away. Jenny promptly escaped.

Two blokes were kissing in the upstairs toilet. Jenny pretended she hadn't seen, and waited on the landing until the room was free. When she came back downstairs she saw Simon passing through the hall towards the kitchen.

Walk over there and talk to him.

He was with a girl, her hair hidden by a fake leopard-skin hat. She had a sexy body, Jenny could tell from seeing the back of her, waist dipped in like some sculptor had taken clay between his hands and squeezed until his knuckles joined together. Jenny hated her instantly, even more so when she saw Simon sink his face down to devour the front of hers, probably smudging her lipstick as she was bound to be the type of tart who wears bright strawberry lips.

Jenny left, defeated, her only partner being the corkscrew with which she managed to escape.

Wine tasted cool against her lips as its semi-sweetness wetted her numbed tongue. A small black cat rubbed ironically against her leg. She poured a puddle of alcohol on the pavement. The cat didn't like it.

Jenny sat on her hands for a while, trying to rescue her buttocks from the hardness of Nina's front door step. She stood up slowly, wiggling her fingers to get some life back in them. The lights were off in Nina's flat, but she couldn't remember if she'd knocked on the door to check if she was home.

'Nina! Nee-nar!' She picked up a piece of mud from the front garden and threw it at the window, making a pathetic dull plip noise. 'Nee-nar!' She found a larger clump, heavy to her hands. She lobbed it at the window but that was a mistake. The shattering of glass woke the neighbours, whose windows opened as Jenny ran off down the street, the wine clenched in her hand. Arm stretched out to one side of her, keeping the bottle far away in case she tripped and fell while escaping from the scene.

Jenny rocked her weight from foot to foot as she waited for an answer to the bell. Explorers in the South Pole had feet as cold as this. Captain Scott and his men had to eat their huskies. Jenny could never eat a dog, not even their own dog Laddie and he really pissed her off at times.

The door opened slightly, revealing an inch more of Sharon as it did so. She stood, resplendent in black rubber dress, trying to pull one side of it back over an exposed mountain of bra.

Jenny held her bottle out. 'I've got some wine.'

Sharon grabbed the offering and slammed the door. Jenny tapped on the wood, waiting quietly for an answer. The door opened up again and Sharon reappeared, the top of her dress peeled completely down.

'I missed my bus,' groaned Jenny. 'I lost Wit. Nina's not at home and I don't know where to go so I came here.'

'Wait there a minute.'

The door pulled shut again. Jenny counted to ninety seven before Sharon invited her inside, leading her past a trail of discarded clothing, tartan shirt, abandoned jeans, before escorting her to a sofa bed in the spare bedroom, and pulling shut the door.

Jenny lay awake with her fingers in her ears. After a while she took them out as being alert and having pains in your lobes didn't seem like a good option. The walls were far too thin. She tried to shut the noises out, but couldn't. Heavy breathing, squeaking, moans. The bed rocking and creaking. Something or someone banged against the wall, and a deep voice started shouting.

A groaning followed, low and resonant. Jenny wondered who was the first person to have an orgasm, was it Adam or was it Eve? She smiled guiltily to herself, proud of the fact that she'd experienced her first act of penetrative sex. She wondered if she'd ever have a proper orgasm herself, and if she did would it sound quite as stupid?

The shouting man had already left by the time Jenny woke up. Sharon seemed more relaxed with him out of the way. They had a late breakfast, sitting in silence while Sharon forced solid marmalade onto her toast. She didn't eat it, just cut it into soldier strips and left them lined up on her plate.

'Was he your boyfriend, here last night?' Jenny ventured.

'I don't want to talk about it.'

'Is he nice?' Jenny stared hard at her. There were lines on Sharon's face. Strain, or worry. Make-up normally hid them.

'He's a bastard and he's married, and I wish I never had to see him,' Sharon snapped.

'So why do you?'

'Because, that's why. Don't bother me, okay? It's none of your business.'

They looked through the Sunday papers, each one occasionally peeping up from the newsprint but never saying anything. Jenny felt somewhat uneasy as she read an article in the Observer about functions of the human brain, giving statistics for the number of people who had become serial killers after serious cranial traumas. She scrutinised the section on head injuries and how lack of oxygen to the brain core can cause irreparable damage. She wondered just how long you would have to go without air, and if it was worse underground, underwater or under sand. She wondered if anyone would ever notice you had changed, especially if you looked the same on the outside and got a place at college.

Jenny was twelve when it had happened. She and Nina were enjoying August away from school, a holiday in that caravan at Bridlington. Nina's parents always asked where they were going and what they were doing as they escaped to the beach and the sea. They dug holes in the sand and sat in them for hours, pretending to be on other planets, other worlds. Jenny scratched away at the wall of her hole with a red spade, tunnelling under the beach until she made a cave of sand for a human to creep through. She crawled inside and then the roof caved in. Jenny twisted round to get back up, but the yellow particles pushed her down, covering her face and spilling into her mouth. She closed her eyes and held her breath as the weight pushed hard against her, sand sifting round her body, filling every air pocket and crevice it could find. She couldn't stretch her lips to scream. All she could hear was the filtering of sand beside her ear.

Underneath the sand. Jenny had lain there, not able to shout as she knew that she would choke. Wondering if lack of oxygen could break your brain, how long it took a body to decompose. A cold object scraped her foot. Burrowing down towards her, cutting through the salted grains. She held her breath for longer as cold metal hit her toe, and then released a wave of air. Vibrations above her head, frantic but nervous in case their digging scraped away her face. Jenny blacked out into a world of nothingness, a void. The darkness cleared and she saw Nina's dripping face as her saviour dug her out.

Jenny was twelve when it had happened, and she was still twelve now.

Detection

Green wellingtons in front of her, mud clinging to their sides. A pirate faced Jack Russell, brown patch over one eye, chewed on a piece of stick beside his master's feet. Jenny held her breath. She could hold her breath longer than anyone she knew. She often practised underwater, just in case.

'Tha's seen that one of Simpson's? Got more meat on it than a feckin' fleshed-up walrus. More pounds of steak on that than on the wife at home.'

Jenny recognised his voice. Jack Turner, a prosperous knacker man with red-blushed face and full-flushed bank account. A good business man with a bad heart from too much cholesterol, which was not surprising if you saw the amount of greasy chips and hot pork pies he ate. Jenny wondered if people who had heart disease were less likely to love than healthy people.

Her leg was getting cramped, muscles pulling at the bone. Go away dog. Don't keep looking under here. If it sniffed her out and bit her then the plan was truly foiled. How could she explain her way out of this? Sorry, Sir, but I'm training to be a motor mechanic and thought I smelt fuel coming from your tank, which is why I'm lying underneath your wagon.

Pairs of wellingtons moved away, followed by four paws. Jenny counted up to thirty, estimating that Turner and his meat-seeking missile pals would be out of sight by then.

Her jacket stunk of diesel, biting her nose, making her drunk with fumes and raw excitement. She pulled herself out from underneath the horsebox, a deep skid mark of mud the only evidence of her ever being there.

Prising open the side door of the long box, she caught a glimpse of white inside. The horse whickered softly, sensing a human presence. That was good, wasn't it? Maybe he'd recognised her when she was standing by the auction ringside, wide-eyed and gaping at the familiar horse. A bit lower in weight, and certainly in muscle, but the essence was still him.

'Any more bids? Going then at seven fifty.'

Jenny had raised her hand, glaring at the leather faced auctioneer in the hope that if she stared at him hard enough then he was bound to see.

'Have we an eight?'

Jenny had waved her hand like semaphore, wishing she had on a petticoat that she could take off and wave like in *The Railway Children*.

'Going...going...'

Stop the train! You have to stop the train! The trees are on the track! Look at me!

'Gone,' the salesman nodded. 'Jack Turner.'

Fuck.

She'd tried to follow him then, but couldn't get past a line of hairy skewbald ponies so never quite caught up. One of his lads led the big horse to this wagon, with her tracking behind, occasionally pretending to read a copy of *Horse and Hound* when she felt she was being watched.

'There's a lad, sssh now.' Her reflection shone back at her from his wide liquid brown eyes, a tiredness round his lids that had aged him by a few more stressful years. Jenny gulped air into her lungs, her heart racing as she prayed that it was him.

'Mister?'

His nostrils flared, a drip of liquid falling. A thin layer of sweat formed on his neck, bringing the greyness of his skin up through the white. Jenny remembered when she first had his winter coat clipped off, and he came out with stripy lines. She'd left a big letter M on his right side rump, like a tattoo made out of hair. It had never grown back exactly like the rest, and was always a few weeks later in moulting when it came round to the spring.

This horse's coat was even-toned, but matted. Perhaps the mane was a little whiter than before, with less streaks of dark grey, but it was a year later, a year older, and it could have just gone light. His legs were paler, less flecked with roan than she remembered. Where was that white mark that had grown back on a grey-blue patch on the knee of his near fore?

The more she checked, the more despondence filled her. She pulled a bottle of nail varnish remover from her bag and promptly went to work.

'Good boy. Just stay still. Don't stand on my bloody hands.'

She rubbed a cloth onto the front hoof, black hoof oil staining her fingers. She cleaned the oil off all four feet, revealing three black hooves, two of which showed evidence of a previous bout of laminitis by the tell-tale grooves of rings, and one white hoof, with a black stripe down the side.

'Good boy. Stand now.'

She pushed as much straw out of the way as she could manage, to get a good view of the hooves. The horse snorted, blinking when her camera flash went off.

'There's a lad.'

A couple of shots of front feet, then the back. You could use the hooves for identification purposes, like an equine fingerprint. The number of times Horsewatch members got their hopes up at a sighting, then went back and checked the files and found the feet were wrong. Mister had four black feet, the front near side fore being slightly bowed to the left as it grew back weird after an accident, always growing faster than the others, though no one quite knew why.

Jenny took a photo of the horse's head and noted down particulars, checking his teeth for approximate age, looking round for scars. When she looked under his tail she understood why such a striking horse could end up at a sale. Two solid lumps underneath, protruding from the tailbone. She sadly made a note. Tumours. That meant cancer. Greys were more susceptible, maybe due to lack of pigment in their bodies.

She gave the horse a mint, breathing up his nose. If she got Mister back, when she got Mister back, she hoped that he was safe. What would she have done if this horse had been him, and she found he was diseased? Was it better to never know where he ended up, to always imagine he was well?

Jenny checked nobody was looking and jumped swiftly from the box, walking away with a sense of purpose, as experience had taught her that loitering was a sure way to get found out. She and Mr Blonde had got into a fight once with a wide man in a field, who they later found was drunk. Jenny had had to lie to the parents, saying the black eye was from a game of hockey, even though she had not played that since school. They could be ignorant of so much, the parents. She would run away when she was smaller, leave big notes in her room and everything, but they never even noticed. She'd hide out in the woods until it got too cold, then walk back in the house.

'I ran away,' she'd say. 'But I forgave you and came back.'

'Your tea's burnt.'

Her mum said that every time. Your tea's burnt. Not surprising as she'd put it in the oven and turned the gas right up. Parents. You could never understand them.

Mr Blonde was waiting in the cafe, in their normal corner by the window with an old poster for Walls ice-cream glued against the glass.

'Much business?'

Jenny pulled up a chair, glancing round the brown-toned room, wedged in by mock wood wallpaper, some of which was drooping from the walls, stuck back up with glue or chewing gum. She scanned for faces, skimming past weathered waxed jackets that smelt of manure and gathered sweat. No known suspects were in view. You could never be too careful. There'd been reprisals against some Horsewatch members who'd rubbed dealers the wrong way. She knew of people in neighbouring counties who'd had their windows smashed, or come home to find someone sitting in their house.

'Just saw one of Turner's, but it's clean. Nothing like it on my list.' She was glad of that, for once. Wouldn't like to tell someone they'd found their horse, but it was going to die.

'Coffee?' Mr Blonde got up to get one. She wasn't a mister, or a blonde, but liked the actor Michael Madsen and was a huge fan of *Reservoir Dogs*. They sat supping polystyrene cups of caffeine, surrounded by smells of animal fat and greasy burgers clamped in fist-squashed buns, and exchanged numbers of suspect licence plates. Registrations of cars that were parked near horses' fields for no good reason. Copies of information they'd pulled off the Horsewatch website on the Internet. Mr Blonde's top source, her Deep Throat, was a truck driver from Ripon. They'd meet up in motorway cafes at midnight, and he would give her lists of wagons with horses that he'd seen. Details of ones that looked illegal, or drove along too late at night.

'There was a car parked near Deacon's yard, two weeks back.' Jenny reported. 'A shitty brown one. Pretty old. Parked down the road for half a day, but nobody got out.'

'You didn't see anyone when it drove off?'

'I wasn't close enough.' Jenny shrugged. 'I think it was a man.'

'Was there much bum?'

'What d'you mean?'

'Men have smaller bums than us.'

'Really?'

'You didn't know? What, you've not seen a guy's naked butt before?'

Jenny blushed. 'I never saw a bum, he... she, never got out.'

Mr Blonde was grinning, her chapped mouth twitching at the side. 'How old are you, girl?'

'Twenty two. Why? How old are you?'

'How old do I look?'

Jenny scrutinised the woman's face, her parchment skin. Lines drawn under the eyes, probably more from wind than age. Too many raw winter's days standing out in fields feeding shivering ponies. Maps of veins across her cheeks, a red atlas of the world.

'Thirty four?' Jenny lied.

Mr Blonde smiled, very flattered. 'D'you know something, kid? You'd make a great detective. Okay, little Jimmy Dean, let's go for a wander.'

That was Jenny's code name. Jimmy Dean. Short for James Dean, her birthday sharer. February the eighth. Aquarius. The star sign of artists and eccentrics and dreamers and visionaries and inventors. As well as bad car drivers.

Jenny followed Mr Blonde to the main building, a large barn, divided into sections. Metal pens with a brief scattering of straw housed tightly held horses in tatty tethers, the oldest, most decrepit pieces of headgear their owners wanted rid of. Yellow numbered circles were pasted to their bums, so anyone remotely interested could check for details in the catalogue. Sad ponies shivered in a long enclosure, halters clamped tightly on their heads, lead ropes dangling straight down like lollipop sticks. A stout black horse was snapping at its neighbour, teeth bared, flashing an eye. Hopeful whinnies, worried squeals. An equestrian purgatory, the inhabitants in limbo while human beings placed bids on their fate.

Jenny weaved through the metal maze, avoiding burly men with sticks, noting down numbers of any freeze-marked horses. It was a mistake, not having a serial number ice-stamped onto Mister's back. If rustlers saw marked ponies it was a mild deterrent, unless they branded them again over the numbers, but that would look so messy you could tell it was a ploy. There was also the trouble of selling the stolen horse for meat, as most slaughterhouses would not accept a numbered animal without appropriate paperwork. But the rustlers were becoming more conniving. Their profits outweighed the risks of getting caught and being sent to prison. They could make three thousand pounds a week out of bent horses on a good spree. A hundred per cent profit, just load your goods into a truck and drive away. Stealing for the specialised market, to order, or else for twenty-five pence a kilo on the bone. It only cost the price of petrol and their liberty if caught.

'Makes me sick to my stomach, sometimes.' Mr Blonde was patting a bug-eyed young Welsh filly. 'I got my first pony at a sale. Over at Lepton. I went there for a saddle but I ended up with Dan.'

Jenny knew the story. A little Welshie, four months old, fresh off the hills, still screaming for his mother. He cost thirty three guineas. Jenny remembered the number as it matched the age of Jesus. Over the seventeen years Mr Blonde had Danny he'd gone from dark blue roan with white blaze and four white socks to pure white with yellow teeth. March the ninth, he'd disappeared, the previous year, along with a Cleveland bay called Eric and a mad ex-racehorse that used to spit at people.

Mr Blonde's eyes were smarting. 'Danny was for life, you know? Some people don't get that. They don't know what they've done.'

They walked round to the sales ring, towards the auctioneer's low rumble. Jenny hated this particular sale, with its remnants of horses and fattened up ponies queuing, worried in the stalls, hoping to attract the attention of someone in riding boots, instead of the beer bellied meat-men in dockers who stood, red-faced and windswept as they eyed up what was fat and what was cheap.

A high-pitched neigh, almost like Mister's voice, but shriller, much more scared. Jenny's eyes settled on the singer, shaking its head, screaming, pulling on a rope as it was led into the ring. Hooves springing off the sawdust, tight stomach sucked in so much you could see into the gut. Barbecue ribs protruded through brown skin, legs twitched like dying spiders.

'Any more offers? Five hundred bid. Five twenty?'

A familiar woman appeared in Jenny's view. She stared at her, half smiling, trying to gauge where she knew her from, as the woman was looking at her in that particular way which showed there must be some connection. School? No, she looked somewhat older, more mature, nearer to thirty than twenty. The riding club, perhaps, or maybe not. She wasn't wearing jodhpurs, not that this should be a clue.

The horse was getting bored of walking round in circles. Dulled feet started to drag. Head lowered.

'Sold then. Five hundred and twenty, to the gentleman in the corner.'

As the red haired woman walked closer, hot cup gripped strongly in clenched hand, Jenny realised it was not a smile she was wearing, but a sneer.

'That's Turner's daughter,' Mr Blonde noted, wisely. 'She's a right mardy bitch.'

As the woman pointedly approached, Jenny remembered where she had seen her before. Her face popping into the light of Roger's box. Her hate as Jenny kissed him.

Anne Mandrake managed to knock into Jenny as she passed, spilling coffee onto her coat. She didn't stop to apologise, as it wasn't accidental.

Mr Blonde was quite intrigued.

'I think I know her husband,' Jenny blushed.

'Well, take a good look at his bum.'

Jenny said goodbye to Mr Blonde in the car park, promising to call later in the week. Then she saw him. The thin singing brown horse, lying like a sad beached whale while men tried to haul him up the ramp into their box. Jenny's stomach lurched. Could horses die if their front legs pulled out far enough, like cats?

'Stop it! Don't do that!' Jenny ran as she yelled, scared and angry. Scared that the biggest man might bring out a stick and smash the horse's head, cull him like a seal and drag his warm corpse up the ramp.

Huddled ponies already in the box, fur rubbing together, sweating up. The dark horse looked Jenny in the eye, seeing her upside down as his head hung off the edge.

The gruff man glared hard at her, his padded jacket bulging. 'What are you squawking at? I own this animal. I'll do what the fuck I like.' Another look. 'Don't I know you from somewhere?'

Jenny hoped he wouldn't remember. She'd spied in one of his fields where he put horses in the summer, to gain more flesh on grass. He'd chased her with a walking stick and a pit bull with a wart.

'Do you have to be so cruel?' She tried to stare them out. Don't blink. If you can out-stare someone you have control. 'That horse deserves better treatment than this, he isn't meat, not yet.' Would they kill the horse right here? Did they have a gun with them? 'I've a good mind to call the RSPCA. I think I'll do it now.'

She reached into her jacket pocket, heart pounding, and pulled out her mobile phone. The dealer blinked. She won.

Addition

Dear Agony Aunt,

I have just squandered my savings on a very skinny horse, which has been up all night with colic. I've phoned the vet to come and see him, but I've got a bad feeling about this. What do you suggest? Can I really afford it?

Jenny B from Leeds

Dear Jenny,

No you can't. Pack in college, hell, you're going to fail anyway, and get a job at Safeways. And go visit a psychiatrist.

Jenny knelt in the straw of Mister's old stable and watched the sick horse mope about, stomach tight against its greyhound ribcage. She was so exhausted from staying there overnight that she could barely recall even bringing the horse home. How she'd managed to persuade a friendly face to give them a lift in his horsebox, coaxing the animal in with over two hours worth of patience and a bucket full of mints. How she'd driven, dazed, in her mum's car, worried that her new horse might get impaled by the blue pony trap he had to travel with. The shafts did seem precariously close. When they pulled the back ramp down at Deacon's she was relieved to see the animal unharmed. As the strange horse sniffed Jenny's kneecaps she decided that he looked rather boring, and that she would call him Brown.

Jenny's stomach rumbled. She was feeling strangely hungry, yet her appetite was suppressed by the acrid rank aroma of the horse's sloppy shits. Soft sinking molehills of excrement were pottered around the dirtied straw or smeared along the walls. A horse's dirty protest.

Jenny wished the vet would come, that the cow he was dealing with right now would hurry up and get well so he could drive quickly over here. Maybe he was lost. You never knew with MacKenzie. Sometimes he'd pretend to be in the surgery doing an operation, when he was really watching a cricket match.

The horse shook his head like Mister Ed trying to talk. His guts were hurting badly, monsters gurgled and spat inside. Jenny wondered why it was that horses couldn't puke, what it would be like if they could? It was bound to look like carrots.

MacKenzie's estate car arrived, bouncing over the rocky yard. A small girl who was supposed to be at school popped her head over a stable door then disappeared again. Jenny hurried over to her vet and led him to the stable, noticing a human shadow ensconced in the passenger seat. MacKenzie pulled a face as he approached the sulking horse. Jenny wondered why the man was wearing a sombrero.

'Que problema es?' He was doing Spanish at night school, and was determined to fly to Madrid for his fiftieth birthday. He ran a hand along the horse's side, moving his ear down close to listen. 'Bonjour mon petit cheval. Avez vous lit Le Petit Prince, Monsieur?'

He was also doing French.

'I bought him yesterday, from a sale. I thought he drank too much water when we got home. I gave him some feed.'

'Poor bugger needs it,' Mad Mac felt the horse's ribs. 'Don't know what possessed you to buy him. He's a wreck.'

'I know.'

'Got a right case of diahorrea. He'll need worming, looks like he's riddled with them.' The vet poked the horse's muck, inspecting. 'No sign, nothing creeping. This is very wet, this muck.'

The brown horse dropped another one, a Niagara fall of steaming waste. MacKenzie concentrated, brought a fresh thought to his brow.

'I'll go get my new partner. We'll discuss it.'

His colleague was pulling something from the boot. As it shut, Jenny focused on a too familiar face, smiling at her, professionally at first, then clouding over with an acute look of embarrassment. Roger Mandrake, the man with cold hands and lizard tongue.

'Hello.' He looked down at her boots. 'How are you?'

'Fine. You?'

'Fine, thanks.'

They walked in silence to the horse. Mad Mac smiled, wearing his matchmaker grin and stethoscope. He ran his hand over Brown's taut stomach, bowed his head and listened to the sounds.

'I don't suppose it was your horse? In Ferrybridge?' Roger cast an eye over the patient, took a quick look in his mouth.

'No, but thank you. For the information.' Jenny blushed.

'No problem.'

'No problemo!' Mad Mac echoed.

They looked solemnly at the horse. It wasn't good.

'Enteritis,' announced MacKenzie. 'Of a very serious kind. An unstoppable form of the runs, where you put food in, and it comes out, put water in, and out again. His whole system is kaput.'

The horse would starve to death, it didn't matter what you fed him. Jenny tried to divert the shock by thinking about Sharon. Maybe she had enteritis, she had got so thin. But she wasn't going to die.

'I treated a young racehorse for the same thing at a yard in Doncaster.' MacKenzie lit his pipe, dropped a spent match into the straw. Extinguished by the damp.

Jenny perked up. If they knew what it was, then they could cure him.

The vet breathed up Brown's nose. 'Had to put it down in the end, it was starving itself from the inside out. You put food in one end, it came straight out the other, just the same.'

Jenny's face, as white as milk.

'If you want,' the older vet put a soft arm around her shoulder. 'I can put your horse down now. Look at him, he's not well, is he? I mean, does he look like he'd get through this? Maybe if he was fitter, had a bit more weight...'

'He's only young,' offered Roger.

'By his teeth, I'd reckon five.'

'He'll die?' Jenny's stomach was pulled into a dog shaped balloon by an invisible magician.

Roger looked uncomfortable. 'Probably. Yes.'

Mad Mac had the equipment in his car, or he could call the knackers if she liked, as then at least she could get money for his meat. Not that he was suggesting she feed bad meat to dogs, of course, but he knew she didn't have insurance, and how else was a struggling student going to pay to get him fixed?

'So is there nothing we can do?' Jenny was annoyed now, angry at herself for buying the horse if it was going to die. She might as well have let the meat-men drag him off in the first place, if they were going to get him now.

'We could try,' Roger offered. 'There's tablets to help decrease movement of the digestive tract, and kaolin to ease his stomach.'

'Expensive and maybe pointless, but...' MacKenzie scratched his nose.

'You could put it on account,' Roger looked hard at Jenny, her pupils widening. 'Pay the bill off in instalments.'

'He likes you!' Mad Mac teased.

'We'll try him for a week, see how it goes.' Roger gave Jenny a hug. She didn't shy away. Sank her head into his shoulder and wished she was asleep, that she had dreamt this. That the brown horse would disappear.

MacKenzie dropped Roger and Jenny off at the nearest pub, and went to visit a yellow labrador called Radar that had managed to get its head stuck down a pipe. The fire brigade were called, but wouldn't go near in case it bit them.

'I'll pick you up in an hour, Roger, okay?' Mad Mac rubbed his plump cherry nose. 'Don't drink too much. We've a heifer at half past two. Don't want you chopping off its bits.'

He also said something about going to the opera dressed as a large yucca plant, but Jenny thought she'd translated that part wrong.

Roger bought her a brandy. She didn't want to drink it, but he made her.

'For the shock,' he said. 'You're looking very pale.'

She downed the drink in one, hands shaking.

'Don't have much luck with horses, do you?' Roger noted.

'I don't have much luck with anything.'

They sat, not knowing what to say. Jenny skimmed round the quiet pub, aware that she had brought some straw in on her boots. She suddenly felt dirty. Smelt of piss, of horsemuck on messy clothes. Maybe she was imagining it. Her senses became more acute in times of stress. Her skin was somehow thinner, more stretched out.

Were people looking at them, her and Roger, thinking they were a couple? Why was she sitting here imagining his tongue inside her mouth, and not the brown horse dying?

He looked so much like Simon. Simon with his mouth on some girl's face, some girl that wasn't her.

'Another?' Roger touched Jenny's glass, his finger curved like a question mark along the side.

She nodded. Grew more brave.

'That woman, at the show... when we... I mean..'

'My wife?' A frown above his brow.

'Yes.'

'She's meant to be my ex-wife, but she won't let me go. Anne... she won't agree to a divorce. Keeps sending the papers back unsigned.'

'She must really love you.'

'Hate, more like.' Roger pulled himself up from the seat, his jeans leaving an impression where he'd been. Warm, leather-look upholstery indented.

As Jenny's gaze trailed the man's lithe body to the bar, she experimented by slowly screwing up her eyes, imagining details. Spotting similarities between him and her Simon. Then she started feeling guilty.

The Savager had claimed another victim. A nine year old mare in a field somewhere near Bramham. Police were following up reports of a Landrover seen parked in the area, but Jenny doubted that would be much of a lead as everyone drove those around there.

He was getting closer. It was upsetting enough that animals were being mutilated or killed, but when the victims were within her local area the fear escalated. Perhaps she should organise a vigil at the stables, take it in turns to stay up there overnight. Maybe call Mr Blonde and take a look at the field where the latest incident occurred. Perhaps they'd find something the police hadn't spotted. All the force seemed to have come up with by now was a guess that this person, presumably male, though Jenny didn't know why they jumped to that conclusion in the first place, maybe had some emotional problems, probably sexual or to do with his mother, and had a deep grudge against horses. If that was the only conclusion they'd arrived at after all this time then Jenny realised that the only way the Savager would be caught was if somebody came forward with information, or if somebody was hiding in a field when the next attack took place. She made a note to herself to buy a sleeping bag so she could start camping out with Brown. It would be great to catch the killer. Might even make the parents proud.

Confrontation

She dreamt again of Bridlington. Hot sand over her body, crushing hard against her chest. As frenzied fingers fought against the grains she realised the substance was slowly changing. No longer seaside solids, but a slide of thickened mud. As she sucked in air to breathe, surrounded by a mass of clinging brown, she realised she was buried underground. In a grave of solid earth.

Jenny woke up gasping. Took a breath. Then another. Heart pumping scared inside her, on the verge of another panic attack. Breathing deeper, long and low, trying to stop herself exploding.

Armadillos could hold their breath for six whole minutes. Jenny could hold her breath longer than anyone she knew, but not for as long as that.

She stared across the room, eyes stinging, ribs sticking hard into her chest. The new horse was going to die. Mister was never coming back, and Simon didn't love her.

Tex lumbered into the classroom. Looked around. The students cowered.

'What's this?' He lifted Marcus's charcoal sketch of a dead body, holding it by the very ends of his stubby fingertips. 'Why does this corpse look so alive? Who is it? Your mother?'

'Yes.' Marcus looked him firmly in the eye.

Tex rocked back on his walking boots, heels bending.

'I drew it last week, before her funeral.'

Tex was uncharacteristically embarrassed. He cleared his throat of phlegm and carried on, inspecting artwork, but keeping quiet. He nodded favourably at Wit's large painting, an apocalyptic vision of the future.

Marcus smiled to himself. He'd made that up. The body was from the local morgue. They had extra human accessories stored away in drawers. He was considering sneaking some fingers out to make a mobile for his room.

Tex reached the desk where Sharon sat, her thin arms resting on a slab of water-colour paper. Covering a weak, insipid painting of two old people, holding wreaths of dying flowers.

'Great stuff,' encouraged Tex, an eager gleam in his eye. He put his palm onto her hand and pressed it firmly.

Sharon burst into tears and rushed outside, slamming the door behind her.

'Time of the month,' Tex teased, shrugging his shoulders. He looked along the corridor but she was gone. He muttered expletives under his breath, then took his place back in the room. Swelled his chest up like a bird and regained control.

Wit watched, rather worried, as Tex went to Jenny's desk. A smug smile on the big man's face as he perused her most recent piece of artwork. A farmyard scene, make out of animal products. Pig shapes made out of bacon, sheep made of wool and old lamb chops, and chicken shapes of glued down feathers with crushed eggshells.

'You can eat chicken,' Jenny's grandad used to say. 'If you have a wing then it isn't meat, it's feathers.'

Tex was staring at her picture. Jenny hoped that he might like it.

'Hey, Horsey... d'you know what you want to do with this?' Tex smiled at her. 'You want to put it on the floor, and jump on it.'

He tossed her picture to the ground, and bounced on it with his size eleven boots. Jenny watched, open-mouthed, as he sprang up and down, meat sticking to his soles and eggshells cracking.

'My office. Ten minutes.'

And with that he left.

An exhale of cigarette breath. 'You're quite an animal lover, aren't you, Horse? You know what they say about that?'

Jenny studied her sock and wondered, if she put one on the left foot and one on the right, and if she did this on a regular basis, would they get a permanent toe stretch at the end so she'd know which one she had been putting on each foot?

'Did you hear the story of Catherine the Great?'

'Sorry?' Jenny glanced up, giving Tex her little orphaned look. The one where the curliest strand of hair on her head lingers innocently over her left eye.

Tex rubbed his tongue against his lip. 'Look it up in a book,' he suggested. 'She was into horses too. Or rather they were into her.'

This man made Jenny feel uncomfortable. Half of the time she didn't have a clue what he was on about, and had a notion that the other half of the time neither did he.

'I'm sorry I've not been here much,' offered Jenny. 'I got this horse, he's sick, he may be dying, but he hasn't got any worse. I have to feed him three small feeds a day, with tablets, so it's all been rather crazy.'

Tex nodded his head. Looked thoughtful. 'What you do in your own time, it's your own business. It should not affect my course.'

'I know. I'm sorry.'

A smile. 'I've killed lots of rabbits, me,' Tex boasted. 'Pellet up the arse and through the mouth. Like they're shitting backwards.' He poked Jenny's papier maché rabbit scene with raised up, stodgy burrows, covered in thick, muddy acrylics. He turned his nose up like it was a moulding rancid nappy. 'No more of this please, it's fucking retarded. No more 'I loved Watership Down, it made me cry and now I want to paint it'. This isn't a course for your old grannies and mad aunties farting about, painting poncey animals every Sunday then selling them at frigging coffee mornings.'

Tex took a big breath and so did she. It was exhausting listening to the man, let alone understanding. He pointed at the office walls, liberally scattered with paintings and sketches, most of which seemed to be exploding bodies or naked, wrenching muscles, along with a colour girlie calendar that was constantly stuck on March because she had the biggest assets.

'Guts,' Tex leaned towards her, impassioned. 'That's what I want to see on my course, Horse. Guts.'

He moved closer, leaving his padded chair to sit beside her on the old scrumpled sofa. Placed his coffee mug on the table to free his hands.

'How long is it now... three weeks to the degree show?' His breath near to her face. 'Now, you might think I'm being cruel, but I'm not. You'll thank me in the end.' Rubbed a sweaty hand on his blue jeans. 'I'm not letting you put up your show.'

'What?'

'If you do, you'll fail. Your stuff's pants. You must know that? It's rubbish. You've done nothing but crap for the whole of this year.'

Jenny's eyes were smarting. Maybe she should have shown him the photographs she'd just brought in to show Marvin? No. He'd take the piss.

'Now, there are two ways around this,' Tex squeezed the girl's arm, a vice around her biceps. 'You can walk away, and leave it, tell yourself that okay, you may have wasted the last three years for nothing, but I bet you've had some fun? Made friends? So it's not a total waste, is it?'

Jenny was getting dizzy, the room contracting round her. The walls were moving closer. The breasts of March loomed nearer.

'Or you can come back again next term, start the third year over, but do some different work. What d'you think?' He smiled at her, saliva crusted in the corner of his mouth. 'But if that's what you want to do, to stay, then you'll have to prove how much you want to. Make me see that you're committed.'

Tex slowly zipped up Jenny's folder, taking his time, staring into her cold eyes as his fingers pulled the metal clasp along.

'Do you get what I'm saying?' He wasn't smiling now. He ran a finger along her frozen chin. Pushed the tip against her pert pursed mouth and forced it through her lips. Pressed hard against the girl's clenched teeth until the pressure made them open. Jenny's throat tensed as the salty flesh rubbed up and down her tongue. She didn't dare to breathe in case she bit him.

He withdrew his finger from her mouth, skimming it slowly down her neck, along the bumps down to a dip above the breast bone. Then he rubbed the wetness off his hand against her top, pushing hard against her petite mounds of breast.

Tex surged from the sofa and carried Jenny's art folder to the door. He placed the handle in her hand, then stood in the way so she had to brush close by him to get out. She felt his eyes following her up the corridor, tracing the line of her bra strap through her shirt. Jenny hurried towards the toilets, and locked herself inside.

The three biggest regrets in Jenny Barker's life:
1. Mister being stolen, and sick Brown being bought.
2. Killing the milkman.
3. Being stupid Jenny Barker.
Tex was going to get her, and her life had turned to shit.

She sat in the thin horse's stable on that Monday afternoon, watching as he nuzzled at some food. He wasn't any fatter, but then at least he wasn't worse. His manure set in runny piles, often a strange shade of green. His urine was thick and milky, which Roger didn't think was very good. He thought the horse was dehydrated.

A shadow in the doorway. She glanced up and saw Wit.

'I thought you might be here.' He looked concerned. 'I tried at your house first.' He lifted up a carrier bag containing a mixed fruit tart. 'What is it with your mum and pies?'

Jenny had to smile.

'He is thin, isn't he?' Wit quietly stepped into the stable. Brown twitched his head up, snorted. 'Do you think he'll be alright?'

'I hope so. I'm not sure really. Maybe.'

'If there's anything I can do....' Wit patted Brown's long neck. The horse sniffed at his knees. 'What happened, with you and Tex? You disappeared. I was worried.'

'Nothing. I don't want to talk about it.' She couldn't. His name made her feel dirty. 'Have you seen Nina? I need to speak to her. I just got her answerphone.'

Wit blushed. 'Um....' He didn't want to say. 'She left college early. I think she was going out. She needed to get ready.'

'Right.' Jenny brushed her coat down, flicked off straw. 'Well I'm off out too, and I'm getting fucking wasted.'

Wit fed the fruit pie to the horse.

Jenny rolled lipstick on her mouth and scrutinised her tense face in the mirror. Her stomach was rolling like a train, thundering as the music thumped below, along with the disembodied voice of some DJ called The Yeti who no one had actually ever seen. Jenny adjusted her short shift dress, pulling her bra straps straight. She tensed her chest so it swelled a little. Bigger boobs. Slightly.

Wit was waiting outside the Ladies, looking sheepish. They walked along the crowded gangway to where a girl was standing behind a counter selling chip butties, with salt and vinegar or curry sauce. They bought a buttie each, though neither of them was hungry. It was comforting holding something in your hand, gave them a sense of purpose. The smell of frying grease and burnt potato fragments wafted through the small hot kitchen, combining with the stench of lager, whisky and urine.

'Have you seen her yet?' asked Jenny, wondering why her friend looked so perplexed. It should be her acting strange this evening, with the sort of day she'd had. She could still taste Tex's skin.

Wit moved closer to her, having to raise his voice so she could hear. The music rising. 'Jenny, about Nina....'

'You what?'

'Nina, well she....'

Jenny smiled. 'D'you fancy her? Shall we have a little talk? I could put a good word in for you.'

'No! Oh just forget it.' He started walking off.

'Wit?' She'd upset him. 'Wit!'

He turned and mouthed something, but she couldn't understand. Jenny sipped some of her vodka. Chilli flavour. Hot. Four more of these and Tex would fade away.

Jenny gazed across the sea of heads and saw Simon walking in towards the cloakroom. Simon, her Simon, he could save her. If she had him, she'd be happy. If she had Simon then the brown horse wouldn't die, Mister would be found at last and Tex would never touch her.

Beams of light cut through the large converted warehouse, lasers above the throbbing mass of dancers. Sweaty bodies shaking to the music, waving arms. Everybody happy. Jenny smiled. She'd talk to him tonight.

Drunk with excitement and much vodka, Jenny hurried down the steps and trailed him to the bar, gulping down the taste of greasy chips as she stood two feet away, waiting for him to twirl around and see her.

She'd speak to him. He'd like her. Everything would be alright.

Three minutes later, a pint of McEwans wedged firmly in his hand, Simon turned and faced her. He threw a smile in her direction.

She'd speak to him. Be braver.

Jenny stepped forward a pace, mouth open. As her eyes caught his she realised he'd not been looking at her, but at someone standing behind. Cold shivers bit her spine as Jenny watched Simon buy Nina a drink. Gin and tonic. He touched her dainty hand as he passed it across. Neither of them had noticed she was there. She was invisible.

Jenny started to shake, her right hand convulsing until Wit appeared and held it tight. He led her away to a chill-out room, where it was only slightly quieter, thanks to linen walls suspended from the ceiling. They sat with a dozen other people, sunk into purple cushions on the floor. Jenny coughed, eyes leaking. Wit wiped her face and chin with his shirt sleeve.

'I tried to tell you,' offered Wit. 'I didn't know what to do.'

Jenny saw shapes forming in the linen, frowning faces, stretched cadavers up on hooks. Her pupils dilated. There were people in the cloth. Laughing at her. And look, there was Jesus, coming off the Turin shroud. White material around him, soft as milk. Spilt milk. Go away, you fucking milkman.

Wit reappeared with an apologetic Nina.

'Jenny, I don't know what to say. It happened. I'm sorry.'

Simon in the background, at a loss as to what was going on. Jenny scrambled up, rushing off, ankles wobbling in stout heels.

'Jenny!'

She ran towards the exit and outside into fresh air, standing a moment to catch her breath. Jenny heard voices, saw Wit and Nina in the doorway. She ran as they moved towards her, heading up the Headrow that cut through the heart of town. She jogged past a couple of newspaper covered winos on a bench near a bank which held much of the Third World's debt.

Jenny slowed to a walk when she saw no one was following. Trying to think what to do next, she started to panic as her last bus had gone hours before. She could hear moaning in her head, soft voices. Her Simon and Nina, making love. Him inside her. Nina. Touching her breasts and kissing those perfect strawberry nipples.

Jenny should have seen this coming. She and Nina had always liked the same things, did everything the same. They had both kissed David Bosco in the coalshed, taken it in turns to have a snog. Jenny rode horses, Nina copied. Jenny became vegetarian, Nina copied. Then Jenny found her with a Big Mac in McDonalds.

Jenny hid near a skip in the multi-storey car park alongside Morrisons. She considered breaking into a car and sleeping in it, but as there were so few cars parked here now she felt sure someone would notice. And anyway, she didn't know how to break in without smashing a window and didn't like to think the owner would lose his no claims bonus. So she hid under some black bin bags and a large sign advertising the goodness of fruit flavoured yoghurts.

Conversation

Mist lifted from the dark silhouette of the Leeds skyline, cold dawning air wafting over the toy town of tower blocks and high-rise offices. Pigeons took off and landed again, shitting in appropriate places. A one legged bird hopped repeatedly round a litter bin, as if chasing its missing leg that was bound to be hiding around the other side.

A small lone shape, swathed with remnants of clinging dust, stood in front of the town hall, where imposing stairs led up to bolted doors. Come wintertime, blackcloaked students would perch crow-like on the balconies inside, waiting to take their walk down to the front, to shake a hand, to step away. Then to patter outside in slipping mortarboards while their families took proud photographs of flimsy pieces of paper that signified degrees.

Jenny ran her hand over the cool jowls of one of the stone lions that was standing guard outside, sadly kissing the end of its nose, avoiding trails of bird pollution which striped the noble head. A lion with a tiger's coat. A bit like her friends, that. Supposed to be one thing, when really they're another.

The lion's face was rotting, ears worn away by weather and eyes melted down to caverns of cold concrete, rainwater tears stagnating in the dip. Jenny walked to the next lion, it was the same but different. He had eyes but not a nose, a flat face of tired stone. His muzzle fell away to nothing. Clenched paws losing definition, losing pride. From the side he was quite ugly.

No horse. No Simon. No degree.

Jenny turned and faced the empty newsagents across the quiet street, boarded up windows defying hopes of food. She was so hungry. She had almost been tempted to eat this stray ham sandwich she'd found in a bin.

'You can eat ham,' Grandad had said. 'If you slice ham thin enough it isn't meat.'

Jenny started to weep, dry tears cutting her throat like

thistles.

'I wish I was a lion.' Jenny rubbed the solid mane, her knuckles bruising. 'I wish I could sit with you all day and do nothing, be nothing. It wouldn't hurt then, would it? Not if I couldn't feel.'

'It hurts to feel nothing.'

Jenny whipped round to see who had just spoken. Nobody there. Only her and the lions.

'Feed your heart to feed your soul.'

'What?' Jenny ran over to the other lion, the one that had a mouth. 'What did you say?'

The stone statue kept silent. Staring. Scaring her. Jenny's head was spinning as she ran off up the road, words echoing loudly, voice rising in strength the further away she got from the calm carved predators.

'Search and you shall find. Hunger and you shall find the food of Christ the Lord.'

Jenny stopped dead in her tracks, shocked. This was some kind of miracle. There was a God, and He was put here especially for her.

She bent down to pick God's gifts up from the pavement. Two packets, and both were cheese and onion, which was definitely a sign. He even knew her favourite flavour, which must show that He listens and watches and doesn't just appear to people whose palms bleed in the centre. She'd never believed the nuns until this moment.

Jenny started to laugh at her own logic. How was she going to tell old Father Flanagan that he should be giving out Walkers crisps to his communicants instead of the traditional wafer hosts? This way people could even choose what Jesus tasted like.

On her way back to the lions Jenny passed a small, crumbling man who smelt of mints and wore a coat so huge and stiff it was walking on its own. He asked her for some money, so she gave him a pound coin. Then she gave him a crisp as he had a Bible in his hand and she thought he'd like communion. As she walked away his voice trailed after her, too faint for Jenny to give it much attention.

'Give and you shall receive. Thanks for the crisp, love. God will feed you carbohydrates galore when you reach the Promised Land.'

Jenny hung around outside college, skulking beside the workmen's skip by the Entertainments Hall, diving out of sight when early morning pedestrians trailed past. She smelt of dried-up sweat and overripe bananas, along with a strong scent of disappointment. Gone was the thrill she used to feel when she would wait for a glimpse of Simon, ready to dash into the lift.

She saw the porter unlock the glass door at the front, the entrance to the tower of glass eyes. When the man went back inside to get his coffee, she ran up the ramp towards the building and spun through the fast revolving doors.

Jenny's heart pulsed as the lift strained upwards. The door pinged open on the seventh floor. She feared Tex but found a cleaner. Took a breath.

The top floor was deserted.

Jenny paced down the corridor, her reflection in a framed painting making her lurch away in fear. Fluorescent light bulbs fizzed as the electricity surged on. Her heels against linoleum, tip tap. Tip tapping.

Tex was the troll under the bridge.

Tip tapping. Tip tapping.

He wasn't here, but she could sense him. His finger wedged inside her mouth. Tap. Tap.

She entered the classroom, went to her desk. Instinct made her flip the lid up. No chocolate inside. A blunt pencil, a broken ruler. Nothing much.

She checked her drawer in the corner, the third one down in a sturdy set of six. Brass padlock firm against it. Damn. She'd left her key at home, in her toolbox, on the floor.

Tip tapping.

Jenny walked towards the sink. Washed her hands clean in cold water, splashed some freshness on her face and started thinking. She had to get her work out of that drawer, all her things, then she could leave.

Down the stairs to the fifth floor.

Tip tapping.

She found a hammer in the sculpture workshop, welded against a table by a melted piece of pot. A splattered person straining from the clay, arms stretched far too long, turned into elephant trunks by some musing student's boredom.

Tip tapping.

Back to the quiet classroom, to the noisy hammer banging against the padlock. Smack. Brass shining, leaping out of the way. Smack, against the lock. Jenny's fingers tight round the wooden handle, nails digging hard into her skin. Indents of white smiles where her fingers pressed the flesh. Against the lock, again, against. Jumping, trying to be free from the ferocious strikes. Jenny's anger rose with every blow.

The nasty troll under the bridge.

Strike! The metal hook bent against the lock, closing like an eyelid. It wasn't going to give. Jenny sighed, deflated.

A shadow in the doorway.

'Hey, you're early.' Her tutor, quite surprised.

Jenny nodded, faint.

'What are you up to? What's with the hammer?'

Her face flushed, hot eyes stinging. 'I haven't got my key.'

Marvin walked towards her, looked at the stack of drawers. 'Why don't you make things easy for yourself and just slide the top one out? That's got no locks on, has it?'

With an ease reserved for grown-ups the man widened his arms, placed one hand on each of the handles of the drawer above. He pulled it out slowly, almost reverentially, like an undertaker lifting a child's coffin from his hearse. He waddled to the nearest table and set it down.

Jenny reached her hand in through the gap and started

pulling contents from her liberated drawer. A photo fluttered to the floor. Marvin retrieved it, nosy.

'Is this one of your horse prints? Wow. So, at last, you brought them in?'

Jenny meekly passed some out. Shots of horses under railway bridges, stark black and white images at suspect sales. Old men with pipes and wet tweed hats, handing over dirty money. Horses being hit with sticks. Tied to lamp posts on street corners, jerking round while fast traffic blurred by. Gypsies on horseback at Appleby Fair, boys trotting up roads on shaggy ponies, bored cars delayed behind. A river of bobbing silhouettes, jet-black hippos of horses in the water, splashing froth.

'This stuff is amazing! I never knew... The Savager, he was on the news before. Dreadful, isn't it? I mean, I'm not a horsey person, but that's just sick. That's a sick person out there.'

A horse serial killer, probably had brain damage. Nobody understood.

Marvin flicked through her notebook, eyes scanning dates and places, staring at obscure photographs, sketches of the equine disappeared. Photocopied cuttings of the Savager. 'You've really captured something with those photos, and this imagery... it's great. Very powerful.'

He scanned through sheets of notes, of hunted horses. Sketches of animal heads, like blazing wanted posters.

March 19th. A dapple grey in Liverpool. His teeth proved him seven years too old.

March 28th. White horse sighted by the M62. In a field under the motorway bridge, with several bay ponies. White horse was not on the missing list, but a 13.2hh bay gelding was identified as Sean, belonging to Mr James Renn from Tadcaster. Successfully returned.

Marvin skipped further down, turning pages full of dates and places, newspaper cuttings and advertisements.

'You've found your theme,' he smiled. 'A quest for truth,

seeking a resolution. Now this is saying something.'

Jenny nodded and said nothing. She placed her work inside a makeshift folder of thickened card, and walked out of the building. She headed home, dress drooping. No one would sit next to her on the bus.

Jenny found Nina on the front step in a comfortable lotus position, strain on her face showing that it wasn't that relaxing a pose to be held in after all. Hiding her shame under a familiar leopard skin hat. Her face was ashen, shadows under her eyes from lack of sleep. She'd been crying.

'Can we talk, Jen? Please?'

She reached for Jenny's hand and was quietly levered up, standing in silence while her friend unlocked the door.

There were two messages on the answerphone. One from a concerned Wit, checking Jenny got home safely, and another from Roger Mandrake. He would visit Brown on Thursday and bring him some more tablets.

Jenny balked. She had forgotten to feed her horse. Irresponsible.

'I can't talk now,' she panicked. 'I need to get to Deacon's.'

'I'll come with you.' Nina's eyes were pleading.

Jenny changed into her stables clothes while Nina sulked around the bedroom, acting as if it should be herself who was upset. She picked up a framed photograph of her and Jenny as children, wearing matching clothes and smiles.

'Everything the same,' she noted. Jenny shrugged.

They hiked the mile to the stables, its trail so familiar to Jenny's boots that they could walk there by themselves. It was twelve years since her first visit, as a shy ten year old with three pairs of socks inside borrowed wellingtons, which still fell off if she ran.

Jenny was treated the same as herds of pony crazy kids, until an incident when she was fifteen, when the hay barn had caught fire. Boys smoking, or something. Soft whispers of flame, tickling crispy bales, and nobody around to notice. Horses were choking in the stable block behind as fumes seeped through the walls. Jenny arrived straight from school, found the stables burning, and without a thought raced inside. She held her breath in hard against the smoke and undid the bolted doors, waving her arms until the horses ran outside. One of them, a liver chestnut beast called Plaslow, reared up and kicked the side of Jenny's head. She fell unconscious outside, with hooves stamping around her, then woke to the sight of the fire brigade and Tom Deacon's ashen face.

Jenny never had to pay for a riding lesson again after that day. She spent the summer helping Tom to build a new line of breeze block stables, behind the gutted barn. The last one along was hers, for free. A home for her and Mister.

Brown's head drooped over the stable door, flies spinning around his face. An eyelash flicked them repeatedly away, but they shot back, undeterred.

'He's looking a bit better,' Nina lied, examining his ribs. The horse's coat was less matted, gaining a shine, but his bones protruded through. Maybe his rump had got more fleshy, with triangles of muscle looming tight against the skin.

Jenny filled the horse's bucket from a nearby tap, and watched him take a drink. She felt Nina hovering at her shoulder as she wrenched open the feed room door and walked towards her bins. Brown's bucket stood on a bench beside the feed bins, with a small note inside, signed by a wobbly, happy face. The horse had already had his breakfast, plus two tablets.

Jenny sighed, less guilty, and mixed him up a small feed anyway. Little and often, that was the key. Too much food would squirt straight through and come out the other end.

'About Simon,' Nina sighed. 'I don't know what to say.'

'Don't say anything then.' Jenny grabbed the bucket, scooped some feed.

'I didn't realise that you liked him so much, and when I did... I was trying not to hurt you.'

'Thanks a lot.' Jenny hit the horsefeed with a spoon.

'No! I mean it. That's why I kept it secret.' Nina frowned. 'I thought, I don't know, that maybe you'd have gone off him by the time you found out. That he was a silly phase, and you'd forget him.'

'How long?'

'What? Me and Simon?' Nina blushed. 'Six months, nearly. It wasn't supposed to be deceit, just secret.' She was genuinely upset. 'I'm sorry. I really am. I don't want us to fall out about this. You mean the world to me.'

'I noticed.' Jenny jerked the bucket up and strode outside towards her stable.

'Listen!' Nina chased out after her. 'We can fix this. I can fix this! Just tell me what you want me to do.'

Jenny halted, bucket adhered to her hot hand. The thin horse wheezing in anticipation as he spotted the mottled feed.

'What I want...' Jenny breathed out, exhausted. 'Is for this horse not to die, for there to be some miracle so I can get my Mister back, for Tex to be hit by a fucking truck so I can get my degree, and for Simon to love me like I love him. That's all. That's enough.'

She pushed past the eager horse into the stable, his nuzzle pressing the bucket, propelling it hard against her stomach. As soon as the food was tipped into the trough, his rubber lips bounced around it, grains of barley grinding against keen teeth.

Nina rested against the stable door. 'What d'you mean about Tex? Have you had words with Sharon?'

'Eh? What's Sharon got to do with it? He won't kick her off too. Not now she's his special student. He always likes her work. It's crap.'

'Jenny?'

'I don't want to talk about it, okay?' Jenny grabbed a pitchfork from the yard and started flicking through her horse's straw, spilling wet muck into a barrow. 'Simon likes you, I understand because you're great. I just wish he'd liked me too.'

'I'm sure if he'd got to know you, Jen, he'd have been mad about you. I wouldn't have stood a chance.'

Jenny perked up. 'Really?'

Kissing David Bosco in the coal shed. Puckered lips, no tongue.

Adoration

Dear Agony Aunt,

My best friend is letting me go out on a proper date with her boyfriend. Do you think this is acceptable, bearing in mind the fact that he is the man I love? We have always shared things before, myself and Nina, but does this mean he is my boyfriend, or Nina's, or both?

Jenny B from Leeds

Dear Jenny,

Who cares? Go for it. And don't forget the condoms. Slut.

Jenny looked out of her bedroom window, having succumbed to so much sleep she wondered if she'd been in a coma after breathing in too long. There were two people in the garden. Unfamiliar, unfamily people. A man and a woman, with a map. Maybe they were tourists.

The couple were no longer there when she went down to get her breakfast. They probably came to the wrong house. She thought she'd come to the wrong house nearly every time she came home. Was it just her, or were everyone's parents weird?

'Mum, there were some people in the garden.'

'That's nice dear.' Mary Barker passed the cornflakes, unconcerned.

'I'm not going back to college. It's all over.'

Her mother poured another cup of tea. 'Nice boy, that Wit. Polite.'

'I said, I'm never going back to college.'

Ray peered over his newspaper, the sporting section.

'Course you are, love. Don't be silly.' Mary's teaspoon chimed against her cup, mixing in two Sweetex, plus two sugars. 'Oh, I hope he liked his pies. Did you get that fertiliser, Raymond?'

His eyes swum round behind thick glasses.

'Fertiliser, fertiliser! You keep going on, don't you? Fertiliser.

You're a minx, woman. A minx. And you!' He looked over at Jenny. 'You'd best get your degree, you've worked bloody hard for it. God knows... you can't just walk away from things. You might want to, but you can't. Responsibility, young lady. That's what this world's about.'

Ray lurched up from his chair, glaring across the table as he retrieved his leather briefcase from underneath the sleeping cat. Teddy yawned, breath stinking, and padded his paws in discontent before replacing himself on a mat alongside the cereals. Ray hastily left for work.

'For the garden,' Mary smiled. 'Fertiliser.'

Jenny had wanted to ask her mother for advice about the Simon problem, but wasn't sure what she should say. They didn't go in much for meaningful conversations, talks on what they really felt. And as for sexual things... when it came to her mum explaining periods she'd simply left a two line note and a pile of panty pads on her bed. Jenny used a couple to stuff her bra.

She scanned the newspaper, disturbed to find another horse attack within a ten mile radius. Then she went to check on Brown.

Jenny had a shower when she returned home from the stables. She rubbed her skin hard with a loofah, smearing moisturiser on her body until it was silky smooth. A thought. What if things progressed with her and Simon? What if he fell for her immediately, instant lust, and wanted to make big love? Hot water bit against her from the shower head, yet she felt icy cold.

The house was empty, the parents both at work. Her mother at the Argos store in Leeds, where customers kept stealing the small blue pens, whilst her dad would sternly oversee events at the local bottle factory. The pair worked hard then took holidays, worked hard then took holidays, worked hard and then bought velvet curtains. Dad changed his car every other year, same make, same colour, while Jenny's mum never changed her car at all.

Jenny searched through her wardrobe for suitable clothes. A dress? Too fancy, far too much. Not leggings, too low key. But her favourite jeans would do, the black ones, with a flattering, close cut top. Not too close, she didn't want him to see the outline of her bra, that would be a touch too inviting.

She sat downstairs in the lounge, watching the clock count down towards the time that they would meet. Outside the Odeon cinema, six o'clock. Jenny raided the drinks cabinet, mixing Cointreau with whatever was the nearest or the strongest. She sat in her father's leather-look chair and tried to feel less cold and worried. Goosebumps wrote white Braille across her arms, words to encourage caution. Warning alarms rang gassy bells inside her stomach, excitement, nerves and fear. She was going to see Simon, her Simon, nearly her Simon. She would have a proper conversation, and they would fall madly in love.

Jenny arrived at the cinema at halfpast five. She checked her hair in the door's reflection, but the wind kept snatching it up like a giant wing. As she watched laden shoppers and homebound workers trail their way along the Headrow, she wondered how many of them could tell that she was going on a date? She wasn't standing here alone because she had no friends or nothing else to do, but because the most important moment of her life, ever, was about to take place, now. She started feeling sick. Maybe she should have eaten a snack before she got the bus to town. Her stomach growled for intake, while giggling glugs of alcohol danced about clapping hands.

Jenny's wrist grew tired from flicking quick views of her watch. The hands were creeping slowly, bored. Simon appeared at four minutes past six, jacket laid across his shoulder, tight white T-shirt tense against his muscled frame. Every inch of him a model of perfection.

'Jenny?' He politely held out his hand. She didn't know whether to shake it or give him her rucksack or coat, so smiled and gave him a quick tap on the knuckles while making a clicking noise with her tongue. Simon looked at her for a moment, no expression, then opened the door into the building. Jenny inhaled as she walked underneath his arm.

'I'll get these, my treat.' Simon bought the tickets, showing his student union card to get a discount. Jenny made an excuse, ran to the toilet. Stomach churning, make-up retouched, her hair landed back on Earth.

They sat in the mouths of scarlet seats in front of the biggest screen. Jenny's stomach lurched throughout the trailers. Digital sound surrounded vibrating eardrums and quaking heart. Her eyes couldn't focus on the credits, as each time she read the letter *S* or *I* or *M* she'd think of Simon, sitting next to her, arms touching, tingling, and him being so close. Her heartbeat was so loud she could no longer hear the words the actors said, only Simon's words, his breath.

'I'll get these, my treat.'

Repeating in her eardrums. He bought the tickets, that meant he really liked her.

She edged her fingers towards the popcorn bucket resting on his firm knee in between them. Digits touched as they reached for fresh popped corn. Sugar tickling her fingertips, her throat. She couldn't swallow, coughed, felt embarrassed for making a noise during a dramatic moment. Simon passed her his large carton of coca cola and she supped, tasting the plastic straw, knowing his mouth had been there too. She squinted her eyes to look at him, trying not to let him notice as she sucked his image onto her keen retinas. He was staring straight towards the screen, not moving, except the gradual rise and fall of his expanding, soft-breath chest. Brows curved above his eyes, intense and thoughtful. His right foot pressing against the back of the seat in front, having to sit slightly sideways as his legs were too long to fit into the normal gap, and he was far too polite to lift his legs over the seat.

Jenny picked at popcorn, trying to stop her stomach from

making bubbling noises. She couldn't focus on the film, it was such an effort to sit still, to keep her heart rate down, to not burp, to be adult.

End credits rolled and the lights gradually came up. Punters left behind them sweet wrappers and crushed cartons kicked discreetly under seats, waiting for the bin bag boy to find where they'd been hidden. Jenny followed Simon to the foyer. He excused himself, went to the toilets, and so did she.

'Fancy getting a bite to eat?' Simon returned, putting his coat on.

Jenny nodded, starving. 'I haven't got much money.' The brown horse ate all of that, what with his feed and expanding vet's bills. 'I could just do with a snack.' Her stomach singing.

Simon escorted Jenny across the road, avoiding lazy buses that paused by traffic lights. They walked past the shimmering entrance of Harvey Nichols, elongated mannequins draped in designer clothes, jewels hanging off their chiselled frames. Simon gave two pounds to a receding woman in a doorway, quietly bedded down underneath her cardboard sheets. He shielded Jenny from cars as they progressed, him walking nearest the road, taking her hand each time they reached the kerb, as if she was his special precious child.

'This means something,' Jenny thought. 'It means that he'll protect me.'

All this time that she had fancied him, she'd never known he was so kind.

They nestled in a corner of McDonalds, staring across two portions of fries, a Big Mac and a beanburger. Cover versions by a cheap George Michael sound-a-like playing repeatedly in the background.

'You like horses then? Nina said you two used to ride a lot together.'

'Yes.' Jenny chewed another chip. She liked how Simon's sentences rose up when they reached the end. It was because he'd been in Australia. Picked watermelons, got a tan.

Simon sucked chocolate shake up through his straw, attentive.

'And you have a horse yourself? Don't you?' Fourlegged beasts were not his forte. He'd ridden a camel once at Whipsnade but the smell seeped through its saddle and hung in a cloud around his face. When he got off it spat at him and then shat on his shoes.

'Yes. He's called Brown.'

'Nina said.'

Nina had said a lot of things.

'My horse is sick, not a disease... you can't catch it.' She didn't want to put him off. 'I have to try to make him fatter. He's too thin.'

'A bit like your friend Sharon? The anorexic.' Simon looked concerned, his eyebrows moving closer.

'She's not anorexic.' Jenny paused, pushed her beanburger around its tray. 'Is she? I know she's skinny. She used to be dead fat, blubber legs.' She blushed, felt bitchy. 'She's been on a right strict diet.'

Simon was not convinced. Jenny found it very telling that he showed an interest in her friends. He cared about her. Simon ripped open a sachet of salt and poured it onto the side of his tray. He flicked at the white granules, then casually tossed some over his left shoulder. The woman on the table behind was not impressed, and gave him an unnoticed filthy look as she spooned particles off her drink.

'What are the plans for after your degree?' Simon pursued a new line of enquiry. 'Have you got anything lined up? Work? A holiday?'

'I dunno... I think Nina will go work down in London. In design. Advertising, probably.' Jenny put her hand in front of her mouth as she chewed, she didn't want to appear messy.

'I'm asking about you, not Nina.'

Jenny blushed. 'I'd like to go on holiday. Somewhere different, get away from things.' Escape.

Simon's face lit up. 'Have you ever been to Italy? It's beautiful. I so love Rome, and Florence. The whole place, it's magical, the sunlight, old buildings, the people....' His voice trailed off. A smile. 'You should go. You'd adore it.'

Then he told her about the person he had loved, an Italian, with long black hair, deep olive eyes and a Mediterranean tan. Her name was Ornella, she was exquisite and quite beautiful. She'd cheated on him though, and got engaged to some Italian.

'Foreigners,' groaned Simon. 'They always stick together.' He cleared his throat. 'Anyway, that's finished now. I'm over her, I've moved on to other things.' Sad-faced, he suddenly looked rather tired.

'That's like with James Dean!' Jenny gushed, feeling as though she understood. 'He fell in love with this Italian actress, Pier Angeli. But her parents thought she was too good for him, this scruffy non-Catholic guy.'

'Did they stay together?' Simon perked up a little.

'Well, no, she married an Italian, Vic Damone, in the same church as she should have married him. She was pregnant.'

'With James Dean's kid? Yet she married this other Vic? Bitch.'

'No,' Jenny recycled facts inside her head. 'She was pregnant to Vic Damone, not James, they'd already broken up.'

'Bloody parents, what do they know?' Simon drummed his fingers on the table top, annoyed. 'They know nothing. They should let their kids marry who they want to. Fucking Catholics.'

'Exactly.' Jenny nodded, keeping quiet about being one of those herself. Poor James Dean. Pier's marriage only lasted for five years, but by the time it ended Jimmy Dean was dead. Pier said his ghost had wrecked her marriage. He was the only man she ever loved, right up until her fatal overdose. Sad that, to love someone forever and not be able to get them back.

Simon had abandoned his Big Mac. 'I could do with a drink,' he mumbled. 'What d'you reckon?'

They headed up to the Dry Dock, a novelty pub that was an

actual boat set in a concrete sea between two roads. They sat at the stern end, supping flamboyant cocktails and oddly flavoured vodkas. Conversation had decreased.

'Should James Dean have challenged him, stood up to her folks?' Simon wondered, sipping tequila. 'Maybe that other guy really loved her, things could have been good.'

'It wasn't, they divorced. She should have married James. True love.'

'True love.' Simon downed his drink in a scorching toast.

'And if James Dean had married her, he'd have been too busy having a lovely life to get killed in that Porsche. They'd have had kids, lots of Jimmies.'

'He wouldn't have been a legend then,' Simon mused, supping water. 'That's just because he died.'

Jenny poked her finger into the petite glass, catching the last dregs of milky Mars Bar vodka on her nail. 'I'm sure he'd rather have been in love than been a legend. If you love someone, you should be with them. It's not fair for things to stop you.'

Simon reached out and touched her cheek, held it softly in his hand, regarding her a moment before leaning closer for a kiss. His lips firm against hers, the taste of salt and chocolate.

'Thank you, Jenny,' he smiled. 'For a lovely evening. You're a breath of fresh air in an overcomplicated world. You make things seem so simple.'

Jenny shrugged, not actually knowing what he meant, but hoping that he didn't think that she was stupid. He gave her another kiss goodnight by the bus stop, then waved and walked away. As she followed the outline of his form walking off towards the deserted university, she realised that she'd missed her last bus home. She stood there, awkward, eyes peering into the distance, hoping Simon would turn around and wave. He'd see her there, abandoned, come back and scoop her up.

He kept walking, hands in his pockets. Disappeared.

Jenny dialled Nina's number on her mobile. What should she say? Tell her how well the evening went, that maybe Simon loved her? Or play it down a little, then scrounge a spare bed for the night?

Nina's answermachine clicked on. Jenny didn't leave a message. She walked towards the cricket ground near Wit's, wind biting her ears but still not caring. Eyes stinging with joy. Her heart was happy now. He loved her.

Wit opened his door, bewildered by the sight of Jenny on his front step.

'I had a date!' she gleamed. 'With Simon. I missed my bus.'

'So you should have stayed at his.' Wit was grumpy, pulled too quickly from his bed. 'I don't know why you bothered coming here. Was it to boast about your conquest? To tell me what you got up to with your man?'

'I missed my bus.' She always did, she should have brought the car.

'Come on then,' Wit escorted her inside, past two bicycles in the hallway and up the slender stairs towards his room. The cheeseplant in the corner had long since died.

'I'll take the sofa,' offered Wit, putting a coat on over his pyjama bottoms. He started beating the cushions flatter, then laid down.

'Don't you have another duvet?' Jenny worried. 'You'll get cold.'

'Yeah, well....' He couldn't look at her.

'I can't kick you out of your bed, that isn't fair.'

'Life isn't fair,' Wit noted. Curled his toes up on the armrest, made them stand in line like soldiers.

'We can both sleep in your bed,' Jenny pulled at Wit's arm. 'Unless you've an objection?'

Wit was silent. He gruffly rose from the worn taupe sofa and led Jenny towards his room. They settled underneath his bulky duvet, staring at the ceiling, impersonating sheep.

When Jenny rolled over to get some sleep she found herself hit with some strange instinct that made her want to turn back and give Wit a big kiss. No reason. She just felt like it.

Vodka rising.

As Jenny tried to fall asleep she wondered who the first person was that invented kissing. Was it Adam and Eve or was that later? Did God ever kiss anyone, or did he even have a mouth?

Jenny started to giggle, feeling warm. She peeled her top off, hoping Wit wouldn't object too much to having naked flesh beside him. She wondered if people ever made love when they were sleeping. What if she and Wit were hard at it in the night, and when they woke up they never knew? Would she still technically be a virgin? Would Simon feel betrayed?

Wit lay still in the hot bed, eyes boring holes into the ceiling. Jenny's breath close by his neck.

Visitation

'You won't forget to feed the cat? And make sure he doesn't go out. I don't want him running off and looking for me.' Mary Barker was concerned. 'And his litter tray needs....'

'I know, I know, I'll clean it out. Don't worry, he'll be fine.'

Jenny passed her mother a beige suitcase.

'And go visit your grandad, will you? Just check that he's okay.'

'Alright, Mum.'

She waved politely as the parents drove away. Bye-bye Mummy. Bye-bye Daddy. Thank God. Now the grown-ups were away she could fulfil her thwarted destiny and become a real adult herself. Simon was coming round this evening. She was cooking him a meal, spaghetti, so who knows what could happen.

The doorbell rang. What had her mother forgotten now?

'Hello Jenny.' It was Nina on the step. She wasn't smiling. 'Can we talk?'

Had Simon told her something? Jenny panicked.

'I'm sorry, Nina. I'm off out.' Quick thought. 'I've got to see my grandad.'

Nina couldn't be shaken off, she followed Jenny to the residential home. They crunched across the gravel towards the sprawling building. Pieces of extra house were built onto the main block, sprouts of brick extensions growing from the oldest part. Each new wing a varied colour, different shades, but containing residents who were uniformly grey. The first time Jenny visited she'd found three empty whisky bottles on the grass. She'd thought they were dropped there by drunken passers-by, until she realised residents had managed to sneak them in, later tossing incriminating alcoholic evidence outside. Not so many bottles now, as most of the windows were sealed shut, since that incident when Mr Kiraljee tried to fly.

'You don't really want to come in, do you?' Jenny queried. 'It isn't very nice.'

'I like your grandad.' Nina had made her mind up.

'He's mad.'

'I know, that's why I like him.'

Jenny sulked. She'd hoped Nina would go off the idea, so she'd not have to see this through. She hated visiting her grandad, seeing what he'd turned into. He always smelt of piss.

The wide-faced matron smiled as they went in. She looked like an over-inflated girl guide, her navy uniform dotted with patchwork badges, souvenirs of where she'd been. Her thick black belt tugged hard against her waist, almost cutting her in half, bending her body like a giant egg timer. She nodded in recognition at the sight of Jenny, and pointed to a red book on the corner table, reminding her that she should sign. The staff liked physical evidence of visitors who'd been, so they could convince the Alzheimer's club that such an event had taken place.

Nina followed Jenny down the magnolia-coated hall towards the lounge.

'Have you spoken to Simon?' At last Nina raised the question. 'I've been ringing him, but there's no answer.'

'He's probably out,' sniffed Jenny. 'It's Saturday. He's maybe doing some shopping.'

Nina wasn't happy. 'He was meant to come and see me.'

'When?' A moment's worry. He'd be at Jenny's house this evening.

'Last night, he never showed.'

'Maybe he forgot,' offered Jenny, happy in a guilty kind of way, hoping that Simon had stood Nina up because he wanted to focus his romantic energies on her. They'd connected, herself and Simon. She could tell.

'What did you talk about?' quizzed Nina. 'Did he say much about me?'

Jenny didn't want to answer. She increased her stride a pace.

'Did he mention that bitch Ornella? The one that screwed him up?'

Jenny wasn't listening. She turned left into the lounge.

Grandad was suctioned to a patterned comfy chair in the corner of the room. Staring out past rows of quiet residents towards cartoons on the television, sound permanently turned down. Like his comrades, he was wearing extra jumpers, a woolly and a cardigan in layers over his shirt. His hands were freezing cold.

'Hello!' Jenny fixed a smile on. 'How are you, Grandad? Alright?'

He grinned with crocodile dentures which clicked against his mouth. He promptly tried to smarten himself up, patting the strands of white that stretched across his head like sieved spaghetti. He was happy to have some company.

'Who is this?' He studied Nina. 'Are you a friend of mine?'

Nina smiled. 'I'm Nina, a friend of Jenny's, remember? I stayed at your old house when we were small.'

'My house!' He nodded. 'It needs a dust. Dirty, dirty! All that dust.'

Jenny pulled up a chair beside him. 'Don't worry about that, it's fine.'

'Will you clean it for me? Sweep the floor?'

Jenny cleared her throat, agreeing, even though the house was no longer his. It had long since been sold off to pay the home his fees.

'You're a grand lass, Mary. We couldn't have asked for a better daughter. It's a shame your mother never got to see you grow.' His eyes were tearful. 'I do miss Lottie, I do. I dream about her.'

Nina looked embarrassed. She started playing with the leaves of a nearby plant. It wasn't real, some sort of plastic.

'Grandad, I'm not Mary. That's my mum. I'm Jenny...'

'Jenny!' The old man's eyes lit up behind his cataracts. 'How is she? Can she visit? Will you ask her, will she come? Can she have a day off school?' He started rocking in excitement, thin knees knocking.

'Yes... of course.' Jenny didn't know quite what to say.

They sat for a while and talked about caravans and ice creams and holidays that they had enjoyed years ago, Jenny starting to become more used to talking about herself in the third person. Yes, it was lovely when they took Jenny up in that big hot air balloon, and oh, didn't she squeal like a cooked pig when they first plonked her on a donkey? How he wished she'd come and visit.

'But you're....' Nina tried to intercede. A look from Jenny stopped her. She wanted Grandad to be happy. Who cared if his memories were real or not, if they cheered him up a little? Glimmers of her old grandad shone through, that quiet man who could lift her on his shoulders, carry her up hills and make her laugh. Give her cocoa at bedtime. With two round rich tea biscuits.

She'd stayed at his house for weeks when she was six, because her mother wasn't well. The doctors called it nerves. Jenny's mum was always crying, so sad it was like someone had died.

'Mary, love?' Grandad leaned closer to her. 'Are you still seeing that chap? Your fancy man?'

'Uuuum....' Jenny looked across at Nina for advice.

'Don't let your husband know,' he chuckled. 'You naughty little monkey! Have you seen my dog? Where's Chipper?'

He'd been dead for twenty years. His yellow Labrador corpse planted in the back garden of the old house. Daffodils growing above it.

'Can you take him for a walk?' Grandad tapped his leg, expecting the dog to come.

'Ta-ra Grandad.' Jenny kissed his wrinkled cheek, catching the taste of Brylcreem from his remaining hair. 'Take care.'

He waved as Jenny and Nina walked away.

'My daughter, that,' he boasted. No one was listening.

Jenny took Laddie the dog out for a walk when she got back. Went up to the stables and checked on the skinny Brown. She decided to inspect her bank balance and consider calling Roger out for another visit, as the horse appeared a little low and lifeless. Laddie chased some kittens around the yard so Jenny took him home. She could not find her mother's cat. He was probably wedged under a wardrobe somewhere upstairs, having a sulk.

Jenny couldn't keep still. She tried relaxing on the sofa, but all she could think of was spaghetti, and how it was too early to cook it, it might be boring, Simon might not like it, and he might not like her.

What if he kissed her again? Did more than that? What if tonight they had sex? Was it too much of a rush? She'd loved him for a year... but could she do it? Do that?

Warning alarms rang gassy bells inside her stomach, chiming that she was in danger. In danger of being touched, or having sex, or both. She started feeling sickly, and thought perhaps it would be easier if she had sex after having lots to drink, as she might not notice it as much, or feel so strange and silly. And scared. She was feeling very scared.

She wanted to talk to Nina, to ask for some advice, but that didn't seem quite right. She wished the parents had given her a lecture about the birds and the bees instead of cats and dogs.

When Simon came here, if they did the sex thing, could she bear to let him see her naked? Would she have to be? She'd always been so embarrassed in life drawing classes, sketching the naked women earning five pounds for an hour, never able to lift her eyes up off her virginal sheet of paper in case she witnessed naked flesh. And Tex would tease her. Bastard. Bastard troll.

Jenny tried to calm herself down with Chris Isaak and two inches of sweet sherry. She hummed along to the tune of *Voodoo* while drawing a rapid sketch of Tex, complete with sweaty baseball cap. She got her Stanley knife out and cut bits off him, taking great relish in slicing off his malevolent right hand. She scribbled over his face in fluorescent marker pen and hoped he'd suffer a slow and painful death or nasty accident within the next five years. Her curse was set. Now time to cook spaghetti.

Three hours later Jenny sat watching candles burn on the expectant dining room table. Sauces boiling in hot pans, bubbling with eager flavour, spitting red. Sixty minutes on, the candles were charred stumps, the sauce was glue, spaghetti string, and Simon hadn't surfaced.

Jenny rang his number. No reply. She kept pressing the redial button, until her thumb was numb with use. She went to bed but didn't sleep. The radiators made gasping, groaning noises, because they knew she was alone.

Jenny tried Simon's number the next morning, but kept getting a whining noise, like the phone was disconnected. Maybe he hadn't paid his bill. Perhaps he had run out of money, and that's why he didn't make it there last night, as he had no bus fare?

Jenny drove her mum's old car to Simon's flat. She parked at a strange angle with the car's arse protruding in the road, and climbed up the stairs to ring the bell.

'What is it?' A scrawny lad peeped through the doorway, organic stubble on his chin.

'Is Simon in?' Jenny's heart raced, worried.

'Erm... Simon!' He shouted, no reply. 'I don't know where he is, I don't really live here. I'm on the floor.'

'I need to check that he's alright. He might be ill.' She almost hoped he was, to give him some excuse. She had this awful feeling, she knew something was wrong. 'Please, can I come in?'

The sleepy youth didn't really have a choice. He stepped back and let Jenny pass beside him, meekly trailing her up the stairs to Simon's room. Jenny knocked on the door.

'Simon? Are you in there?'

'He's probably asleep. I haven't seen him. I were out all day yesterday, didn't get back till late. Who shall I say has called?'

'His girlfriend,' Jenny stated. The young man looked quite surprised. His mouth dropped open, about to say something, but he thought better of it.

'Simon?' Jenny pushed the door with her wrist and it rolled open.

'Fucking hell! He's been burgled!' The lad gulped. 'Shit!'

All of Simon's things were gone. An empty bed remained, with two stripped pillows staring out like blinded eyeballs. Jenny checked inside his wardrobe, and found only bare Formica.

'His CDs, his stereo,' wailed the squatter. 'I'd best check all us other rooms. God knows what else they've took.' He ran out, worried.

Simon's desk was cleared of everything, only scribbled ink-blots remained. His bookcase was lined with dust, not books. No sign that he'd ever been there. Almost as though he were a figment of her imagination. A wishful fantasy.

The stubbled youth came back. 'I don't understand,' he said. 'No one else has had 'owt touched. I don't know what's happened.'

Jenny sank down on the bed, exhausted. That same feeling in her guts as when she found Mister's empty stable. She lifted a pillow onto her face to check if she could smell him. Just a touch, a memory, Simon's scent. His skin against the linen. She clutched it to her, she wouldn't leave it, couldn't.

She spotted litter in the bin and hoped to find a clue. Two opal fruit wrappers, an odd sock with a large hole, and a blue envelope with an airmail sticker on. It was addressed to Simon, written in a swirl of eager curves. A female hand, thought Jenny, too impractical to be a man, too eager and romantic. There was nothing left inside it, the letter gone. She flipped it over, but found no return address. The postage stamp was Italian.

Jenny drove home in a blur, scavenged pillow secured in the front passenger seat, safety belt strapped across it like a person. The envelope lay gloating on the dashboard.

She pulled into the driveway, surprised to see Mr Price the next door neighbour standing there with Teddy the cat wedged in his arms. The man was rooted to the tarmac, as if he was forced to stand still for a task and couldn't move. He looked remarkably uncomfortable. This would probably mean trouble.

Jenny tried to think of some excuse as to why their pet had been skulking around his garden, digging up expensive bedding plants, transferring his prize Koi carp from the fishpond to the patio, leaving them there to gulp their last. The number of times Mr Price had been around over the years, dead fishes firm in hand, or making the Barkers witness their dying breaths after the cat had laid them out to dry. No wonder Teddy was meant to stay indoors.

Mr Price held his arms towards her. 'I've got your cat.'

Jenny smiled, relieved that the man's tone wasn't angry. 'Thanks. I thought he was hiding under a wardrobe, stupid thing.'

The man was quite upset. 'I've been waiting half an hour. You weren't in.'

'No. I was out.' Losing Simon.

Mr Price held the cat further towards her. It occurred to Jenny that she'd never seen Teddy as quiet as this before, especially around the neighbours whom he generally despised.

'It's Teddy,' Mr Price said, squeezing the feline. He didn't know where to put himself. Crimson rising up his cheeks, for some reason a wash of tears filled his eyes as his arms began to shake. 'Teddy's dead,' he moaned. 'A double glazing van ran over him. The bloke didn't stop. He drove over Teddy and sped away.'

Mr Price placed the cat in Jenny's arms. She stared down, confused. 'He doesn't look dead,' she noted.

'He's very dead. Really. Look.'

He squeezed a paw. No reaction. Jenny examined the static cat. He still looked like Teddy, it wasn't like he was damaged or anything. He wasn't even bleeding. There was a tiny speck of blood on his nose, but he could have done that anywhere.

She patted his head softly. 'I'll take him to my vet. He'll see to him. He's a good vet, isn't he Ted? We quite like him.'

Jenny moved her face down to the animal's breathless, cat food mouth. Tongue peeping out between his teeth. No movement.

'He's really dead?'

'He was dead half an hour ago,' groaned Price. 'And he's still dead now.' The man started to walk away. 'Unless his name is Lazarus.'

The three biggest regrets in Jenny Barker's life:
1. The disappearance of Mister, and now Simon.
2. Killing the milkman.
3. The flat cat being dead.

She gently placed Teddy on the front doorstep and left him there for fifteen minutes. He was still dead when she came back to check.

Simon vanished, and now the cat deceased. It was not a brilliant day. This was going to mean big trouble, and she was bound to be to blame. She should have checked the cat was safely in the house, not being squashed outside. Maybe she could put Teddy's body in the garage and hope the parents ran over him in the car when they drove in? Then she could act dumb and shocked and it wouldn't be her fault.

Perhaps they wouldn't notice he was dead. Perhaps she could leave him on the kitchen table and pretend he was asleep. Or perhaps not. The dog kept jumping up and trying to have its wicked way with him, surprised that the cat had waited ten years before deciding it found Laddie so attractive.

Jenny moved the cat to a safe place. She'd looked up the meaning of 'necrophilia' in the dictionary, and imagined it meant the same for animals too.

She went to have a long lie down upstairs, hugging Simon's

scented pillow. The phone rang. She didn't answer.

Information

Dear Agony Aunt,

How can everything change so quickly from bliss to disaster? One minute I'm with the man of my dreams, then next thing I know, he's vanished off the face of the Earth, and my mother's cat is dead. She loved that cat and I loved Simon. What do you suggest I do?

Jenny B from Leeds

Dear Jenny,

What can you do? You can't organise the world, you just have to move along with it. Don't get too disturbed over your boyfriend, he isn't like your horse - he WILL turn up. You cannot steal a person. And as for your mother's cat... it's fucked.

The parents arrived home.

'We've had a lovely time!' beamed Mary. 'Scotland is so... Scottish.'

Anxious, Jenny rose from the bottom stair. 'The cat's dead.'

'That's nice, dear.' Mary shut the door as her husband put the cases down, groaning at the extra weight of Edinburgh rock, not the real kind that tastes of sugar and has Blackpool written down the centre, but that strange Scottish stuff that tastes of cinnamon and crumbles up like chalk.

Her mother eased out of too tight shoes. 'Oh, my feet! Where's Teddy boy? Where's my little lovey?' She looked stern for a moment, a frown above her nose. 'You did remember to feed the animals? You haven't let them starve?'

Laddie came running out of the kitchen doing the obligatory wagging of the tail routine before diving back behind the washing machine.

'Mum, listen. I've got some bad news. Very bad.' Jenny spoke slowly, pointedly, wishing she could make herself sound slightly more upset. She stared at the front door handle as she spoke, fixing her eye level to maintain an even voice. 'There's been an accident. Teddy....'

Her mother's arms swam through the air in semaphore panic. 'Where is he? Is he hurt?'

Jenny cleared her throat. 'A double glazing van ran over him. Mr Price found him, brought him round. Teddy's dead, Mum. I put him in a dustbin bag and left him in the greenhouse.'

Mary Barker exhaled a horrendous blubbering wail and her husband dutifully hurried to the greenhouse. He returned with the dustbin bag and a handful of cucumbers.

'She's right,' Ray nodded. 'He was dead. Look.'

He pulled Teddy's lifeless form from the black bag. It still looked like Teddy, but a whole lot stiffer, and with a flopless tail.

Mary started crying and ran off up the stairs. She glared down at her husband.

'You don't care, do you, Ray? I can tell you're not upset.'

'It's just a cat, love. Not a person.'

'But he was!' Mary's words bit through him. 'He had a human soul. He was a reincarnated spirit, born again.'

Jenny had forgotten that part.

'Right!' Ray snorted. 'He had the soul of your precious Bernard. I don't know why you didn't call him that and have done with it. Why did I stay with you, woman? All these years. You drive me up the bloody wall.'

He slammed the door as he left, and Mary locked herself inside the toilet. They left the suitcases in the hallway, and nobody unpacked.

The brown horse wasn't well.

'He's not looking any fatter,' Roger mused. 'His eyes are a bit more perky, but...'

'Can MacKenzie come and see him?' Jenny asked. 'He might know what to do.'

'Meaning I don't?' Roger raised an eyebrow, stern.

'He's been a vet for longer, he might think of something else. I don't want him to die.'

Roger nodded, sighed. He was looking tired today. He said he had wife trouble. She'd been following him around. Turned up in a farmer's field when he was breach birthing a cow. And he'd been up too late last night with a grey mare in Sherburn, slashes on her side that were put there by either vandals or someone worse. Lines across the skin like fishes' gills. Little open smiles of red, sewn up with spider stitches.

'The Savager?' Jenny asked. 'Another attack, this close? Did you contact the police?' She felt guilty at her excitement.

'No. I thought about it, but the horse's owner was in a state, and anyway, I don't want to get involved. I've got enough problems already.'

'But if it's the Savager, he may have left a clue? They might be able to catch him.'

'It was probably just kids, messing about. The mare's going to be fine.' Roger didn't want to talk about it. 'We should do some blood tests on your horse, see what's going on.' He pulled a syringe from his medical bag and rummaged for a vial. 'There could be something that we've missed.'

Jenny winced as he inserted the needle into her horse's scrawny neck and starting drawing blood. Brown flinched, nervous. Flipped his head round to check what was going on, then let his lip droop down.

'And while I'm here...' Roger suctioned on a thin pair of rubber gloves and bent down to scrounge a recent sample. He pulled a palm full of dung into his hand and expertly pulled the glove off, catching the waste in an air pocket in the middle. He dropped it into another bag. 'I'll get this tested, and give you a call when I've any news.'

Jenny thanked him and watched him leave, admiring the shape of his back as he walked, the straight line of his shoulders. She was still looking when he glanced round, both of them feeling awkward that they had been caught staring, so each giving a little wave to cover up.

He reminded her of Simon, and it hurt.

Jenny wiped muck off her shoes, checked her hair for straw and caught the bus to town. It was lunchtime, so Tex should be in the pub, guzzling his pint and chewing soft cheese sandwiches.

Her heartbeat quickened as she approached the college building, head down, hair in her eyes as a disguise. She passed Sharon near the lower gallery, where freshly painted walls stood awaiting future artwork, fierce expectations to be hung on bald blank space. Jenny looked away, not wanting to be noticed. Simon was right, that girl was far too thin. Her face was like a skull, and clothes hung off so limply, as if dripping from a wire hanger. A person made from pipe cleaners. She didn't eat enough, she'd stopped. As Jenny went up in the lift, she felt guilty that she'd not realised earlier that Sharon wasn't well, as opposed to just not hungry.

Jenny got off on the seventh floor where the second years normally were. There was nobody around. Deserted. It was too near the end of term. She tried the office, but that was shut.

She couldn't stay long, Tex would come. Someone would see her, ask her what was wrong. She climbed the stairs to the top floor, peeping around the door to check the coast was clear. She'd written a note for Wit, to tell him not to worry. He'd been ringing up a lot.

Jenny placed her letter in the pigeon hole for people whose surnames began with S, because Wit's surname was Stanton. She eagerly checked the Bs, for Barker, praying that Simon had left a message. The box was empty.

She had a thought. What if? Yes. There was an envelope addressed to Nina, and she recognised his writing. How could he write to Nina, not to her? That wasn't fair. She took the envelope in her hands and flipped it over. Damn. Not only had he not written a return address on the back, but he had licked the flap securely down. Jenny held it towards the light, trying to make out any words on the inside, but the paper was too thick, a clotted cream. She poked her thumb nail underneath the rim, trying to ease it open without a tear. The glue had sealed it firmly, and as the back ripped open, paper stretched along the tear.

Feeling guilty, Jenny peeped inside the envelope, not wanting to read the contents, just to search for an address. A moment's scrutiny revealed a pristine upper page. No address, just a scrawled message. Something she shouldn't read.

Jenny tried flattening the back of the envelope down to make it look intact. She placed it in the pigeon hole, wishing she'd never found it, wishing she'd had the guts to read the thing. The envelope looked battered, scratched by nails and wet with fingerprints. This wasn't looking good.

She picked it up again. It had so obviously been tampered with. Maybe she could put the note in a new envelope, trace Simon's writing on the front? She couldn't tell Nina that she'd opened it.

'Hello stranger, where've you been?'

Jenny hid the note in the back pocket of her jeans. Tight against her bum.

'Nina... hi.' Jenny cleared a guilty throat.

'What have you been up to?' Nina asked. 'We had a big meeting about the show. You should have been there. Tex was fuming.'

'I'm not... I'm not submitting,' Jenny sighed. 'I'd fail, so why bother?'

'But you can't!' Nina was stunned and awkward. 'All this time, your work! I don't get it. You can't give up now, that's stupid.'

'No,' Jenny looked hard at her, determined. 'My work's crap, and it's finished. There's nothing more to say.'

'Jenny? Jenny!'

Nina's words floated after her. The lift arrived. She left.

'Blue Hotel, on a lonely highway. Blue Hotel, life don't work out my way...' Jenny was in her bedroom, singing along to the sad strains of Chris Isaak when the front doorbell rang. She took a breath and went downstairs.

'I told you, Nina. I'm not coming back.'

She opened the door, surprised to find Marvin outside. He looked concerned, his carrot hair was somehow more subdued.

'We need to talk,' he offered. 'What's this about you not putting up your show?'

Jenny blushed, skin burning. How could she explain this to him? Would he believe her if she mentioned Tex's threats? Why should anyone believe a thing she said? They'd think she was confused and had misinterpreted his words. Those art tutors were bound to stick together.

She led Marvin into the kitchen, giving herself something to do by making a pot of tea. What if Marvin already knew what Tex had done, if they had laughed about it, come up with a dual plan? Good cop, bad cop.

'I've got an idea,' ventured Marvin. 'Tex is right, your artwork isn't up to what it should be, for whatever reason that may be... but those photos, the ones you showed me, I think we should go with them.'

'You've spoken to Tex?' Jenny worried.

'We had a conversation, but he's judging you by what he's seen, so we'll have to change his mind.'

'I don't want to talk to him.'

'If you've had a falling out, get over it. I want you and your photos back in my office, now, so we can go through them and sort this out.' Marvin thudded his mug of tea on the breakfast table. 'Then I want you to write a short piece on themes, styles, and where the work is headed. Get it feeling solid, then you can talk to the external examiner when he comes in next week. We'll get a show up on that wall.'

Jenny nodded, mute.

'Are we sorted?' Marvin was determined.

Jenny sat in the front seat alongside Marvin as he drove them into town. His driving made her nervous, with his thin

106

hands waving around. There was a free-range rabbit in the footwell which kept trying to chew her laces, and excreted black buttons of crap when they skid round roundabouts.

Jenny followed Marvin through the college, him gripping onto her portfolio in case she changed her mind and fled. Her eyes kept glancing at the office door when they got inside, expecting company. Her small frame perched on the edge of the sofa like a bird, ready for flight.

Marvin extracted Jenny's photographs and laid them across the desk, making preferential piles.

'What about having these ones on the wall?' He pointed at a spread of images. 'Think of some text to go with them, you can get a strong black font in reprographics. And maybe get this one blown up larger, as a centrepiece? You do your own prints, don't you? Fancy getting busy in the darkroom?'

Jenny glanced across, then nodded. Marvin was content.

'We'll get you through this, Jenny Barker,' the man smiled. 'I give you my word on it. I'm just glad Nina came to me, said there was something up.'

Jenny started to feel guilty. Nina, Wit, Marvin, they'd all tried to help her. What had she done for them?

Marvin found some fresh sheets of card and started measuring for mounts, checking the picture sizes, crafting frames with his sharp knife. He nicked his thumb, fresh smear of strawberry blood staining a corner. Jenny tried to clean it off with an eraser, but that only spread the mark.

The office door creaked open and Tex's bulk appeared.

'You busy?' He looked at Marvin, avoiding Jenny's eye.

'Give us half an hour. D'you want to see these? They're great.' Marvin held up the nearest print.

'Another time.' The troll shrunk from the office. Jenny stared after him, unblinking, until he scuttled out of view.

Termination

Jenny sat, guilty, in her bedroom, clutching a pair of fresh washed jeans. If only she hadn't been so thoughtless, hadn't wedged them in the jam-packed laundry bin, ready for the washing machine to chew and churn. She tried to fit pieces of the sodden cream shape back together, but the paper was far too pulped to resemble more than squirts forced from an icing bag. Now Simon's words were gone, ink stains washed away by Persil automatic.

Jenny had decided to own up and give Simon's letter to Nina. After all, her friend had helped her, talked to Marvin, got her artwork sorted out. And how had she repaid her? By liquidising Simon's last words of goodbye.

Butterflies flew round Jenny's stomach as the afternoon clocked down, minutes ticking towards the evening of the degree show. She was tired from lack of sleep, from staying up overnight the previous week working long hours in the darkroom. She'd lost track of what was night or day, confused by fluorescent light bulbs in the black, time capsule space. Stark images developing in the tanks, fresh photos for her folder.

The students had started to bend under the strain. Wit wasn't smiling any more, and Nina was distracted. Tall illustrator Tree had been turning up quite drunk, and Sharon suffered an epileptic seizure. She'd been standing by her blank wall, preparing to put her work up, when suddenly she started fitting, spasms like an electric current surge. It was lucky that Tex had been there, ready to thrust a ruler into her mouth to stop her from swallowing her tongue and choking. He drove Sharon to the hospital, where they thought the attack was brought on by too much stress. Jenny had been to the doctor's surgery herself as she was having problems sleeping, and when she got exhausted she couldn't stop the tears. The doctor gave her some tablets and a smile.

Jenny ruffled through clean clothes inside her wardrobe and

decided to wear a long terracotta dress, rivers of soft flowing material. She scooped her hair out of her face and affixed fresh make-up.

'Jenny, are you ready?'

The parents were waiting in the hallway, her mum wearing a skirt, her dad a frown.

'You look nice, love.' Ray made an effort and took Jenny's cold hand. 'Right, let's go see what you've been up to.'

The college gallery was cluttered with chatting people when the Barker clan arrived. Uncomfortable exhibitors in clean pressed clothes, supportive friends and family mushrooming round them. Tables topped with wine graced the way in, eager first year females handing a glass out to each guest, mumbling red or white, red or white in friendly monosyllables. The air smelt of stale cheese straws.

'Which is yours, then?' Mary Barker was quite keen, but also intimidated by what she didn't understand. She averted her eyes from a painting of a naked, exploding man with giant testicles, then spotted a video installation with images of rotting meat.

'I'll show you round,' offered Jenny, strategically planning to show them a weaker display before she got to hers. Sharon's wall, perhaps, with its anaemic water-colour women wearing pastel coloured sweaters.

Jenny's eyes danced about, searching out familiar faces. Looking for his broad shoulders and short dark hair. She spotted Wit supping red wine in the corner. Mary waved and hurried over.

'Is this your work Wit?' Mary spied his wall space, awash with nightmare images, a dark inferno of humanity, a myriad of detailed scenes. 'That's nice,' she offered. 'Nice colours.' She looked through his glossy book of illustrations, each picture reduced down and placed with text. 'Impressive!' Mary glowed. 'Did you see this, Jenny? Wit's things are in a book.'

'Self publishing,' Wit explained. 'With the help of my computer.'

Jenny sidled up to him, feeling awkward. 'Odd this, isn't it? Where are your parents? Are they here?'

'They couldn't make it.' He didn't look at her, embarrassed.

'You're lucky,' Jenny grinned. 'I feel like I'm eight years old. Like my folks are having to take me into school.'

'Jenny, which of these are yours?' Ray was losing interest, though he was enjoying looking at the small circular photographs of each student, pinned on the walls beside their names.

Jenny spied the shape of Tex approaching, a willowy woman affixed close by his side. Her hand in his, their fingers woven together. Jenny wanted to move out of the way, but was fascinated. She stood her ground, safe with Wit at her right arm.

'That's one of my tutors, Tex,' she stated, almost wanting to say more.

'Enjoying yourselves?' Tex nodded at Wit's half empty glass. 'You want to get yourself a refill. Celebrate.' He looked at Wit as though he knew something. A secret. 'Have you met my wife?'

Jenny was surprised. The woman was pleasant and attractive, with a soft friendly face.

'It's good to meet you.' Jenny smiled, felt awkward, had to move away. 'Come on, let's see my work.'

Jenny led the parents to a wall near the gallery window. Her photographs stretched along the length of it in frames. Black and white images, strong statements that made the viewer look again. 'Wanted' posters with missing horses, mug shots of suspected thieves and illegally parked vans. A series of prints called 'Disintegration' charting the life of an unknown horse, images of a pregnant mare, birth of a long legged foal, adolescent fillies kicking heels, through puberty, through illness, re-birth, and finally death. Mary Barker looked away. The final image was disturbing. So too were the Savager reports, a notebook filled with notes and sketches, incidents of crime.

The parents did not know what to say. Tears welled in Mary's eyes and Ray passed her a tissue.

Jenny glanced at Tex canoodling in a corner with his wife, both full of childish whispers, a firmly welded couple. She looked past them and saw Sharon, tired, leaning against a wobbly canvas screen. Her skin milk white under a sad black dress, wire arms straining to hold her empty wine glass. Her hands were shaking, her eyes focused on Tex. She wandered out of view.

'Do you want to see Nina's work?' asked Jenny. 'She's done these designs for bags and stationery. Very practical, great colours.'

Marvin appeared beside them.

'Hello!' he beamed. 'You must be Jenny's folks.' He extended his hand, shaking theirs with long fingered cotton gloves. 'She's such a talented photographer. You must be very proud.'

Ray and Mary nodded in agreement, watching other gazers scrutinise the pictures, realising that they were really rather good.

'I'm glad I got you that camera.' Jenny's father kissed her cheek. 'You've done right well, lass.' He smiled, pausing a moment, as though the words were hard to say. 'Maybe now you can get yourself a job.'

The students maintained polite smiles and inhibited their swearing until their families had seen enough and gone, clutching cheap photocopy catalogues as souvenirs of the event. A handful of genuine art lovers and talent scouts stayed longer, conspicuously noting down the names of students with the most interesting work.

The gallery lights were dimmed and the party moved upstairs, leaving a trail of crunching crumbs and mislaid glasses. The artwork sagged without an audience, leaving shadows on the walls like sunken eyes.

Tree stood in the corner of the lift laughing as he travelled up and down. No one ever saw him get out. Jenny helped to carry the remaining wine bottles upstairs, swaying behind a swaggering line of singers.

'We're all going on a summer holiday...'

How many years had she heard that song, through infants, middle and high school, someone always sang it, badly, when they broke up for six weeks of wanton freedom.

Jenny realised that everything was over. In a week's time she'd take her photos off the walls, make sure her desk was clear, then walk away. The students would eagerly exchange their home addresses and promise to keep in touch, but the phone calls would gradually dwindle and the Christmas cards would cease. In the end they would forget each other's names.

Most of Jenny's friends were on the top floor supping beverages and dancing to the music. Marcus was getting down in a big way to the chorus of Madonna's *Express Yourself*. He'd put on a kilt for no obvious reason, as he wasn't Scottish and he didn't have good legs. Jenny reckoned there was a lot more to Marcus than she'd realised.

She found Nina puking in the toilets, crouched over a bowl.

'Are you alright?' Jenny was worried, her friend was very pale.

'Too much wine.' Nina wiped her mouth, dousing herself with water at the sink.

'Are you sure?'

'Of course I'm fucking sure!' snapped Nina. 'It's that cheap shit plonk they bought us.'

'I liked it.'

Nina glared at Jenny. 'Well, you're easy to amuse.'

Jenny started to walk away, annoyed at her friend's tone. Nina reached for Jenny's arm.

'Jen, I'm sorry. I'm feeling pretty shitty.' Nina's eyes were bloodshot. 'You'd have thought that he'd have shown up for my degree show. He was supposed to care about me.'

Jenny couldn't look at her.

'Not a word,' Nina sniffed. 'The selfish bastard. What did I do, hey? Why did he run off?' She saw that Jenny was uncomfortable. 'Don't worry, I'm not blaming you. I mean, he didn't fall for you on your night out, did he? If I'd have seen that coming I'd have never let you go.'

Jenny reddened. 'But you said if he got to know me, he'd be mad about me. You did, you said that.'

'I was trying to cheer you up.' Nina blew her nose, needing cheering up herself. 'I owed you that at least.'

Jenny watched her friend splashing water on her face. 'Well, thanks. I had a lovely time.' She and Simon had connected. She knew that. 'I don't suppose that you've got his address? Where his parents live?'

Nina gave her a cold look. 'If I did, then he'd have been here, wouldn't he? No, I don't know where he is. He could be dead, for all I care.'

Jenny felt bad about the letter. She left Nina alone, worried she might let something slip that she'd regret. She wandered along the corridors, depressed. The elation of the evening giving way to weariness. She came across Marvin on a lower level, together with his white rabbit that for some reason was wearing a false beard while being pushed along on an old skateboard.

'Good show, Jenny!' Marvin smiled, skidding the rubber wheels.

'Yeah, thanks.'

Three years, and this was how it ended. With a hangover and a rabbit. She thought of Nina hunched over the toilet bowl, dripping sick, and went upstairs to check. The toilet door was locked now, the engaged sign twisted round.

'Are you alright in there?'

A moan.

'I'm sorry about Simon disappearing.' She was, for both of them. 'He should have come tonight. But I loved your show anyway, it was great. Did your family like it?'

Jenny crouched down on the ground and tried to peep under the door.

'Nina?'

A strange shadow on the floor. Some broken glass. Jenny

peered closer and saw a pair of skinny legs. They did not belong to Nina.

'Hello?' She tapped the door. Something was wrong. 'Are you alright?'

There was a faint rustling, a fumble with the lock. The door pulled open and Sharon's face peered out.

Jenny sighed, relieved. 'I thought you'd had another fit.'

Sharon shrugged, skin pulled tight against her cheekbones, faint as sun bleached parchment. Monochrome as one of Jenny's photos, standing there in black and white. She wobbled in the stall, slow swaying, all at sea. Red dripping from her arms like uncorked wine. Blood pumped from jagged cuts across her wrists.

'Sharon, Jesus!'

Ruby droplets created gems on the tiled floor. Jenny grabbed some paper towels, panicked.

'Hold these down. Jesus, Sharon! Why?'

Jenny pressed blue paper onto Sharon's wrists, gripping with her hands to stop the flow. The blood was unabated, soaking through the blotting pad, the soft redness turning purple.

'Oh God, oh God!' Jenny's hands were shaking, but Sharon was perfectly still, except for pumping blood.

'I only got a third.'

'What?' Jenny could hardly hear the whisper.

'I only got a third.' A single tear glistened as it slid down Sharon's cheek. 'I slept with Tex, and still only got a third.'

'You what?' Jenny slotted the words together. Did she mean a third class degree grade? That meant she'd passed at least.

'He said... he said he would... A third! And he made me a whore.'

Jenny gulped, distracted. The blood flow wouldn't stop.

'Wait here,' she pleaded. 'Keep the pressure on with these.' But how could she, how could Sharon keep the pads firm without another pair of hands? Quick thinking, Jenny pulled the outer toilet door open and wedged it with her foot. Grabbed onto Sharon's wrists again, pressing hard she walked backwards into the corridor, her feet stepping tentatively as she felt for solid ground. Leading the drip white, red drip girl towards the laughs and music, as though beckoning a child forwards for a surprise.

The room fell quiet when they entered. Shocked silences and faces, then a low mumbling as people wondered what to do. Several mobile phones were pulled from pockets and an ambulance was called.

The police arrived before the ambulance. They wanted everyone's co-operation, so everyone got out of there as quickly as possible. Certain substances were flushed down toilets. Jenny and Wit absconded with a carrier bag of crisps.

'Should we go with her?' Jenny watched as the ambulance men appeared, wrapping a blanket round Sharon's shivering body while they loaded her inside. 'Is she going to be okay?'

'Hope so.' Wit was quiet and very drawn. He held onto Jenny's hand as the vehicle's flashing lights whirled around, tyres screaming as it pulled out of the car park.

Jenny was feeling sick now, shocked. She remembered Nina, but couldn't see her anywhere. She must have gone already.

'Can we go to the hospital?' Jenny's words were hanging in cold air. She kept seeing Sharon's face, her slivered wrists. That smile of lipstick red across the skin.

Wit led Jenny along the tarmac towards a taxi rank. There were some shadows in the distance, people fighting. The shapes of Tex and Marvin waving fists beside a car. Tex's wife shouting ignored protests into the wind, then stomping off, head down. Marvin slid into the driver's seat, Tex's thick hand grabbing after him. The door slammed shut. Tex howled.

Wit and Jenny walked along, neither knowing what to say. Letting their tapping shoes do all the talking.

Jenny and Wit sat in plastic bucket chairs in the emergency waiting room, trying not to look like they were watching as walking wounded from fights and car crunches came in.

'Weren't her family there tonight?' asked Jenny. 'There should be someone here, her next of kin.'

'I thought they lived in Australia. Didn't they emigrate?' Wit remembered seeing a postcard at Sharon's house with a smug-faced koala bear, and a real crocodile skin bag.

A nurse they'd talked to earlier walked towards them.

'How is she?' They spoke in unison.

'Much better,' the nurse smiled. 'We've stopped the bleeding and stitched her up, but we'll need to keep her in.'

'She lost a lot of blood,' sighed Jenny, the taste of it still sticking to her tongue. The sight of broken flesh burned on her lids every time she shut her eyes. The young nurse nodded calmly.

Wit and Jenny left Sharon fast asleep with tranquillisers and bandaged wrists the size of boxing gloves. They collapsed into the back of a taxi cab, still reeling from the attempted suicide. Wondering if Sharon had really meant to die.

Jenny stared blankly through the back window as they trailed through the streets away from Leeds Infirmary. Past darkened shops and offices, and the lions that told her things.

Excursion

Wit had a girlfriend. He had filled his parents in with the details when they'd been quizzing him last Christmas, his brother Walter goading in the corner near some tinsel, current woman drooping from his arm.

Annabel's family owned a textile company in Doncaster, and she was interested in the whole concept of design and the environment. She'd met Wit during a talk on primitive tribal art and intercontinental accounting at college. The only problem with their seemingly perfect relationship was that Annabel did not exist.

Wit had never expected that his folks would have to meet her, but they were adamant. Walter was always teasing that Wit had some big secret he wouldn't tell the family, which was indeed true, but it was actually the fact that Wit was doing art, when everyone thought he was studying a degree in accountancy.

'So that's why they weren't at the degree show?' Jenny mused. 'I thought it was strange, I mean, everyone was there, except for Sharon's...'

Their friend was still in hospital, her suicidal phase apparently extinguished, classed as another cry for help. She'd been moved to a ward for problem eaters and was having therapy. Jenny had been to visit her, and taken in some grapes. She had watched Sharon eat seven of them, no pips.

Wit nodded, tired. 'And now, they want to meet her, my gorgeous bloody girlfriend. I wouldn't ask, but...'

'It's fine,' Jenny smiled. 'I quite fancy not being me for a while. My life's got too messed up.'

The occasion of the meeting was Wit's parents' silver wedding anniversary, an event to be attended by all relatives, beloved and friends who could be bothered turning up. Wit had groaned that Annabel was too busy, but his mother put on that face of hers which always made him change his mind.

'So, was it Marbella or Fuengirola?' enquired Jenny.

'Better go for Paris, really. They think that Spain's too cheap.'

Jenny nodded, scribbling information on her notepad as they travelled down by train. She normally took the coach when she went anywhere, National Express with student discount, so this journey itself was fun, with electric doors and landscapes flashing by.

'How long have we been together?' Pen poised.

Wit calculated. 'Eight months. No, nine.'

Jenny nodded, turning her head to the right so she could look into the window and casually inspect Wit's reflection, instead of staring rudely at him, mouth agape. He didn't look like Wit. Literally. He'd dyed his hair dark brown and subdued his spikes flat with a layer of mousse. He'd even taken his earrings out, as well as all the metal work that normally hung around his face. When he wasn't looking she peered closer, trying to see if there was a hole in his eyebrow where that gold ring used to be. She wondered if he was too hot in that suit, small beads of sweat making a necklace round his collar. She'd never seen her friend looking so smart. He normally wore jeans and a tight T-shirt above his rippling tattoos. Now he looked like a bank clerk, or a nervous job interviewee. Not Wit.

They had fabricated stories, past times that they had had. Jenny found it ironic that she should pretend to be someone else with Wit, when in reality he was one of the few people she could be herself with, and not profess to be any more than that. As they laughed over the fun they'd had on their imaginary holiday, Jenny thought again how great it would be to have Wit as a brother. She'd always wished she was not the only child at home. She often asked why her mother didn't have more kids, only to be given a blank stare followed by a few minutes daydreaming while the woman imagined something in such detail that it made her smile before subsiding into tears. Jenny never mentioned children in front of her father though. He'd storm off out to work.

'Why didn't you tell your folks you were at art college?' pushed Jenny. 'I don't understand. You're brilliant. I mean, you got a first! I bet they'd be so proud.'

Wit looked up over his magazine then lowered his eyes again. 'You don't know my family,' he muttered. 'They wouldn't be impressed.'

Jenny wriggled in her chair, distracted. What was it with Wit? The only student to get a first class degree in their whole year, and he wanted it kept secret? When she had got her mark on that Monday after the show she couldn't shut up about it. A second class degree but a first class feeling. Marvin had beamed at her, suggesting that she apply to the Royal College of Art, try for an MA in photography. When Jenny told the parents about her grade they splashed out on a Chinese meal, and even ordered seaweed.

A dark green Mercedes met them at the station. Jenny was sure this must be a mistake, that they should get the bus, but the driver took hold of her case, determined, and locked it in the boot. Jenny slid into the back seat with Wit, disoriented.

'Won't this cost a lot? It's much smarter than a taxi.' She worried, fumbling in her purse. A finger touching the cocktail stick she'd saved from the Dry Dock, a souvenir of that special night with Simon. She took it out for a moment, savouring the smell caught on the wood. The little crushed umbrella.

Wit smiled, amused. 'I should have warned you. My family, well, you'll see.'

They were driven away from the main town, down thinning roads towards soft country lanes. Jenny had always expected Wit to be townie, not to have come from a world of Constable landscapes and long fields. She was surprised she never knew this.

The Mercedes turned into the gravelled drive of an impressive, white stoned mansion, a fringe of ivy hanging from the roof, standing proud like a National Trust monument in impeccable emerald lawns.

'Wit, that's not...I mean, you don't?'

'Home sweet home.' He shrugged, rather embarrassed.

'Wow.'

The only time Jenny had seen such a house was when she visited Castle Howard and bought postcards and the *Brideshead Revisited* soundtrack. She was in shock. She'd never known Wit was as affluent as this. It didn't fit his image in the least. She looked at him and wondered who he was, if the Wit she knew was an invention.

His mother met them at the door, smelling of gardenias, kissing Jenny on the cheek and calling her Annabel in a soft, well rounded voice. An imposing woman, mid-fifties, with an expensive skincare regime to stop her getting any older. Wearing a plain but classy dress, she was immaculately made up, with hair that was freshly set each morning and glued there for the day. She took Jenny by one of her long-fingered hands, with a scattering of rings and muted nails, not calluses like Jenny's mother wore. She led the girl across a long marble-floored hall, drowning her with compliments and smiling at Wit as though he had won a prize.

Jenny blushed, remembering that when she first met Wit, she'd assumed that he was less well off than her. She had even apologised for having her own horse, as if that made her snobby, when in reality it only made her poorer. She tried to catch Wit's eye, but his were downcast.

A short fat man called Norman carried Jenny's case up to her room, freshly aired and laced with elaborate white trimmings and pastel flower arrangements. Jenny rubbed the petals for a scent. Nothing. They were made of silk. Quite fitting for a family built on pretence.

Wit was housed in a bedroom further down. Very proper and correct. Jenny sat in her guest room, deciding what to do, wondering if she should go and have a talk with Wit, practise being Annabel or something. But he was probably too busy concentrating on being Wit. Not Wit, William. She had to call him William.

A knock on the door. 'Annabel? Are you decent?'

Jenny cleared her throat. 'Who is it?'

'It's me, stupid. Let me in.'

Wit was smoking in the corridor, wafting air around his hand rolled cigarette.

'Smoke alarms,' he moaned. 'Like bloody boarding school. And Walter's on the lurch. I think he suspects something.'

'How can he?' Jenny panicked. 'We've only just arrived.'

'Yeah, but he reckons something's up.' Wit stepped inside and shut the door behind him. 'Separate rooms, you and me not being together, it's all very prim and proper.' Wit eased the door open a crack, saw a shadow further up the plush pile carpet. 'I tell you, he's spying. He is such a sad bastard, he's got nothing else to do.'

'He's out there now? Nearby?'

'I think so.' Wit took a drag of his special cigarette.

Jenny giggled. She whispered in her friend's ear.

'Hhmmmmm,' groaned Wit, a grin licking his face. 'Baby, baby. Oh, God, I really love you. '

Jenny tried not to laugh.

'I love you too, William. Oh yeah.'

'Annabel, you're beautiful. You make me....' He turned his nose up.

Jenny rubbed her hands over Wit's sweater to make a rustling noise. Loudly kissed her hand, mouth snapping, while Wit banged his heels against the door. He pulled his arms around her and lifted her off the ground, back straining. His buttocks knocking against the wooden door frame. An eager banging of elbows, suppressing giggles. They moaned like alley cats with fish.

'Oh yes, yes, yes!' they laughed, Jenny trying to imitate the sexual noises she'd heard behind Sharon's wall. A thought hit her. The plaid shirt on the floor, the shouting, the bedstead thrusting against wallpaper, ripping shreds. She had heard the sex of Tex.

Footsteps hurried away up the corridor. They peered outside and saw Walter departing.

Wit winked at her. 'Great orgasm,' he smiled.

'My pleasure.'

He kissed Jenny softly on the cheek and left her to get changed.

By eight o'clock that evening the Stanton house was filled with a trail of relatives, close, distant, and some so distant they were social miles away. Gifts littered the long tables, though Jenny found it hard to believe that any of these presents were going to come in handy, as surely a couple who'd been married as long as them would have amassed all their required possessions.

Mrs Stanton unwrapped another brandy bottle.

'Oh, I love it, it's divine. Isn't it divine?'

Or a pot-pourri ornament, in the shape of a fox's head.

'Oh, I love it, it's divine. Isn't it divine?'

Sometimes she alternated words. Divine, gorgeous, super, smashing, lovely. Jenny thought the word expensive would be more appropriate.

Wit had transformed himself in a black, well-cut tuxedo, and as he beamed proudly at the sight of Jenny in her glistening red dress, back cut so low that she couldn't wear a bra, she stared up at him and thought how handsome he'd become. How happy she was to hold his hand and walk while heads and faces turned and smiled approval. She wondered if anyone could tell that Annabel's dress was laced with magic and that when she took her slippers off they were replaced by wellingtons.

Jenny was glad Wit hadn't inherited his brother's characteristic of licking ladies hands when introduced. The pock-faced Walter kissed her skin in such a way that she could feel his spit. For someone as rich as he, his tongue felt very rough.

'It's wonderful to meet you,' Walter drooled, moistness collecting on his lip. 'William's never brought a girl back home before. You'll have to come more often. Especially when I'm around.'

Jenny reddened and started coughing, feeling the eyes of Walter's bleached-blonde girlfriend, sharp fingertips pushed tight into her man in case he went astray. Her cold protective stare bored into Jenny, through her dress to her lower class skin. Jenny tried to disguise her Yorkshire accent, to speak in proper sentences and reply when spoken to. Wit picked up on her awkwardness.

'Relax. You're the most beautiful woman here.'

Jenny shrugged. 'Your brother's girlfriend hates me.'

'That's only because she knows Walter wants to fuck you.'

A canapé dropped from Jenny's mouth, rolling across the floor until it was spiked by a stiletto.

'Wit, don't! That's horrid. You can't speak like that.'

Wit gave his leering brother a radiant smile. 'What a prat. If he didn't have money, he'd be nothing. No one would want to know him.'

'He might be interesting.'

'Jenny, he collects stamps.'

'Oh, right.'

She rested her head on Wit's left shoulder as they swayed in time to the music. Most of the evening Wit's father had been singing away on the karaoke machine that Walter had brought as a gift, which went down very well with him, but no-one else.

Jenny clung onto Wit as the music slowed a pace, not sure what they should do, how convincing a couple they were supposed to be. She felt Wit's parents watching with approval as his arms tightened around her waist and their bodies fused together.

Jenny wanted to ask Wit if he'd heard any news of Simon. If he knew his home phone number or where he could be reached. As their slow dance continued she decided not to break the spell, and make believe that she really was in love.

Wit stared hard into her face. Brought his head closer down and kissed her, softly first, quite nervous, then with enriched enthusiasm. Jenny could feel his heartbeat through his jacket.

Jenny closed her eyes and thought of Simon and imagined how it would feel to have his hands on her, to be lying close beside him. As their tongues twisted together she could sense memories of Simon's mouth, the taste of candy floss.

'I shouldn't be drinking,' Jenny laughed as the music swirled her round. 'I'm not supposed to.'

'Who says?' grinned Wit.

The doctor. No alcohol with her anti-depressants. She couldn't tell him, he'd think that she was mad, or that she'd try to slit her wrists like Sharon. Jenny led Wit off to a corner and downed some more champagne. She was more than a little drunk. An elephant-size drunk. She kissed him, burped, felt silly.

'Let's go for a walk, Wit. I need some air.'

She led him across the gardens, past ponds of giant fish, and they stood alongside statues on the lawns.

'You're one rich guy, Wit,' Jenny smiled. 'I wouldn't mind marrying into this.'

'Wouldn't you?'

'Sure. The landed gentry... isn't that what you call it?'

Wit shrugged. 'My father earned it. He's good at business. We're not like the royal family.'

'So you'll never be a lord then? Lord Wit?'

Her friend blushed a little. 'Well, a baronet. One day, maybe. It depends on things.'

'Things?'

'If people die.' Wit put his hands back in his pockets, juggling with change, hoping Jenny wouldn't notice he was nervous.

'People always die.' Jenny was staring at a bush, becoming dizzy.

Wit lit up a long cigar. 'Baronet William Maximillian

Fitzgerald Stanton the Fifth.'

Jenny giggled. Wit, a man of means. One who ate Branston pickle sandwiches every day because they were the cheapest.

'I love Wit,' she grinned. 'Not William.'

With that she kissed him, swirling with emotion. Her hands manoeuvred underneath his jacket, keeping warm. He clung onto her, protective, and they stood, moonlight paling them like the surrounding statues, those static solid people without memories or lives, until Jenny put her palm in his and led Wit to the house.

That night she had a dream. Simon was there with her, whispering in her ear, unmemorable words, but tones tinted with love. She felt his warmth beside her, the taste of his salt skin against her tongue. His lips melded to hers, hot breath, their bodies touching. She could sense him when she woke. The bedclothes felt so warm, as if he was still there. A transparent indentation on the sheets.

Wit was waiting on the patio, Cheshire cat grin across his face as he pulled up a chair for his new girl.

'Morning Annabel,' his eyes fluttered. 'Did you sleep well last night?'

She beamed, excited. 'Great, thanks. I had a lovely evening.'

Wit couldn't stop smiling. Walter kicked him underneath the table.

That Sunday was the hottest day they'd had all year. The Stanton clan sat out on the pastel patio, chatting nonsense. Every time Mrs Stanton asked Annabel a question Jenny would pretend she was asleep on her sun lounger, soaking rays.

Wit and Walter played a game of tennis on the court. Jenny couldn't understand why Wit turned down the offer of a spare pair of Walter's shorts and a clean T-shirt, as he reddened with effort stretching to reach the ball, streams of sweat under his dampened jumper. At one point Jenny was scared that he would faint, his flushed face looked dangerously close to combustion.

Match lost, Wit went to get freshened up and they caught the next train home.

On the way to Leeds, Wit admitted that the reason he'd kept covered was not because he didn't want to show off his impressive muscles, but because his parents would go berserk if they knew he had tattoos. Every summer when he went home he'd wear a coat over his short-sleeved shirts and pretend that it was raining. He'd stopped swimming in the pool they'd had installed, saying he had acquired a fear of water. They gave him money to see an analyst. Wit spent it on the unending supply of dope he kept amongst his paints.

When Jenny returned to her house later that evening, she saw a Landrover parked outside, black metal trailer hooked onto the back. Roger was sitting smoking in the front seat, his elbow resting on the door frame. He smiled when she walked up to him. Then said he'd found her horse.

Reunion

'Is it really him?' Jenny's heart pulsed fast with fearful anticipation as they drove along the motorway. 'Are you certain?'

Roger shrugged. 'As sure as I can be. It's been that long since I've seen him. But when she jumped him over that wall, he kicked up his heels just the same. I'd always noticed that.'

Mister would do this little twist move with his feet, bending his hooves up and sideways, to be clear of any bricks. He hated to knock walls, ever since that solid one at Bramham when he had scraped the skin off his left knee.

'But what can I do?' moaned Jenny. 'I spoke to my insurers before, when I thought I'd found him, and it's too complicated.' She could remember their words exactly. If a horse is repossessed, in a legal situation, then the animal becomes the property of the insurers until the insured client pays back the money originally paid out in the initial claim.

Jenny had already spent her insurance money on the brown horse, the one that was going to die. The scabby one who didn't have insurance so would be a one hundred percent loss of money.

'I thought you'd be happy,' Roger groaned as they took the turn-off towards Manchester. 'Have you brought a photo? Registration forms, something to show he's yours?'

'Yes.'

'So stop worrying then.'

'It probably isn't even Mister,' Jenny sighed as they steamed onwards. 'Just a horse that looks like him.'

'Whatever.'

Jenny fidgeted. She gazed in the rear-view mirror and saw that the murky brown saloon car which had been with them since Leeds was still trailing behind. 'She should overtake, stupid woman,' Jenny moaned. 'It's not like we're going fast.'

Roger looked at the reflection. The muscles in his cheeks tensed as he focused on the driver. He pressed the accelerator.

'What is it?' Jenny could tell something was wrong.

'Nothing.'

'What's the matter?'

'I keep seeing my wife everywhere,' Roger sighed. 'It's my imagination. I mean, I see her all the time. Sometimes in places where there's no way she can be. Getting paranoid or what?'

He turned off at the next exit. The brown car carried on along the road and drove away. Roger started to relax as they continued on their journey, then pulled into a quiet stable yard.

'I said I'd come back later,' he explained as they walked into the courtyard, the outside lights on now the day was fading. 'Told her I needed more time to think about it.'

'Hello!' A fair haired woman in her early twenties popped her head over a nearby stable door. 'Decided you want him then? Brilliant.' She slid open the bolt and came outside. Jenny eagerly peered over, but was quickly disappointed. The horse standing there was black.

'Tracy, this is my friend, Jenny Barker.' Roger nodded. 'She wanted to see him too.'

'Great!' The girl was friendly. 'He's a smashing horse, I'm sorry I've got to sell him, I really am.' She looked quite genuine. 'But I'm off to college in the autumn, and I can't keep this up. I've got too many on.'

Jenny moved closer as they walked towards some stables at the end of the quadrangle. 'How long have you had him? How old is he?'

'Erm, I'm not sure about his age, but I've only had him for three weeks. Don't know why I bought him, really. Well, there was a dealer bidding for him, I thought he might go for meat... and he's a nice sort, aren't you boy?' She led them into the stable. The grey horse whinnied, eager. 'He's a bit cold-backed, he bucks, but he's got a real jump in him.'

The grey horse nudged Jenny's belly and pulled a face, stretching back his plump pink nose. Jenny sank against her horse's beating chest, rubbing the curls of fur that spun in opposite directions, creating swirling carpet patterns on his front. The horse gulped with constant whickers, running his face over her hair, licking her neck and arms. Snorting with breaths, ribcage expanding against his lightened skin. Delighted black hooves stomping on the straw.

'What's going on? You know him?' Tracy started to feel awkward. Roger gently led the girl away. He explained the situation, occasionally interrupted by squeaks and whinnies coming from the horse's stable.

Tracy was in shock. 'Shall I call the police? What d'you think will happen... I mean, is he mine... or hers? I paid for him, I didn't know that he was stolen.' She hardened. 'What proof is there he's hers?'

Roger pulled out a photograph, Jenny and Mister at a show. Tracy checked it closely, worried.

'I didn't know,' she sighed. 'I bought him, so he's mine.'

Jenny stepped out of the stable, stunned. Mister banged his kneecaps on the door, snorting loudly, scared that she was leaving. She had to go back to calm him down. Tracy watched, realisation sinking in.

'I could ring the auctioneers,' she offered. 'Try to find out some background. Which dealer, where he came from.'

Roger smiled. 'That would be good.'

'I didn't know that he was stolen.'

Roger squeezed her arm. 'You did great, you saved him from the meat-man, didn't you? And now he'll be back where he belongs.' Roger gathered up his business sense. 'I'll give you what you want for him, pay you back for what you've spent. The insurance claim, it's complicated. This way will work out best.'

Tracy watched as Roger brought out his cheque book.

'Or I'll get you cash if you want. I could come back tomorrow?'

'I trust you,' Tracy smiled, looking back at the singing horse with the pale girl. If she didn't know better, she'd have sworn the horse was crying.

They loaded Mister up and headed home, with Jenny still in shock.

'How much do I owe you?'

Roger concentrated on his driving, squinting at bright headlights in the road. 'It doesn't matter.'

'I'll pay you back. Get a job. Two jobs! I'll pay you for him.'

'Whatever.'

They drove along in silence, Jenny's elation transformed to tiredness. Too much thinking had wearied her, the excitement was now exhaustion. They would have to take her horse back to Roger's stables, as Deacon's was full up, and anyway, the horse was Roger's now, despite his insistence that he wasn't.

An owl screeched as they pulled into the deserted yard, horses dozing in their stalls. The moon smiled down as they led Mister from the trailer to a stable. Jenny shook straw apart with her numb hands to fluff up his yellow bed. She couldn't stop looking at him, scrutinising details. That small scar across his knee, his long mascara lashes, and those black circles around his eyes, like eyeliner painted on.

She rang Mr Blonde on her mobile, she knew that it was late, but the woman never slept. Mr Blonde choked with emotion.

'I still have to keep searching,' the woman sniffed. 'I'll get my babies back one day. You find everything in the end, you see. You only have to look.'

Roger had wandered off. Jenny couldn't find him.

'Roger?'

The stables were strangely ominous in the dark. Jenny could hear noises further down the dusky drive, behind the surrounding wall, unseen. The trees were breathing. She felt someone was watching, heard the rumble of a close approaching car. She glanced round. Roger's Landrover had gone.

Jenny hid in Mister's stable, nestling beside him, shaded from the door. Heavy tyres rubbed along the rough yard, getting closer. The clank of a metallic door, followed by flat firm footsteps. A long grey shadow snaked its way over the door.

'Hello?'

Roger peered into the stable and spied Jenny hiding there. She sprang to her feet, hoping she hadn't looked too foolish.

'I thought we could celebrate.' He lifted up a bottle of wine. 'It's chilled, fresh from the off-licence. Unless you've to rush home?'

'No, that's great. Thanks.'

Roger pursed his lips together as he struggled to uncork the wine with an attachment on his penknife.

'Harder than birthing a cow,' he joked. 'Glasses, glasses...' There were none anywhere. Roger led Jenny into the feed room, mice running across the floor as he flicked the light switch on. Jenny watched Roger's broad back as he carefully washed two chipped mugs in the sink, then briskly shook them dry.

'A toast!' Roger poured the wine out, right up to the rim. 'To happy homecomings.'

They clinked their mugs together. Jenny wasn't as tired now. She had found her second wind and felt like she was dreaming. All the times she'd imagined finding Mister, she never knew that she would soar as high as this. Her head buzzed and she grew taller, full of air.

'I don't know how to thank you.' She sat next to Roger, feet dribbling off the feed bins, heels tapping against the chiming metal.

They said nothing for a while, just sat supping white wine, each of them listening to the other's breathing, hearing tiny movements of their clothes as their chests rose up and down. The scratching of hiding mice, the bombing of a beige moth into the light bulb, assorted equine snorts outside.

Roger lowered his face close to Jenny's mouth. Her lips began to tingle as she pulled back slightly, nervous.

'You've got a nice wheelbarrow.' She felt embarrassed.

'Thanks.' Roger smiled. 'I've just re-greased the wheels.'

Roger leapt off the bins and grabbed the barrow, pushing it

towards her. It was nothing special, only reinforced metal with fat rubber tyres and an old sticker on the handle.

'Fancy a ride?' Roger gulped the remnants of his mug. He tipped the wheelbarrow up so particles of shit and straw fell out, and offered it to Jenny. She got in, giggling, feet raised high above the ground as he pushed her outside into the moonlit yard. Horses' heads protruding from the stables, checking on the noise. The couple laughed stupidly, quite drunk, and bounced along the bumpy concrete path. Roger veered off towards the hay barn, where sleepy cats yawned in the nests they'd made from bales.

'Going, going!' he jested. 'Gone!' Roger tipped the wheelbarrow with unexpected force, catapulting the rider into a prickly pile of straw. She sprawled around with barley seeds and straw chaff in her hair, and promptly started sneezing. Roger moved forwards, laughing at her as he rocked backwards on his heels. Jenny lurched up and grabbed his arm, throwing herself back down with him beside her.

They smiled into each other's faces, warm breath caught between them, their bodies inching closer, bit by bit. A black cat investigated, its whiskers tickling Jenny's fingers as she laid still beside the man.

The three biggest regrets in Jenny Barker's life:
1. Killing the milkman.
2. Simon deserting her, the swine.
3. Not losing her virginity to the increasingly attractive Roger Mandrake.

Jenny nudged towards him and the cat scattered away, leaving the writhing humans to move closer. Heat rising from their bodies in the keen collision of clothing as fabrics rubbed together. Weave upon weave, harder, faster. Roger wrestled with Jenny's top while she picked straw from his hair, caressed his neck, softly biting his skin. She could feel the pump of his adrenaline as blood rose to the surface, soft metal splinters sucked up by her magnetic mouth. Her top wedged onto her head, making her laugh as she couldn't see and her arms were splayed upwards, like she was in a bank stick-up. Another tug and it was off. Jenny cupped her hands over her bra, embarrassed that Roger could see. He smiled at her, kissed the skin between the mounds. It tickled.

Roger's jeans slithered down his legs revealing sage-green boxer shorts. His legs were hairy, like a faun. Jenny laughed, felt silly. Straw rubbed against hot breasts as he rolled her over onto her front. Licked his way up from the base of her spine to the nape of her neck, easing that tight knot of tension. She moaned, part ecstasy, part itch. Her head dizzied with fear and excitement as he ran his fingers down her buttocks and peeled away her pants. Her insides were cold and shivery, as if her blood had turned to meths. When he eased her back over and sucked debris from her nipples she felt like she needed the toilet.

He pulled her hand down towards his crotch but she wiggled it back up along his stomach to the splattering of hair upon his chest. Roger moaned as she squeezed his flesh and sucked the underside of his neck. Salty, sea water skin. Ripples pulsed through her body as her head started to spin. Roger rested his face on hers and chewed the bottom of her ear. Jenny was glad she hadn't put in any earrings.

Roger started his round trip again, round her neck, round her breasts, round her waist... ending up at that triangle of fluff that Jenny would rather he hadn't seen. She could not see the attraction herself, but he was in there like a cat at double cream. Jenny stared through the doorway at the night sky while his tongue licked into work, and tried to concentrate on counting stars. If she looked down at the bobbing head between her legs she would have a giggling fit.

Think of something else. Pussy. Cats. Pussy cats. Different colour cats. Ginger... oooooh. Tortoiseshell, yes, more. Black,

black, black, God, yes. Grey and white, oh God, that tickled.

Something different. A quick glimpse down as she felt his tongue run up her skin, his spit dribbling cold into her navel. His fingers twitched within her, sending the contents of her stomach lurching, wine splashing around. Cats and dogs. Woof, woof, his finger really tickled. Don't laugh.

Faster, deeper, loosening her muscles. If only inserting tampons felt as good as this. Don't. Laugh. Closing her tingling eyes, she saw stars and planets painted on her lids. Pluto. Saturn. The North Star. Northern. Up north. Up. Up more. Deeper. More. Finger flesh inside her face. His skin, her taste. It reminded her of fish.

Think of things to stop you laughing. Miserable things. Ethiopia, famine, disease, war, overpopulation, bonking, condoms, AIDS. Fuck, she hadn't thought of that. She presumed the fact they'd gone as far as this was a sign that penetration would occur? How could she sit up now and ask if he'd got condoms? Could she say the word out loud? Would he think that she was dumb, or a ridiculous drunk tart? Would his manhood be insulted?

When Jenny looked back down at Roger he was doing something unspeakable inside the front of his boxer shorts. This was it then. This was officially it. Jenny watched in awe and some surprise as her new acquaintance stood up all on its own, extinguishing the credibility of her old biology textbook.

She inhaled when he entered her, the pain like a hot cut. Feeling a strange force pushing within, pressing tight, pulling and sliding like an odd plunging device. Damp heat of rubbing skin aiding the suction. She gulped back the taste of sick as it burped into her windpipe. Roger raised himself above her, not wanting to squash her deeper into the straw, her body sinking away the more he sunk inside her. She watched him groan with effort as his buttocks clenched in rhythm with his panting, pounding heart. One two, in out. One two, in out. The motions sent her numb. Jenny tried to think of a word to describe it. No.

She couldn't think of one. Her left leg cramped, and she was stuck.

Sweat rained from Roger's face. Loud groans came when he climaxed. Jenny made a soft cooing noise, aware that she'd been conspicuously quiet.

'Are you okay?' Roger stroked her chin. 'Alright, love?'

Jenny nodded and tried to smile, but felt awkward and strangely guilty. Warm liquid trickled slowly down her leg as she sat up. A dull pain grew inside her. She was suddenly very dirty, conscious of the muck around them, of streamers of thick dust hanging from the rafters, and the horse-shit piled outside.

She grabbed her clothes and hurried to get dressed, covering up the strawberry rashes scratched onto her by straw. She couldn't look Roger in the eye on the drive home, even though she wanted to. They kissed goodnight on the outside step and Jenny ran upstairs.

She locked herself in the bathroom and splashed her body clean. Stared into the mirror to see if she looked different, more womanly, alluring. But she just looked more tired.

Excavation

Dear Agony Aunt,
I'm in love with Simon Marles, but I've just done it with the vet. He's
nice, he brought my horse back. What do you suggest that I do now?
Jenny B from Leeds

Dear Jenny,
Did you like it? Do it again! But think about the Pill.

The parents had gone on a last minute cheap package holiday to Spain, leaving Jenny to take care of the house and Laddie the leg-humping dog. She'd waved them off to Leeds Bradford airport, and then Roger came round.

He looked quite worried.

'What's wrong?' Jenny panicked. 'Is it Mister? Is he okay?' What if he'd jumped out of the stable to come look for her and had got crushed on the road?

'He's fine.' Roger hugged Jenny to him, kissed her childish, pouting mouth. 'Tracy rang. There's no lead on the dealer. He'd bought the horse from someone else, and God knows how many times he'd changed hands before that.'

'Will you come inside?' Jenny glanced round the front garden for prying neighbours. She didn't want to be reported, to have Mr Price spragging to her father, saying that she'd brought a man around. He was bound to be snooping about, as there were workmen in his garden, and he wouldn't trust them to get on with things unguarded.

They went through to the kitchen. Laddie scuttled over, took a look then padded off. He'd not been the same since Teddy's death, he seemed rather confused. He kept barking at the greenhouse and sniffing round the compost heap. He'd tunnelled through to the neighbour's garden in search of his missing friend, and brought back a garden gnome instead.

Roger sank into a chair. 'There was an incident at Tracy's

yard.' He sounded like a policeman. 'They're not sure... they think it was the Savager.'

'What!' Jenny immediately felt ill.

'It's alright, the horses are fine. The Savager was disturbed. He'd been in a stable with a horse, but it broke out, made a disturbance. Tracy was there.'

'She was there? And is she...?'

'Concussion, a few bruises. A black eye.'

'You've seen her?' Jenny couldn't take this in.

'We spoke on the phone. Then at the police station.'

'Wait, you went to the police station?'

'I was the last person to see her.' He shrugged. 'Well, I mean, we were. I could kill a cup of tea.'

'Fine, yeah.' Jenny filled the kettle. She was stunned. 'So what did the police say, do they know who did it?'

'No. Look, it could have been a burglar, an intruder.' Roger shuffled on his chair. 'It might not be the Savager at all. That's supposition. It could have been a jealous boyfriend. Got any biscuits?' He clearly wanted to change the subject. 'How's Brown?'

'Thin.'

'We got the tests back. He's anaemic. Very. His red cell count's far too low. And there's microbes missing in his belly that help digest the food. The good bacteria, which break components down...'

Jenny wasn't listening. The Savager. If they hadn't brought Mister back that night, if they'd not gone over straight away, and Tracy wasn't there... Mister could have been murdered.

'Jenny, are you okay? You've gone white.' Roger squeezed her hand. 'Come here. Let's take your mind off things.'

They made love in the parents' bed, as her cramped single was too small and she wasn't keen on carpet burns. Jenny wrote a post-it note to herself to remember to wash the sheets. She lay in Roger's arms while he smoked a menthol cigarette, which made his kisses taste of breath mints.

'You are so different to Anne,' he smiled. 'Why couldn't I have met you first, wiped out the last three years with her?'

'Your wife?'

'Ex-wife.' He inhaled a tired drag.

'You got the divorce then? Great.'

'Well, no. Not officially, but nearly.' Roger extinguished the cigarette stump and rolled towards her. 'It's difficult. Believe me, she's pretty strange.'

'People say I'm strange,' Jenny ran her fingertip along his shoulder blade. 'Is that why you like me? I've got the mental age of twelve.'

'Give over!' He squeezed her stomach. 'You're a sweet kind of strange. She's creepy, a proper rabbit boiler. I mean, when I first met her I thought she was great. Older woman, experienced....'

'Better than me?' Jenny thought she should make more noises.

'No. Just different. She got a bit demanding, too possessive.'

Roger said he should have seen it coming. That Anne had been obsessed with him from their first meeting, when he'd driven over to see her sickly sheep. She'd never taken her eyes off him when they sat eating roast lamb the following Sunday, him at one end of the table with the mint sauce, her at the other with the mustard. He had wondered at the time if the lamb chops they were eating had belonged to the specimen he'd examined. If he had just eaten a patient.

'Her dad's a slaughterer,' Roger explained. 'You may have heard of him. Jack Turner? He bought her a pony for her thirteenth birthday. After the summer holidays he had it killed for meat. Unlucky for some, hey? He wouldn't let her get attached, you see. But she got attached to me.' He ran his hand through Jenny's hair, pulling strands across her face. 'Knacker kid, that's what school bullies called her. They put bits of liver in her desk, with pony pictures on it. Kids are cruel. She wanted to go to the riding school, but they wouldn't let her in.'

Jenny turned over, awkward. She hadn't wanted sentimental details.

The front doorbell rang.

'That might be her!' teased Jenny. 'She's come round to get us.'

'Yeah, right.' He sank back into the mattress. 'No, it's probably your parents, forgotten their passports or something.'

Jenny propelled herself from bed and grabbed her clothes.

Wit was in the driveway. He had just started to walk off when the front door opened up. He smiled when he saw Jenny, but his face was strained and troubled.

'Hi! I'd just decided you were out.'

'No, I'm here. Come in.' Jenny quickly straightened her shirt, brushed some hair out of her face. 'It's great to see you.'

'I thought maybe something was wrong?' Wit followed her inside. 'You've not called me since the party.'

'That was great!' smiled Jenny. 'I had a really good time.'

'Really?' Wit was glad.

'God, yeah. And that house! You're a dark horse Wit, aren't you? I didn't have a clue.'

'So we're fine then? You're not pissed off at me?' He moved closer towards her, wanting her to stand still for a moment, instead of fluttering around the kitchen like a sparrow.

'It's been crazy,' Jenny grinned. 'I found Mister, my horse. I got him back! It's incredible.'

'And it's him this time?' Wit's face darkened a moment. 'For real?'

Jenny grinned. 'I didn't go mad and nick the wrong horse, if that's what you mean. Yes. It's really him.'

'That's great. I'm happy for you. Jenny....' He took a breath. 'I've got something to ask. I mean, we get on, we have a laugh... and I thought... well... Could we go on holiday?'

'What?' Jenny darted round, hearing footsteps upstairs.

'Remember when we were in the first year?' Wit cleared his

139

throat. 'We said that after our degree, when everything was over, we'd go bumming it round Europe. The whole group.'

'I forgot.'

'You and the rest of them, it seems, or else they're just too skint. But I thought, Europe. Inter-railing. Going off on an adventure.'

'It's a great idea but I'm broke. I've got my poorly horse to feed, and Mister...'

Wit's eyes lit up. 'I'll treat you. We can get someone in to see to Brown. You must know people?'

'Yeah, but....'

'No buts, Jen. I've already booked the tickets.'

Roger appeared in the doorway dressed in navy boxer shorts. Wit's mouth dropped open.

'Wit.' Jenny started blushing. 'This is Roger. My... vet.'

Roger reached his hand out to shake, but Wit kept his arms clamped firmly by his side.

Wit stuttered. 'Right, well, I have to pack. I'm off. I'm going. Nice to erm... See you later.'

Wit raced to the front door.

'Wit!' Jenny went after him. 'William, stop!'

He was already heading up the road. Jenny saw Mr Price watching from the bushes, and quickly shut the door before he spotted the masculine form of Roger standing close behind, half naked.

'He fancies you,' smiled Roger.

'Give over. Wit's my friend.'

Jenny peered out of the front window until she saw Wit rounding the corner, where he disappeared from view. His departure made her anxious.

'I'd better go after him.' Maybe Wit could take Nina or Sharon to visit Europe? They could both do with a tonic.

Roger snaked his arm around her waist, spread kisses along the back of her smooth neck. Jenny decided Wit could wait till later.

Jenny lay sunbathing in the garden after Roger left. She tried to read a book but couldn't concentrate, and Thomas Hardy's heroine Tess seemed to be having too dark a time for such a sunny day. The words shimmered on the page like insects. She couldn't focus.

The dog kept barking at the fence.

'Laddie, shut up.'

He was giving her a headache. There was too much action taking place next door, with constant banging and drilling. Following the murder of the last of his rare pond fish, Mr Price had decided to forego the wonders of the scaly deep and install a larger sun deck with assorted furniture. Jenny wished he could have picked another time to get his workmen in. She needed peace to help her think. There was something troubling her, but she didn't know quite what.

Jenny went round to find Wit at his house. The door was locked, and when she looked through the front window she couldn't see signs of anyone, just an old abandoned sofa and an unemptied waste bin full of cans. She felt a surge of deja-vu.

She clicked her mobile on to phone Wit's parents' house, but got a strange, crackled response. A woman who appeared to be his mother quickly answered, her voice spiked with an abruptness which made Jenny start to panic. When she asked if Wit was there the woman made a muffled noise, and the receiver was passed along to someone else who put it down. Jenny tried calling back later but this time nobody answered.

When Jenny returned home she realised Laddie was also missing. She went round to Mr Price's to see if he had seen him, but her neighbour wasn't there. His garden was a hive of activity, with two bare chested workmen and a cement mixer all ready to fill the pond. Jenny was surprised how deep it was. She scanned across the garden, unaware of a pair of eyes watching her from under the far hedge.

Mr Price came round at six o'clock. He looked more vexed

than normal.

'You'd better come fetch your dog,' he started. 'He's in my back garden.'

Jenny followed him round and looked across the grass. She couldn't see Laddie anywhere. Confused, she turned back to Mr Price, who was staring dreamily at the remains of his fish pond.

Then she noticed it. Sticking up through the set concrete. A miniature collie's tail. It wasn't wagging.

Price was distressed but completely in control, as if he had a dog cemented into his fish pond every day.

'He must have been hiding somewhere and gone in when they weren't looking. They filled it in and went off to the pub. He'd set by the time they got back. Now I've got to pay for them to come back tomorrow and chip him out.'

Jenny couldn't think what to say or do. She called Nina, who wasn't in, and Wit still had not returned. She didn't want to worry Sharon, and Roger was unavailable in surgery. There was no one left to turn to.

'Grandad?'

Jenny had to talk to someone and tell them what had happened. She had to practice on somebody before the parents arrived home. 'Grandad, can you hear me?'

It had taken a while for the nurse to find him, and was now taking even longer to get him to talk out loud down the receiver.

'Grandad, it's me. Jenny.'

Nothing.

'I wanted to see how you were.' If his week had been as eventful as hers. Get horse back, lose virginity, kill dog.

A throaty growl emerged. 'Who is this? The government?'

'Grandad, it's Jenny. Remember? Mary's daughter.'

'Do you poo your pants?' He said that softer, in case a nurse was listening.

'I grew up, I'm twenty-two now. I don't wear nappies anymore.'

'Mrs Arberthough is eighty-two and she poos her pants.'

Jenny cracked a smile. 'Right, Grandad. I really needed to know that.'

'It's something we all have to look forward to. They listen, you know. To the phones.'

'Who does? The nurses?'

'The government.' He whispered, softer. 'I think they want to steal my pension. Wait there, I'll go and get my wife.'

'Grandad! Hello? Are you still there?'

A long silence. The sound of the receiver dangling, tapping on the table leg. Jenny was about to hang up when she heard his voice again.

'Hello,' he growled. 'Who is it?'

'It's Jenny!' This was ridiculous. She must have been stupid to think he could have offered her advice, helped her to ease the news of dog death. 'Your granddaughter!' She felt guilty at her annoyance, took a breath. 'I was just ringing for a chat. The dog died, he's been killed...'

'What dog? I haven't got a dog. Are you trying to say I've got a dog?'

'No!' groaned Jenny. 'Mum's dog. Laddie, you know, the little collie.'

'Can I come and see him?'

'No, he's dead.' Now Jenny was confused.

'Can I come and see you? In my car?'

'Yeah, course you can,' sighed Jenny, weary. 'You take care, Grandad. Don't be messing with those nurses.'

With that she put the phone down. No advice on what to do about the dog, or how best to break the news, but she felt like a better person, and it helped.

Jenny heard the parents' pull into the drive. She'd been psyching herself up for hours now, with the help of wine and brandy. The car doors slammed. Shit. They were going to murder her.

Mary Barker fluttered into the kitchen, complexion browned by the sun and an over-enthusiastic application of foundation.

'Look at me, Jenny!' she beamed. 'Aren't I looking healthy?'

'Not like Laddie,' sighed Jenny, nodding over to the table.

Mary Barker let out a horrific scream and dropped everything she'd bought in the duty-free. Dark puddles of alcohol seeped through the carrier bag as she stared at the lump of concrete with a set of squashed paws, a static tail and a snout sticking out the front. Jenny thought it was lucky that when her mother fainted she didn't land on the broken grass.

Recrimination

Jenny's parents kicked her out. Not because they blamed her for the dog death incident, though they found that rather careless, and called her selfish for not taking better care of their last remaining pet. It was because of a pair of dark green boxer shorts they found under their bed. Ray Barker was a Y front man, and he was quite appalled.

'You hussy! You did it in our bed!' He'd snarled at Jenny and then glared at his wife. 'You and him... the pair of you!'

Jenny felt bad about this, even worse now they'd found out. But the reaction was extreme. Ranting. Recriminations. The parents in a screaming match about sex and betrayal. Jenny had hoped they might be happy, they'd seemed delighted when Wit had come around, when they thought he was her boyfriend. They weren't delighted now.

'If you're going to treat this place like a cheap hotel for hookers, then you can pay for it by the hour,' Ray spat. 'Else get out on your own, and do what the hell you like. But in this family....'

Her mother had tried to calm him. That only made things worse. Jenny packed everything she could into a rucksack and two suitcases and thundered down the drive, red-faced, eyes burning. Shamed. It was only when she reached the bottom that she realised she didn't know where she should go. She phoned Nina, but her friend was out. Roger was in, so she went to live with him. That seemed fair and reasonable. It was his discarded underwear that caused the problem in the first place.

Roger lived in a rented cottage near Fairburn Ings, a place so quiet the only interruptions were the squawks of moorhens and thunder flaps of swans. The occasional chimes of an ice cream van on its way to feed birdwatchers by the water. Jenny went to watch the birds to calm herself, but after a while it made her feel more restless. She was cut off from her friends, miles away from anywhere. The buses seemed to run by the day, not the hour, and she was stuck at home. Only it wasn't her home, not really. It was just a place to stay.

Roger was very pleased to have her there, and at first Jenny found it quite exciting. Pretending to be a grown up, doing the cleaning, cooking meals. They had a romantic dinner every evening for the first week, but then ran out of candles.

It was a fifteen minute walk to where Mister was stabled, and Jenny was glad of that at least. She'd spend as much time as she could with him, taking him out for rides around the cool shade of Ledsham woods. Up past Ledston Hall, by the overgrown cross country jumps in North Park, where she rode when she was younger. There used to be lots of them on ponies then, rivers of kids trotting along the country roads. Now it was just her, and the only person to talk to was her horse, grey ears twitching like mice as he listened.

Jenny worried about Brown, who was stuck over at Deacon's. She telephoned every day, making sure he was getting the right tablets and proper feeds. She needed to be there. It wasn't reachable by bus, and Mister would be exhausted if she rode him that far, he'd wear away and become as thin as Brown. Jenny had hoped that once she got Mister back safely everything would feel fine. But now she was more troubled. The brown horse needed her, and she missed stroking his gawky neck and seeing his silly sunken face.

Jenny thought she should be happy. Everything she had wanted, she had got. Her missing horse, a man who loved her, independence from her folks. She looked at herself in the mirror and wondered what *fulfilled* was supposed to look like.

She missed college, missed her friends, far more than she'd expected. She found herself getting up in the middle of the night to pack her art-tool box ready for the next morning. It was over a month since they'd finished, and each day she got more bored. She wanted things to be like before, with Nina, Wit and Simon.

Reality was dreary, and it was heavily sinking in. She'd

queued up at the dole office, filled in the appropriate forms. A woman with a painted smile asked what she did, what line of work she hoped to find. There was nothing resembling design or photography on the computers or the boards, which boasted opportunities for factory work in Bradford, fruit picking in a field, fish and chip shop fryers, care assistants, bar staff and early morning cleaners. The polite advisor suggested that Jenny should try another career option. Perhaps shop work would be good? They were often taking staff on at the Asda. Jenny stewed in mute annoyance. She'd struggled through her A levels, through a year doing an art foundation course, three more hard years for her degree... and this woman told her to try something she could have done straight out of school? What would she have suggested to Turner prize star Damien Hirst? Go work in a meat factory, if you like working with dead things?

Jenny got some more anti-depressants and tried to be more positive. She sent copies of her photographs to magazines and newspapers, hoping to drum up a bit of interest. She tried to make herself feel settled, putting up some pictures in her room. Roger didn't like them.

'What are you doing?' He ripped down the newspaper reports, part of Jenny's collection from her old bedroom wall. 'What's this Savager stuff for?' The articles upset him. 'There's some nutter out there attacking horses, and you want to rub it in? I've got enough to deal with at work without reminders about this! And look, you've used drawing pins. You've made holes everywhere.' He rubbed his finger over the heavy wallpaper, flattening it down.

'I'm sorry.' Jenny realised a mistake had been made.

'Keep them in a file or something, if you must.' Roger calmed a little, embarrassed by his outburst. 'I mean, it's not exactly Monet is it? We don't want this up as decoration.'

'No. You're right.' Jenny felt like a child now, not a lover.

'Okay?' Roger hugged onto her, stroking her auburn hair. 'I didn't mean to shout.' He picked a tatty clipping from the carpet and tossed it in the bin. 'And now Mister's back, you don't need to be part of Horsewatch, do you? No more sneaking about in fields.'

Jenny remembered she had to ring up Mr Blonde, thank her for the sack of pony nuts she'd sent as a welcome home present for Mister.

'Right, I'm off for a shower.' Roger grinned at her. 'You can join me if you like.'

Jenny collected up her newspaper cuttings and put them out of the way. The phone rang.

'Hello?'

No one answered.

'Hello? Roger's house.'

Still nothing.

'Anyone there?'

The phone was clunked down the other end. Jenny dialled 1471, but the caller's number was withheld. Roger appeared, wrapped in a toga towel.

'Who was it?'

'Dunno. Wrong number?' Jenny shrugged. Maybe it was her grandad, but then he didn't know where she was. Or her mum, who couldn't think what to say.

Roger weaved towards her.

'Okay gorgeous... so how about that shower?'

He took hold of Jenny's hand and casually lifted the phone receiver off its base, leaving it to buzz and whine while they went upstairs.

A postcard arrived from Wit. It had been stuck on the parents' fridge for a week before they realised that it wasn't meant for them. Mary Barker redirected it, and wrote *hello* on the bottom.

Wit was in Paris. It was great, but he wished Jenny was there. He'd drawn a smiley face, saying next stop Amsterdam.

'Let's make Chris Isaak happy,' Jenny mumbled,

remembering that evening in Hyde Park, lying on damp grass under the sky, naming stars and singing gloomy love songs.

She missed Wit. She should have gone on holiday. She so needed a rest, an escape from everything.

'We could go somewhere,' Roger offered. 'Abroad, if you like. I've not been away since...' Since his honeymoon with Anne.

'I can't afford it,' Jenny sighed, distracted.

'It's a present. I'll pay, I'm earning.'

The phone started to ring. He picked it up.

'Hello, Roger here.' A silence. 'Hello?' Furrows deepened on his brow. 'Aren't you going to speak to me?' He saw Jenny watching. 'Well fuck off then.' He thumped the phone done. 'Bloody kids.'

The look on Roger's face told Jenny he knew it wasn't. They stared at each other, neither knowing what to say, each realising that the other one was worried.

'Could be a fault on the line?' suggested Jenny.

Roger shrugged. 'A bad connection.'

The phone rang again, shrill cry cutting the silence. Roger didn't bother to answer it this time, just pulled the cord out from the wall to stop the ringing.

'Come on, let's go somewhere.' He was more determined now. 'Anywhere you want to. You name it, I'll go out and buy the tickets.'

Jenny didn't have to think for long. 'Italy?' Simon said it was beautiful. 'I'd love to go to Rome.' A worry. 'But what about Brown and Mister?'

'Trust me, I'll take care of them,' said Roger. 'I've got it all in hand.'

Roger was true to his word. He shipped Mister to a grassy field for a vacation, convincing Jenny that he was better off out at grass than cooped up in his stable. He offered little Debbie Dakin at Deacon's a daily wage to take good care of Brown, promising a bonus if the horse put on any weight. Then they drove to Manchester airport and got a flight to Rome.

They stayed in bed the first morning, eating breakfast off the sheets and barricading the door to stop an incensed Italian cleaning lady breaking in with soap and towels. Roger taught Jenny the technical names of muscles and bones as they explored each other's bodies, guessing at their foreign pronunciations. In the evening their faces dripped with spaghetti as they ate out in the town, warm air blowing against them, feeling free. Savouring each special taste, each moment, making the most of everything, knowing that soon it would be over.

Jenny wandered round Rome in a daze, staring at sun-baked buildings and listening to the whispers on the streets. They sat in quiet, soft-toned cafes supping cappuccinos, eating ciabatta and drinking local wine. They tossed silver coins into the Trevi fountain, hoping that one day they would return. Pigeons fluttered around them as Roger told Jenny he loved her. She said the same thing back, worried that the words had made her flustered. As he kissed her, Jenny couldn't decide if what she felt inside was genuine love or indigestion. The aftertaste of olive oil stayed in her mouth, along with a scent of cold cooked chicken.

I love him, I love him not. She pulled petals off one of the red roses that Roger gave her. I love him. She really liked his smile. I love him not. She didn't like his temper. I love him. She liked how he cared for animals, it was good to have a vet on call. I love him not. Jenny ran out of scarlet petals. She started on another rose.

They visited the Colosseum and got the full guided tour with tales of gladiators and traitors, Christians and lions. The sunshine burnt Jenny's nose and forehead lobster pink, drawing the letter *T* upon her face. As they walked round the Pantheon the echoes were so strong that she could hear Romans chatting in the background, like a constant Walkman buzz. She imagined merchants standing in the hollow circle, doves flying overhead up to the roof. Deep Italian voices, or maybe Latin.

Canis est in via, she remembered that from school. Funny that all she could remember from a picture and word book of the sad tale of Pompeii was that the family dog was in the street. It probably barked like crazy when Vesuvius erupted. Canis est in via. Watch out, the lava's coming. Nobody noticed though. The people didn't know tragedy was upon them until they turned to rock.

How strange, Jenny thought, that no one sees bad things happening until after they occur. There must be a system within human nature that shuts out signs of the inevitable.

Their dog was turned to stone. She could see him in her head. Smile set solid on his bewildered canine face.

Shivers ran down her spine as for a moment Jenny believed completely in reincarnation, and knew that she'd been in this place before. The sounds, the smells, she knew them. They were deep inside her. This place, it meant something. It had to be significant.

Roger had gone to buy some souvenirs when she saw him, standing by the doorway to the hall. Jenny froze. A golden halo rose above his soft dark hair as sunlight filtered in from the street outside.

'Simon.' She couldn't shout. His named glued on her tongue.

He stepped out into the square, melting into the crowd as she went running, shouting this time, catching glimpses of the back of his head as she ducked through tourists and lively Italian vendors.

Jenny stood in the centre of the market place, people sprinkled around her, some looking at her like she was crazy, until realising she was foreign and therefore bound to be confused.

An old lady with a basket of strawberries tugged at her arm. 'You English?'

'What? Yes. Sorry.' Jenny glanced around. Nowhere. Gone.

'You lost, yes? English lady?'

'Yes,' Jenny was dizzy in the heat, panicking as she saw Roger approaching. 'I lost him.'

Roger took Jenny's hand.

'No lost! He came back!' The strawberry seller held out a bowl of fruit. 'You buy, for pretty lady.'

Roger agreed. They watched the woman wobble off.

'Is something wrong?' He led Jenny to a bench, aiming for some shade. 'You look like you've seen a ghost.'

Jenny chewed her lip, thoughtful.

'When they threw Christians to the lions,' she started. 'Did they tell them the name of the lion that was going to eat them? Or would they never know?'

Sunstroke, that's what the doctor called it. A little too much sun. Fair people were susceptible, it seemed. Jenny asked if it could make people hallucinate. See things that were not there. The man gave her a shrug. He said that it was possible, especially with wine. He told Jenny to lie in a bath of cold water for two and a half hours, and to wear a head scarf outside. His brother had a store, apparently, where they sold excellent headgear. You could buy a cotton head square with the Virgin Mary on top.

Jenny went out and bought some postcards, sending one of the Pope in mohican hair-do to the parents, a sculpted horse to Nina, a city view to Sharon and a naked woman to Wit via his home address. She supposed he'd get it some day, when he stopped travelling around.

She and Roger waved at the Pope in St Peter's Square but Jenny wasn't sure that it was really him. You couldn't tell at such a distance, and her eyes had been playing tricks.

'How do you feel? D'you need a drink of water?' Roger was dutifully concerned.

'I'm fine.' Jenny's nose was stinging.

'And you're having a good time?'

'I'm loving it.' It couldn't have been Simon, Jenny decided. It must have been the hot sun and the red wine.

'Would you like to come back here again, say, maybe next summer?' Roger took hold of Jenny's hand. 'And we could go to Florence too, I hear it's beautiful.'

'Yeah, I'd love that.' She liked Rome.

'But a really special holiday,' offered Roger. 'I mean, a honeymoon.'

'What?' Had Jenny heard that right?

Roger got down on one leg, his bare knee scratching on the cobbles. 'Jenny Barker, you're the one good thing that's happened to me in years. I know this may seem fast... but will you marry me?'

Jenny's stomach lurched. That was definitely indigestion.

'But...um... you're still married. Your Anne won't....' A thought flashed through Jenny's mind. She was jealous of his wife, each time she heard the woman's name it got her back up. What did that mean, emotion-wise? Was it proof she was in love?

Roger was adamant. He had a plan. 'This way we'll be rid of her! If she realises I'm serious about you, that we're a long-term couple, then she'll see that things are over for me and her. It'll speed up the divorce.'

Roger's bent leg was shaking now.

'So, what d'you say?'

Jenny became aware of several pairs of eyes watching them.

'I'll think about it,' she offered.

'Is that a yes?' Roger squinted against the sun.

'Okay.'

Roger scrambled to his feet and took the stunned girl in his arms. As they kissed amidst the pigeons a nearby gathering of nuns from Dunstable started to clap and a small American boy called Chip sang snippets from *The Lion King*. Coins were tossed in his direction and one of them hit Roger on the back. He picked it up, rolled it in his palm, then put it in his pocket for good luck.

Roger bought a sparkling engagement ring, crusted with coloured gems, from a small jewellers at the back of their hotel. It seemed a lot of money, but then most foreign countries had figures with loads of noughts. He placed it on Jenny's vibrating finger over their linguini dinner, while a prompted violinist stood beside their table, his bow screeching against the tightened strings.

They lay awake on the last night of their holiday, safe in each others sun-kissed arms. When Roger went to the bathroom, Jenny cuddled up as close as she could to the warm patch where he'd been. People can really grow on you, she thought, enjoying the closeness, the comfort, the growing familiarity.

She listened to running water, to the tooting traffic in the hot city street outside, and imagined herself in a long white dress and veil, walking down the aisle, seeing him waiting at the front of the church, fingers drumming against his leg with nerves. The back of his head, dark hair cut close against his nape, resting just above his collar.

Jenny's mum was waiting outside Roger's cottage when they got back from the airport. Her face milk-white, eyes red.

'Your grandad's dead.'

He'd been sprucing himself up in his bedroom, trying to put Brylcreem on his hair, only he'd used barbecue lighter fuel by mistake. Then in some freak accident he lit a cigar and set his hair on fire. But it wasn't this that killed him. He had a heart attack.

Communication

That night she dreamt of wedding days. Of walking down the aisle in crisp icing sugar dress, feet tapping in a pair of pointed shoes. Her future husband standing patiently, his broad back turned towards her. Sunlight glittering through stained glass windows, catching coloured motes in the hot summer haze. The bridegroom turned and it was Simon.

When Jenny woke she couldn't breathe.

The holiday was over. Grandad's funeral took place without much incident. It rained, the parents were upset, Jenny and her mother cried a lot, and the mourners ate egg mayonnaise sandwiches in the church hall. Jenny's father had calmed down, and her mother offered to lend Jenny the car. She never used it. Never went anywhere.

'Are you alright?' Nina stood by Jenny at the graveside, looking down over damp earth, the hole where her grandad lay. 'I never see you anymore.'

Jenny shrugged, glancing at Roger in the distance, leaning against his Landrover, smoking a cigarette. 'Yeah, well, I'm kind of miles away.'

'We should go out,' said Nina. 'Catch up on things. It's been too long. How's Brown, and Mister?'

Jenny sighed, wiping her nose. 'Brown's okay, a bit fatter, but Mister....' She'd not seen him since their return from Rome. She had asked Roger to fetch him back from grazing in this mystery field, but he was adamant that the horse should stay exactly where he was. He said it was safer, that he was well out of the way. When Jenny pushed Roger further he got angry.

'We'll go out,' decided Nina. 'Friday. Get into Leeds and you can stay at mine.' She took hold of Jenny's hand. 'I'm really sorry about your grandad. He was fun.'

'Yeah, thanks.'

Roger pipped his horn, impatient.

'I'd better go.' Jenny scraped some soft mud off her shoes.

'Are you sure you're alright?' Nina was concerned. 'I don't know... you're looking older.'

Jenny shrugged. 'I grew up.'

She kissed her friend on the cheek and walked over to Roger. During the drive back to Fairburn Ings neither of them said a word.

They'd had a row the night before. Jenny wanted to meet up with Mr Blonde, check out a local Horsewatch lead. There'd been a mention of the Savager.

'I thought you'd dropped this!' Roger barked when he found her Horsewatch notes. 'You women, you're just trouble, I think you make things worse. What are you playing at, pissing about in fields? It could be dangerous. And haven't you got better things to do?'

He drove off in a huff. Jenny got her notes out of the dustbin when he left, hid them underneath her socks. Maybe it was the photos that upset him. Some were pretty gruesome, and as a man whose job was to preserve and rescue animals, they must have made him sick.

Roger apologised once he got back home at dawn, blood splattered on his clothes. He said he'd had a nose bleed. When he climbed into bed beside her the sheets stained with crimson patches, a fresh pattern of poppy petals.

She loved him. She loved him not.

Nina and Jenny met up at Indie Joze in the Victoria quarter of Leeds, and sat at a round silver table in the partitioned section of the echoing arcade. They drank a pitcher of ice-cold margarita, each scowling at the salt rims on their glass.

'Did you get a card from Wit?' asked Nina, digging out a slice of lime.

'Yeah, from Paris. Then one from Amsterdam.' He was no doubt replenishing his dope supplies, and watching busty ladies through the windows.

Nina was grinning at her.

'What?' Jenny checked her chin for dribbles.

'You and Wit... you're as bad as Mulder and Scully,' Nina's lip curled slightly. 'Out looking for aliens, yet you can't find what's in front of you.' Nina noticed someone. 'Here she is!'

Jenny glanced across, saw Sharon arriving. Nina pulled her up a chair.

'How are you doing, girl? Feeling better? You look well.' Nina tipped some pound coins from her purse. 'Drink?'

'No thanks. Well, coffee. Choca-mocha if they've got it.'

'Sure that's not a Chumbawamba?' Nina caught a waiter's eye.

Sharon gave a gormless look. 'What? The hairy thing from Star Wars?'

'Good to have you back, love.' Nina smiled. 'Right. I've got to go and have a piss. I seem to go every half-hour.'

Nina headed inside the cafe to the toilets.

Jenny couldn't think what she should say. She mixed lime and ice in the bottom of her glass until the straw went out of shape.

Sharon broke the silence.

'Thanks for visiting me in hospital.'

'No problem. I hope you liked the grapes.'

Sharon's drink arrived. Thick froth.

'Seedless,' noted Jenny.

'Yes. They're better without pips.'

Jenny supped up her last dregs.

'I might be going on holiday,' said Sharon. 'To go and see my folks.'

'That'll be nice. Koala bears.'

'You know, they sleep during the day. They just come out at night. Nocturnal.'

'I went to Rome,' Jenny said. 'With my....' Fiancé? Not too comfortable a label. 'With Roger. He's my vet.'

Jenny wanted to ask Sharon why she'd done it, why she'd

tried to kill herself. Whether a cry for help or not, it seemed a drastic measure.

She felt Sharon's gaze upon her.

'Did neither of you know?' Sharon's eyes were burning. 'Didn't you notice that there was something wrong with me? That I wasn't eating. That Tex was on my case. Why didn't you ask me then how I was feeling? Couldn't you see what was going on? Were you so stuck in your own world you couldn't tell?'

'I, um... well. Yes. No.'

'You know something, Jenny Barker? You can be really fucking stupid. But I guess I'll have to let you off, as I think you saved my life.'

Sharon wiped chocolate gunge off her top lip. Put on a smile as Nina walked towards them. Her right hand started to shake. She slid it underneath the table, fingers clenched.

'I'm sorry,' offered Jenny.

'Who's sorry?' Nina sank into her chair. 'God, you know, my wee's so yellow. It looks like Lucozade.'

Sharon smiled at Jenny. The conversation over. They sat and sipped for the next hour, then Sharon had to leave as she felt tired. Jenny and Nina both gave her a hug, for the first time since last Christmas when they bought each other presents. They watched her walk away.

Jenny was distracted. She'd picked up a colour out of the corner of her eye, and it was fluttering. She bent down beside the table, reaching for the yellow flyer on the floor.

Madame Biruschka Bennett - medium to the souls.

Seances and readings, any time, any place.

If they come at all, they come to the best.

There was an address in Harehills. They decided to go along for a laugh.

Madame Biruschka was originally from Birmingham. She was too small, too round, with far too much skin on her face, sagging down like a Shar-Pei dog's coat, wrinkling along the body like a ruff of velveteen. Ready for peeling off in one from bum to head. The woman's drooping skin was coated with wallpaper strips of thick solid fake tan, and a couple of bulky rings on every finger. She wasn't surprised to find the two young women on her doorstep.

'Come in luvvies,' she cheeped, her voice rather high for someone who looked as if she should sound like a ship's bell. 'I knew you were coming.'

They followed her through a hallway dotted with Iron Maiden posters, with a stink of burning incense and unwashed socks. A black cat sat by the open kitchen door, trying to look spiritual.

Madame asked them for ten pounds each then led them into a darkened room with purple walls, glowing candles in the corners and a long wooden table centre stage. Three people were sitting round it, pensive. A middle-aged man in a grey suit huddled next to a thin woman with dyed hair, both avoiding the keen gaze of a young man in motorcycle leathers. Two vacant chairs stood patiently at one side, near the psychic's empty throne.

'Creepy,' whispered Nina as they sat. 'Think they've been waiting for us?'

Jenny looked over at the youth opposite, a blue tattoo painted across his head in the shape of a roaring dragon. He said his name was Andrew.

Madame Biruschka shot him a look of warning. 'We have no names here, my lad. Only the names of the dead souls of our parting.'

She sat at the head of the table. Closed her eyes.

Nina giggled softly. Jenny nudged her to be quiet and act somewhat mature. You'd think that Nina would take this more seriously. It wasn't like they hadn't dabbled with the occult before. When her precious guinea pig Pumpernickel died during that cold winter, icicles sticking to his nose, they had spoken to the dead pet via their home-made Ouija board.

'Can you hear me?' They had asked.

The template moved across the letters.

'Eeep Id.' Came the reply.

'Are you in Heaven?' They had asked.

The template moved across the letters.

'Otf Sig Ba.'

Both Jenny and Nina vowed that they hadn't pushed their hands along. The animals were with them. Solid proof. For creatures cannot spell.

When Jenny came back from her daydreams Madame Biruschka was moaning a deep tone, resonance growing stronger as she reverberated. The scrawny woman next to Andrew started swaying her head from side to side, trying to get more involved with the proceedings.

Sweat seeped from the psychic's forehead, brown stains dripping on the cloth, bouncing as she banged her soft stomach against the table edge.

'Talk to me, darlings. Tell me who's there.' She breathed out slowly, asthma wispiness scratching against her windpipe. 'Feel the power. Come through the heat into our world. Let me bring you to the light!'

Madame Biruschka grabbed hold of the hands of nearest sitters Andrew and Jenny, making them both jump in fright. She swayed from side to side, her neck somehow managing to stay set in the same place like an expert Indian dancer.

'Feel the rhythm of the dead. Hear their voices.'

The rest of the circle started to join hands, Nina squeezing Jenny's in mock fear and exaggeration. Andrew swallowed his mint in a bid to concentrate. The man in the grey suit smiled as he wrapped the meek thin woman's palm inside his.

'Yes, please, tell me.' Madame's face glowed bright behind a flickering candle. She let out a deep sigh. 'Yes, I hear you.' She raised her hot hands higher, dragging her neighbours' arms up, revealing sweaty armpits of black hair.

'Yes! Yes! Come, now! Come! Come! God, yes!'

The watchers glanced around, the thin lady quite embarrassed, casting her stare down on the table. Jenny blushed, jaw dropping. Nina struggled not to laugh. Madame's eyes snapped open, boiled eggs of white, the irises disappearing up the top and rolled right round inside. Jenny's stomach lurched.

'Does anybody here know Doris?' Madame's voice had dropped a tone. No answer. 'Dora then?'

The man in the suit chirped helpfully. 'I know a Dennis.' He leapt up as the Madame's eyes rolled back. She dropped forwards, exhausted.

'She's gone. She says no one would know her. No-one cared anyway. That's why she killed herself.'

Jenny felt sick. Poor Doris. Nina tried not to smile as Madame walked around the room, winding her shoulders back to ease the stiffness. As she patrolled her area she stopped swiftly behind Andrew, placing gold-tinted hands firmly on his muscled shoulders, lurching him upwards as if hit by a suction force.

'Your mother says you've got to sell your bike,' snarled Madame. 'Or you'll be joining her much sooner than you think.'

Andrew gulped, mouth gaping. He tried to say something, but the words stayed in his gut. Nina looked at Jenny, surprised. Jenny shrugged, nonchalant, acting as though she'd thought this woman was genuine from the start.

Madame Biruschka sat back down in her place and the circle of hands resumed. The woman rocked from side to side, humming softly, like some Mama Queen from a sixties hippie peace camp.

'I don't want to ask her name! Don't you know it? If you can't feel her presence why are you with us anyway?'

Madame rocked faster, reddening with effort, and was jolted back on her chair by an invisible vacuum suck. Her eyes flashed open, pure unseeing white.

Her voice began to deepen, slowing, slower than a record on its slowest speed, slower than the most bored cricket commentator in the world.

'He wants to talk to Jenny.'

Nina gripped hard onto her best friend's hand as Jenny raised her head.

'Jenny? Jenny? Can you hear me?'

A sickness rose from Jenny's stomach to her mouth. Peas and carrots. Peas and carrots. She wanted to say something but her lips had stretched too tight.

Madame sweated profusely, words flowing out with watered salt.

'He says he's sorry he had to leave so soon, that he wished he'd known you better.' The woman groaned with effort, wrinkles flowing as she spoke. 'But remember those special times you had together.'

Nina prodded Jenny's side. 'Who is it?'

Madame swayed closer, heat rising from her head, moisture sticking damp hair against her discoloured forehead.

'He wants you to know he really loved you. You have to know that.'

Jenny forced words out of her mouth, a high-toned whine like she'd been sucking on a hydrogen balloon.

'Whoooo?'

'He just wants to say goodbye properly,' Madame started to twitch. 'And asks you to remember him.'

'Who?' High and low pitches in unison, a chorus of inquirers.

'Don't ever forget that Simon loved you.'

Madame's eyes flicked themselves shut as she collapsed onto the table.

Simon's dead.

Jenny stared out into space, hardly able to see for the steaming sweat that rose, frightened, from her face.

Simon's dead.

She squeezed so hard onto Nina's hand that the girl began to scream and punch her to be let go.

Simon's really dead.

Shocked by a wave of cold, Jenny was hit by spasms as she released Nina's bruised hand. As she expired under the table Jenny saw Simon's face smiling in front of her.

When Jenny came back round Nina was kneeling alongside, rubbing her arms and crying softly. Madame had gone upstairs for a rest and said they could stay downstairs until they got their act together.

The group dispersed when they saw that Jenny was alive. Andrew put on his motorbike helmet and sped off into the night. The man in the suit invited the thin woman to get an Indian take-away.

'It's bullshit, Jen,' Nina and Jenny went outside, neither of them able to feel their feet on the pavement as they walked. 'She's a con artist, it's not real.' Nina tried not to look disturbed, but she was ghostly pale. 'He can't be dead. He isn't. And why would he have a message for you, it's not like you're his girlfriend.'

Jenny's eyes were glazed. 'He loved me.'

'He hardly knew you.'

Jenny glared at her, upset. 'He loved me! You heard.'

'This is stupid, Jen. For fuck's sake, he was my boyfriend, he ran out on me! If anyone should get a fucking message then it's me! He isn't dead.'

'He is.' Jenny walked on ahead, fresh air making little sense of what she'd heard. She dug her nails into her palms, indenting white half-moons deep down into the skin. She wanted to wake up, to be asleep, to be anything but here, right now, with this new information. Simon Marles is dead.

Nina followed, confused and raging. Angry if Madame Biruschka was a fake, and even angrier if she wasn't.

'He was my boyfriend Jenny!' growled Nina as she walked. 'I asked him to go on a date with you to cheer you up. That's all it was.'

'He loved me.'

'You're deluding yourself! You're so stupid. And selfish! You don't care about me, you don't care about anyone except for baby Jenny Barker and her precious little life! God, you really make me sick. What about me, hey? What about me!'

Two youths leered from a car window as they passed by.

'How much for a quickie, love?' A jeer.

'Fuck you!' Nina ran after them, snarling as they sped off up the road. She looked around and saw Jenny had gone, her shape in the distance, jogging off towards Hyde Park.

'What about me?' Nina whimpered, then turned, headed for home.

The rain began to pour, incessant strips that blended with Jenny's tears as she ran, faster, wanting her heart to pop with effort and end it all. Her clothes darkened a shade a minute in the rain, from beige to brown to black.

She'd seen Simon in Rome. She'd convinced herself that it was nothing, sunstroke, wine, a similar Italian who possessed the same slow walk. But now she knew much better. Simon's ghost had followed her, he was waiting for her somewhere, until they could be together, two reunited spirits in the void.

Jenny padded towards town, being splashed by tooting taxis as she walked. She sheltered in a doorway near the City Varieties, reading old, sodden, brown-edged posters for shows that people probably hadn't bothered to go see. The old music hall was dead and so was Simon.

She should have guessed this, known that loving him would lead to doom. Don't love anyone, don't love anything, because they always die. James Dean in a car crash. Sal Mineo stabbed to death. Natalie Wood drowned deep beneath the sea. All of Jimmy's co-stars, all the rebels that weren't without a cause.

Jenny walked up the lamplit Headrow, past bank machines with red signs that boasted they were closed, sealed off with toughened plastic and a smug satisfied smirk. She ran her hands over the front of one and knew that all the money in the world was useless because whatever she did, however rich she became, she could not buy Simon back.

She saw a pigeon with a white head hopping about near the beer barrel man statue in Dortmund Square, probably installed in honour of drunken Germans who brought some free beer into Leeds. She wondered why the pigeon's head was white, and if she'd ever see the bird again. She picked through a litter bin to find something for it to eat, throwing some half digested chips in its direction. It flew off.

A red car nearly knocked Jenny over as she walked across the road, not looking or caring and indeed rather hoping that the driver wouldn't stop. She stood in the road for several minutes, watching headlights pass.

The stone lions were waiting for her outside Leeds town hall. She stood nose to nose with the nearest one and listened hard for its soft voice. Fatigue was biting her muscles as she rocked, sending herself into a trance. She wished this was a nightmare, that she would wake soon, find herself curled up safe in bed with the man at home that she was loved by.

Madame Biruschka said he loved her. Simon. People had to love you, didn't they, if you cared so much yourself? How cruel to have such feelings for someone else if they didn't have them back.

'So what do I do now?' she asked the lion. 'Where can I go from here?'

Words echoed round the concrete square, sending pigeons to the rooftops.

'You've got to tell me,' Jenny pleaded. 'Please.'

The lion stayed silent, unresponsive. Maybe it was thinking. Jenny began to cry again, wanting to speak secretly but her throat was pulling tight into a scream. She doubled over, gripping her stomach as she coughed. Nauseous as her insides rebelled against the shock and rain and alcohol that they had endured until now. Marching up her throat in protest, spitting globs of fury at her feet. Jenny wiped her face, weeping harder

165

as her nose began to drip.

'You've got to help me now!' she squealed. 'I think I'm going mad.'

A panda car arrived and two policemen walked over. They tried not to laugh as they dragged Jenny away, asking where she lived, only to be curtly told she lived in Hell. They drove to the station and put her in a cell to sleep it off. They considered pressing charges for being drunk and disorderly, but she wasn't doing any harm and quickly sobered up. Within an hour she was showing the custody sergeant how to do some magic tricks. The one where she escaped from a pair of locked handcuffs didn't work, but that was only because they weren't the special magician kind.

'My boyfriend died. I just found out,' she told them. Pity crossed their faces and they had a whip-round so she could buy herself some flowers and a nice box of Swiss chocolates. A kind policeman drove Jenny to her parents' house at three-thirty in the morning.

Jenny was glad she still had her own key as she crept in through the back door and slithered up the stairs. She didn't put the lights on as everybody was asleep, but wished she had as she collided with a cupboard in her bedroom that she hadn't known was there. The drink must have distorted her perception as she was sure her bed was facing the wrong way.

She woke early the next morning with less of a hangover than expected, but more of a sense of loss. She remembered Simon and wondered how she'd cope. Funny how you can not think about someone for a long time and then think of them every minute.

She sat down at the breakfast table and poured herself some fruit juice.

'Can you pass the toast please?'

The toast was duly passed along the table, and Jenny had it on her plate ready to coat with lemon marmalade, so much better than the bitter orange, when she became fully conscious of the silent faces watching her. A surprised Chinese man and woman, with their grinning burping child.

Jenny realised that this was not her family.

Desertion

The Yeungs were more surprised than Jenny at this sudden, curt appearance, but once she explained who she was, and how she lived there, then the tale fell into place. Even so, Jenny was rather perturbed that the parents had moved house without even telling her they'd put the house on the market. Mrs Yeung was kind, considerate even, as she gave Jenny her mother's phone number and suggested that she rang her to find out what was going on.

Roger came to pick her up. He was rather tense, annoyed. Said he hadn't had much sleep. As Jenny sat beside him in the Landrover one thought went through her head.

Simon Marles is dead.

Roger dropped her off at the cottage and drove away towards the veterinary surgery. As Jenny unlocked the front door she got a sense something was different. A soft scent hung idly in the air, the fragrance of vanilla. Jenny walked from room to room, picking up the flavour, finding pockets of air where the smell was more intense. A strong aroma in the tidy bedroom, hanging limp above tight sheets.

There were two wine glasses on the draining board in the kitchen, and a pair of matching mugs. Jenny lifted the metal kettle off the stove, water splashing angrily inside it. The base was still lukewarm.

Jenny rang her mother's number. Mary Barker wasn't surprised to hear from her, but seemed a little flustered. She shrugged off accusations of running away from home by saying there was a letter for her daughter in the post. She would ring Jenny back soon and arrange a date to meet. To sit down somewhere quiet and explain what was going on.

Jenny felt abandoned, like that little child eating Woolworth's Pick and Mix, left completely on her own. No newspaper articles. No being reunited with her parents. Not even an eager Mrs Tapper, squeezing hard onto her hand.

Not forgotten this time. Dumped.

Jenny visited Brown and gave him a lunchtime feed. She spent hours in his stable, watching him guzzling water and sniffing straw. His belly was slightly rounder, more compact. She hoped he was getting better. She couldn't bear for him to die.

The afternoon yawned along, flies buzzing. Jenny parked the car in a local supermarket car park, and rummaged through their bursting paper bank. She pulled out reams of newsprint, searching obituary columns for a sign of Simon's name. She sobbed as she read poems to mourners' loved ones, saying how special they were. How missed. How they were forever caught in thoughts. She couldn't find Simon's name, so maybe he was living? But then, she couldn't find her grandad's either, and she knew that he was dead.

What had Simon died of? Why? How could a fit, perfect, twenty-six year old not be living any more? A sudden stroke? A heart defect? It seemed too quick for cancer. An accident perhaps. A car crash? Jenny shuddered at the thought of his pulped body, leaking blood.

James Dean had died aged twenty-four. It happened.

She tried to stop herself from thinking. Tried to change the subject. She drove around the countryside, peering into fields. Searching for a familiar flash of grey until the dusk ruined her view. Why wouldn't Roger tell her where Mister was? What if he'd sold him, if he was lying to her?

There was something that felt wrong.

When Jenny returned to Fairburn Ings the phone rang, impatient. The rooms were empty, ominous in their stillness.

'Hello. Mum?'

Nothing at the other end.

'Roger, is that you?'

Jenny recognised the silence. She didn't expect to hear a voice.

'Will you fuck off! Stop ringing us.'

Jenny hung up. She had poured herself a brandy when the

phone started again. She answered it, annoyed.

'Yeah?'

A woman's voice. 'Do you know where he is? Do you know what he's doing? What he did last night?' A questioning pause. 'He's a bad man, he does bad things.'

Jenny clunked the phone down, shaken. Then she unplugged it at the wall. Sank into the sofa and blocked her thoughts out with TV. Saw fragments of a local news report, another Savager attack. She saw the horse was grey.

The clock was chiming eleven when Roger returned home. He found Jenny sitting in the kitchen, nursing two china mugs.

'Was someone here last night?' she asked. 'When I was out with Nina?'

Roger approached to kiss her cheek, then stopped. The words sank through a brew of beer into his brain.

'What, you're allowed to go out with your mates and I'm not? Fantastic! I work all day, supporting you, I really flog myself, and you give me a bollocking for having a couple of cups of coffee?'

'I just meant....' Jenny started to feel ridiculous.

'What?'

'Nothing. A woman called. I thought...'

'You thought what?' Roger moved towards her, head tilted like a plastic nodding dog on the back ledge of a car.

'I thought, maybe your wife...?'

'That bitch!' He couldn't hold his anger. 'Why would I want her in this house, I hate her, she hates me! She just wants to destroy me.'

'And us.'

Roger looked at Jenny with repulsion. 'It's because of you she does it,' he growled. 'It's you that set her off.'

The troll under the bridge.

Jenny couldn't understand. 'But, you'd broken up, you weren't with her anymore.'

'No, but she was still with me. She won't give up.'

'Maybe,' Jenny had a meek suggestion. 'Maybe we should call it off for a while, have a break or something.'

'You want us to break up?'

'I need some time to think,' she mumbled. 'Stuff's happened, and I, I just don't know any more. I don't know what to do.'

Roger was spinning round the room, holding onto the side of his cheek as if it was destined to fall off. He stared at her face, searching for emotion instead of that blank wall of skin and cold as ice cream mouth. He reached out for her hand.

'Look, I'm sorry I've been moody, it's the stress. I love you.' He ran a finger down her chin, trying to make her smile.

Jenny watched the sparkles of her engagement ring as it spun around her finger, punishing the skin. Roger massaged her hand between his sticky palms, telling her that he loved her and that they could work this out.

She pulled her hand away. 'I don't love you enough.' She concentrated on the floor as she spoke, on a cat-shaped coffee stain. 'I thought I did but I don't.' She'd worked this out at the paper bank, looking for Simon Marles' name. 'I would have died to save Simon, but I wouldn't die for you.'

Roger paced up and down. 'Don't be so melodramatic! You didn't even go out with the guy.' His fists tapped the top part of his legs. 'You go out with me.'

Jenny set her teeth together. 'But I'll always love him more.'

His hand slapped hard against her face, fingers pink, like twitching prawns. She stared at him, face burning.

'Why are you with me anyway?' he snorted. 'For your precious bloody horse? This... relationship... it's just some kind of thank-you?'

Jenny's lip quivered. A trickle of warm blood. Roger saw he had her trapped.

'That's it, isn't it?' He shook his head, defeated. 'Well, I know what I'm worth now. Half a ton of horse meat. Maybe I'll sell him to the knacker man. Cut his heart out and feed him to the dogs.'

Jenny was shaking. 'You wouldn't hurt him? You're a vet.'

Her heart rate quickened, scared. Her face drained ghostly pale.

Roger softened. 'I'm sorry, babe. Forgive me? Please?' He took hold of her hand. Kissed it, then her cheek. 'I do love you. I do.'

'I know.' She shivered.

'I don't want to lose you.' His voice was cracking as he tried to hold back tears, his arms still shaking.

'I'm sorry, Roger. I really am.'

She hugged onto him, numb. Felt guilty. All this hurt, it was her fault. He'd been so good to her, finding Mister, giving her a home when she got thrown out of her parents' house. And now she'd turned him into this.

The troll under the bridge.

'Are we going to be alright?' He looked at her, eyes pleading.

'Of course we are,' she lied.

He led her up the stairs and into bed. Jenny lay staring at the ceiling once Roger had gone to sleep, listening to his soft snores and her hard heart.

He's a bad man. He does bad things.

She searched for a valid reason as she pulled her clothes from bedroom drawers, flinching with the sound of every creak. She scribbled a quick note, saying she was sorry, that she needed time to think. Begging him to keep Mister safe until she could buy him back.

She crept down the wooden stairs. Took the door key from his coat pocket and let herself out of the front. She posted the key back through the letterbox, with her abandoned ring.

She pushed the car along the street for half a mile, so that he wouldn't hear the engine starting. Drove through dark deserted, roads. No idea where she was going.

Procreation

Four weeks and nine days.

Four weeks and nine days and three hours.

Four weeks and nine days and three hours and two minutes.

Jenny glared at the calendar on the wall of Nina's flat, willing something to happen. This wasn't normal. She'd never been this late before. Never. Well, except during her A levels but that was because of stress and anyway you can't get pregnant when you haven't had sex in the first place, unless you live in Israel. As the weeks had gone by then she'd started to hold aspirations of becoming the second Virgin Mary. She'd seen the signs. She'd felt a strong desire to go to church and sniff the incense and insincerity. She even went to Mothercare to see what the Son of God was wearing that year.

But this was different. This time a biological transition had actually taken place.

'Bless me Father, for I have sinned. It's been three hours and thirty-seven days since I had my last bloody period.'

Maybe she should ring Roger up, warn him that she'd made a mistake taking the Pill, that somehow it hadn't worked.

'Hello Roger. I'm pregnant.'

He would persuade her that this was for the best, that the foetus was a sign of unblemished love, and that they should get married. She would agree, of course, as she was signing on, had no current job prospects, only enough money in the post office to keep the brown horse in hay and feed, and if the parents had a home where she could stay they would never let her live there as an abandoned, unwed mother.

'Hello Roger. I'm pregnant.'

In a fit of jealousy, thinking it was not his kid, that she had cheated on him, he would put her to sleep with an injection he used for aged dogs.

Jenny lay on the floor in Nina's bathroom and tried to

remember what people in her situation would have done fifty years ago, before the National Health Service and the Pope. There was something obscure about a bottle of gin. Mother's ruin, they called it, and it wasn't because of alcoholism or spending too much grocery money on drink. You needed lots of hot water, she remembered, as she set about her work.

She stood in the shower with the water on full pelt, burning her freckled skin lobster pink, making it smell like bubbling mussels on Blackpool stalls. The gin idea was abandoned as it tasted nasty, so Jenny swigged back raw vodka with a Russian drunkard bear dancing on the front, and decided this new cure was rather fun.

She threw up in the toilet bowl. Heaving and sweating, ears buzzing as her eyes spun round in circle vision like some Cinerama show in Disneyland. As her head throbbed in vile rebuke she wondered if she'd sicked the baby up yet, and if so, would it be big enough to spot it in the bowl? Like one of those green plastic parachutists she used to dangle out of trees. Little plastic people floating down out of the sky.

Four weeks and ten days.
Four weeks and ten days and five hours.
Four weeks and ten days and five hours and six minutes.

'Hello Roger. I'm still pregnant. Why don't you marry me and give me back my horse?'

Bad idea. Instead she'd try Plan B.

Jenny sprang off the rusting gate onto Tom Deacon's big roan mare. Lead rope clasped tightly in her hand as she squeezed legs against the horse's sides. They trotted round the field, Jenny bouncing ridiculously as they lumbered about, the animal's wide back hot against her sticky jeans. The horse jumped over a clump of yellow ragwort and Jenny nearly fell off. Afterwards she wished she had as that might have done the trick. The puffing horse started sweating so Jenny slid down, dejected, and cooled the mare with a sponge dipped in cold water.

Four weeks and ten days and six hours and two minutes.

Jenny dangled her legs over the tree branch and looked to the ground beneath. Plan C would have to work.

'One banana, two banana...'

She counted up to ten and changed her mind. Then jumped, landing hard on the ground, unhurt but slightly shaken. She hopped up and down on the spot before climbing up again.

'Three banana, four banana...'

The fourth time she leapt from the old oak tree Jenny let out of wail of agony, making the watching horses gallop off in panic. Pain shot through her body. Shit. Now she'd really done it.

'How did it change your life, being in a wheelchair, Miss Barker?' The newspaper reporter would ask.

'It made me understand my destiny and justify my sense of self worth.'

'How has it changed you, as an artist?'

'It has increased my celebrity,' she'd smile. 'Now I am a force to be reckoned with. A person of disability with ability. And my story can be seen soon on screen, with the forthcoming release of the movie, *My Broken Foot.*'

Jenny's blackened foot was in a bucket of cold water when Nina returned home from her new design job in Leeds.

'I sprained it,' Jenny explained. 'When I jumped out of a tree.'

Nina put her portfolio on the table. She wasn't really listening. Jenny hobbled after her as she went into the kitchen.

'It would have been nice if you could have started cooking something,' Nina snapped. 'I'm knackered. You could help more, do jobs in lieu of rent. And can you ask Roger to stop ringing me at work? God knows how he got my number.'

Jenny shrugged. She'd left Nina's new business card pinned

up in Roger's kitchen. Easy mistake.

'I have to rub ice on my foot every two hours.' Jenny tried to divert the conversation. 'That's what the doctor said.'

'Great.'

Jenny watched her friend, hunched over their second-hand microwave, stabbing the plastic wrapper of a frozen Fisherman's pie. She wasn't as much fun as usual, Nina. She was getting rather boring. She was letting herself go a bit, she'd put on a little weight.

'I think I'm pregnant, Nina.'

Nina nuked her anaemic meal-for-one.

'I said, I'm pregnant.'

'Isn't everyone?' Nina snatched the food out and prodded it with a fork. 'That's all we need, isn't it? Another mouth to feed? I only just got my job.'

'I can work. Anyway, I might not have it.'

Nina glared at her. 'It's Roger's? Well then, tell him, and sort yourselves out. And stop him ringing, he'll get me fired.'

Jenny sighed. 'I'm not going back to Roger. I decided.'

Nina pushed the meal away from her. The lightweight plastic carton fell, unwanted, to the floor.

'Your kid's father's alive! You should be grateful, what if it was Simon's, and he'd left you on your own....'

'I wish it was his,' Jenny sighed. 'Because then I would still have him, a part of him.'

'You're ridiculous!' Nina snarled. 'He was my boyfriend, not yours. You don't care how much I hurt, you don't understand.'

'I'm sorry,' Jenny shrunk back, awkward.

'Just get out!' yelled Nina. 'I'm sick of looking after you. I've got to take care of myself.'

'But, Nina....'

Her face was masked with hurt. 'Want to know something, Jenny? I don't like you anymore. I wouldn't call us friends. We've grown too far apart for that. We're not teenagers now. You need to be responsible.'

Nina picked her house keys up off the sofa.

'When I get back, I need you to have gone.'

Nina walked out of the room. She slammed the front door shut behind her.

Jenny moved her things round to her mother's, a small but pleasant terrace in a quiet part of Meanwood. She sat in the living room, unable to take her eyes off the stuffed ginger cat in a glass case on the fireplace. Teddy had come home.

Mary Barker told Jenny the whole truth.

She'd left her husband. It had been coming on for years. They'd stayed together as dutiful parents until Jenny left the nest. They hadn't expected her to turn round and come right back.

'I don't understand,' Jenny mumbled, stunned, wanting to share her problems with her mother, not to be handed even more. 'Why couldn't you tell me this before? Why didn't you say you were moving house, separately or whatever, and divorcing too, if that's what's going on?'

'You're not following what I'm saying,' groaned Mary. 'We need some time apart, your dad and I, to get things in perspective. To re-evaluate our lives.'

Like her and Roger, Jenny thought. That meant it was over.

'Where's Dad then?'

'He's got a new job in Manchester. A bigger firm. It made sense for him to move. I'm staying here in Leeds with all my friends. When I miss him enough to join him, then I'll go.'

'But you can't be splitting up!' Jenny wheezed. 'Have you seen reports on broken homes? It's unsettling for the children. If you two break apart right now I might have psychological damage.'

Mary laughed. 'Oh, Jenny, you're incredible! You're not a child anymore. You may act like it, but your birth certificate is proof you're not.'

'I've never seen my birth certificate.'

'Well, believe me, I have.' The woman softened. 'Our family was a mess, Jenny. We've held it together with bits of sticky tape and glue. I've got to get things back to how they were before.'

Mary Barker poured herself a drink.

'When Ray and I got married it was really special. You may not understand this.' She stopped herself. 'We were desperately in love. But he was off at work, at conferences, doing his own things, and leaving me to mine. Let's say I got distracted.'

Jenny sat, engrossed, scarcely able to believe this was her mother talking, grey eyes glazed with sincerity.

'I met another man, who was loving, kind. Gentle, even. And he was always there. I saw him every day and, well, we sort of got involved.'

'Sort of?'

'Okay, okay, so I had an affair.'

Jenny was shocked. 'What, like a fling?'

'Well....' The woman sighed, memories filling her face, adding a spark of youth she'd missed for a decade. 'It went on for seven years.'

Jenny sat in silence, completely floored, cold shivers snapping at her spine and cold ice cooking on her swollen foot. Something her grandad said came to her mind. Some fancy chap.

'You're leaving Dad for him? Is that why you're splitting up?'

Mary Barker shook her head, half laughing at the impossibility of it all. 'It was years ago, too many. I wish it was now, because I never stopped loving him. There's not a day gone by when... no. It doesn't matter.'

'Why are you telling me this?'

'You have a right to know.' Mary lit another filter cigarette. 'He was married with two young kids so he couldn't leave his wife. Not then. Things were more awkward see, you couldn't leave a woman on her own. Not like now, with benefits and day-care.' She took a long, impassioned drag. 'We thought we'd wait until things got settled, then we could work it out. I'd have gone anywhere with him if he'd asked.' Mary shrugged, starting to wonder herself why she was going through this scene. 'I thought I owed you this, to explain why things with me and your father were never really right. Why he can be so distant sometimes. He's a good man, Ray, you know. He loves you, in his way. There's not many would have put themselves through that. Anyone else, they would have left, but no... he stuck there with us. Made sure we were looked after.'

Jenny sat in total silence and listened to the rest. Everything made perfect sense. Her mother had been in love with Bernard Sykes, the tragic milkman of her youth. He delivered more than bottles when he came a-knocking at their house. He had a special interest in what lay waiting there inside. His sperm was quality gold top, whereas the man called Mr Barker was later found to be infertile, sterilised semi-skimmed.

Transfusion

The three biggest regrets in Jenny Barker's life:
1. Killing her father, the milkman.
2. Simon Marles being dead.
3. Losing her virginity to Roger Mandrake.

So, she'd killed her dad when she was six. She hadn't meant to. It wasn't her fault. Would God keep making her pay until she died?

Of course he would.

What if Jenny's mother knew it was her who had knocked Ernie Bernie down? Sent him flying onto his deadly crate of milk. Cold glass piercing his heart, red blood seeping along that blotting pad of snow.

Bernard Sykes. Jenny Sykes. Her father.

It all fell into place. Those first six years of her existence, playing happy families with Ray, the eager dad who thought she was his daughter. Then Bernard's death and her mum's attack of nerves, the polite code for a breakdown. That's when Ray stopped smiling at his daughter, because she was someone else's little girl.

Jenny lay in bed, fully awake, scrutinising Ernie Bernie's image. Her Mother had found a photo, carefully preserved, and gone to Boots to make a copy. As Jenny stared deep into his fair-haired, charming face she could see herself behind that smile, catch the same look in his eyes. She wished she could remember what his voice had sounded like, but each time she closed her eyes and imagined back she could only remember bottles and that battery powered whizzer van. Whizz. Clink. The sound of glass. Clink. Two pints today please. Clink clink. Whizz.

She missed him. She didn't know him but she missed him anyway.

Jenny gazed into the plastic bucket full of blood, watching Mad Mac siphon it off into a waiting pristine bag. Corpuscles splashing, platelets swirling in the rush.

'From a slaughterhouse,' explained the vet. 'If we can infuse him with fresh blood we can build his cell count up. Give him a fighting chance.'

'What if his body rejects it?' Jenny worried. They'd tried Brown on an iron tonic, but it wasn't working fast enough, he needed extra help.

'It's worth a try,' MacKenzie shrugged. 'A more aggressive approach.'

He'd already put the horse on a course of steroids to aid his muscle growth. Not much noticeable change in his bulk so far, but an altered temperament. The previously docile horse was more belligerent.

The vet placed a twitch on the gelding's nose. Strong leather wrapped around his muzzle, pulling tight, pressure increasing as he twirled the attached stick. He handed it to Jenny.

'Don't let go.'

Jenny held onto the smooth wood with sweaty hands, fingers shaking as the horse started to snort. The end of his nose squeezed like soft clothes in a mangle, deadening the nerves in his top lip. He didn't seem to mind it. Stood stock still.

MacKenzie pressed an injection into the underside of the base of the animal's neck to insert a pliable duct. Inside it he poked a thin tube leading from the bag of blood, then held the crimson packet up above his head, letting gravity go to work. Jenny watched as soft drips of blood filtered down into the horse.

'God, it really makes your arm ache,' moaned the vet, getting tired of this already. 'Have you got a saddle handy?'

Brown started to fidget as Jenny passed the twitch stick to the vet, lack of hands relegating the blood bag into his pocket. She returned and flipped the saddle on the horse. He bucked, cold-backed and angry, just like when they let him out into the paddock for a run.

'The steroids are working!' MacKenzie grinned. 'Told you we'd see a change.'

They'd had to move Brown into the isolation block to keep him out of trouble. It was a good idea to have the horse away from public view, especially as some meddling bugger had reported him to the RSPCA, saying he was being maltreated and starved. Mad Mac put them to rights. But since the steroids the horse was more aggressive, he'd started biting, breaking skin. Once he'd picked up little Debbie Dakin by the hood of her parka, and bounced her up and down outside his stable door like a dancing marionette.

Jenny tightened the horse's girth, his taut teeth snapping. MacKenzie wedged the blood bag underneath the saddle pommel at the front, packing it firmly between the horse's withers and the gap. Blood slowly seeped like lukewarm jam towards the duct.

'That should do it,' MacKenzie nodded. 'Better than standing there all day. Clip another blood bag on when that one's done. See how you go along.' A knowing look. 'I hear you don't want Roger turning up? What's that about? He wanted to come today, watch what I'm doing with your beastie.'

Jenny blushed. 'It's personal.' Roger had shown up unannounced a couple of days before. She'd hidden in a feed bin until he drove away.

'Right then,' the vet started to pack up his things. 'I don't really want you messing about with needles when I'm not here. You might leave air in the syringe, cause an instant heart attack.' He nodded to the blood bags. 'So when you've done with these, you can either squirt blood into his mouth, make him ingest it, or mix the rest into his feeds. A bit at a time, mind. He might not like it.'

Jenny thought he would. The horse liked hamburgers.

The stables' phone started ringing as MacKenzie drove out of the yard.

'Hello, Deacon's,' Jenny chirped.

A pause at the other end.

'Hello?'

She kept getting calls like this. Soft breathing. Probably bored kids on holiday, nothing better to do than mess around and dial.

'Look, this is silly.'

A male voice interrupted. 'I've got your horse. Come back to me, please, or you won't see him again.'

'Roger? Stop this. What are you going to do to him?'

'Meet me, please. He's fine, Mister's fine.' A sigh. 'I'm not, I need you.' He sounded very calm and polite, the phone wire hiding his feelings. 'We need to talk about this. About us.'

Jenny quietly put the phone down, worried. She knew that he was angry with her, hated her even, but he still kept ringing. He was trying to drive her mad.

Dear Agony Aunt,

I'm feeling guilty about Roger, about hurting him so much. I'm scared about the baby, what I'm going to do. I wish Simon wasn't dead. I wish I hadn't killed my dad. Is this my punishment? I need to know things will get better.

Jenny B from Leeds

Dear Jenny,

You brought bad luck into the world, and it stays with you. The only escape is death. Come back to the Five and Dime, Jimmy Dean, Jenny Dean. Come back to the Five and Dime.

Jenny sat in the cool isolation block, watching her strange horse sup from a bucket of fresh blood. There were four large stables in the building. Three were stored full of meadow hay, the other one housed Brown, gnashing behind a row of metal bars. His kneecaps knocked against the bolted timber door, a constant tapping noise.

The window at the back of Brown's new stable had been boarded up with planks. He'd smashed through the original pane with his hard head. Jenny stuffed old paper sacking in the hole until she could decide what to, but the horse ate his way through most of it, standing in the middle of the stable with a large sack hanging from his mouth. Tom Deacon put planks over the hole where the glass used to be, and metal bars across the front of the stable to thwart further escape attempts. Jenny made sure she kept the shovels far away, in case the horse got clever and tried digging his way out.

Maybe it wasn't just because of steroids. What if the horse had a disorder? Some schizophrenic cells that had erupted in his brain, turning him from a placid, loving soul into a tortured sadist.

She thought guiltily of Roger. How he'd got down on his knee when he proposed. The Rome landscape in the distance, romance wafting around them. She'd fallen deep into his mellow, soulful face and kissed him until her lips went numb. Funny how they felt the same with pleasure as with pain. She wondered if there really was a difference. Pleasure. Pain. It was becoming the same thing.

'You still love me, don't you Brown?'

She knew the horse despised her too. He looked like he could kill her, padding round the stable, snorting blood out of his nose. Throwing his head up into the air, eye whites rolling as he caught a dangling joke-shop plastic bat with his left ear. It bounced up and down on stretched elastic, trying to escape the teeth that followed it around, snapping playfully until they caught a wing and bit it off.

'You wouldn't hurt me, would you?'

Jenny knew he would, one day. She hurriedly picked up his empty bucket and rushed from the stable, shutting the door fast before the rearing animal got out. He was getting worse, she could tell. She watched for a moment as Brown focused his attentions on another of his rubbery winged friends.

She washed the bucket in the tack room, staining the sink pink before swilling everything away in a torrent of cold water. She scrubbed her hands with coal tar soap. You had to wash the blood off. If she had any cuts in the skin, any little nicks, then the blood might get inside and mix with hers, and she would lose weight off her thighs, her chest, along the fleshy part of her arm until all that was left was bone. She wished she could kiss her horse and make him better, but now she couldn't even touch his face.

Two kittens rolled around on the floor while she flicked splashes at them. Father, Son and Holy Ghost. She remembered how she and Nina had baptised the horses, years ago, when Mister got sick with that infection in his foot. They'd got the rosary Aunty Pat gave Jenny for her First Communion, dipped it into unholy water buckets and splashed it on the horses, making the sign of the cross on each animal's head.

Father, Son and Holy Ghost,
I baptise the thing I love the most,
So God will keep you safe and well,
Then you'll go to Heaven, not to Hell.

Jenny often wondered about the animals, if they would become angels. Up in the big sky with her grandad and the rest. With that donkey she met on the beach at Bridlington, which must be dead by now as it was so long ago since she had seen it. Could things stay alive forever if you still saw them in your head? Could she make Simon breathe again if she concentrated very hard?

Jenny closed her eyes and focused. On her lids, the blurring face of a smiling milkman. In her ears, his milk float hum.

The kittens crept into the isolation block when Jenny wasn't looking. They hid in shadows by the door until she walked away, then started to explore. They found some hay to sit on, but that wasn't very interesting so they climbed up on a box of brushes and jumped down off the side. They did that a couple of times but it got boring.

Brown stuck his head over the stable door and snorted at the mottled animals. They looked up, amused, heads on one side to see who was in the air. The male kitten moved off first, squeezing a speckled tongue between his lips, crawling through a gap under the door into the deep forest of yellow straw.

Jenny heard the commotion when she came back from the shops, ice cream drizzling down her hand. She ran into the building, cornet dropping in the dirt as she watched the brown horse shaking what appeared to be glove puppet cat, banging it against the metal bars that jailed him in. A sickening crunch of bone as Brown bit his teeth closer round the shape before spitting it on the floor.

If horses ever could be sick, it was bound to look like cats. Jenny didn't want to see inside the stable. But what if the kitten was somehow still alive? Not to check would be as bad as killing it. She bent over in a tight ball as Brown reared up, narrowly missing her back. A hoof bounced off Jenny's buttock as she grabbed hold of the fur bundle, ducking out of the stable to check on what it was. Yes. It had been a cat. But it wasn't anymore.

She tried mouth to mouth resuscitation but there wasn't much of a face left to blow down. She tried her hand at heart massage but all that did was make it squishier. She laid the kitten down and wondered if she could pretend it had run away. Would somebody notice? They hadn't noticed when she'd done it.

'I ran away,' she'd say. 'But I forgave you and came back.'

'Your tea's burnt.'

Dead kitten on a pyre of straw. Make it burn and disappear. Disappear. Destroy the evidence, like an overcooked meat pie.

Jenny remembered there was something she had overlooked, which had four legs and a miaoow.

Using carrot deterrents in a bucket to keep her safe, Jenny let the horse bite at a mouthful, then grabbed his headcollar and

186

tied Brown to the bars. She kept glancing over to check on him while scrutinising his stable for any signs of cat.

The search was about to be abandoned when she noticed it. There under Brown's foot, as though the horse was wearing a new style of ermine boot. Only this one was made of cat. Jenny was surprised that she only felt marginally ill when she peeled the squashed animal off her horse's hoof. The indentations had made it almost circular, not like a cat at all. It was more of a fluffy polo mint, with the face of a hammerhead shark attached onto one side. Jenny kept looking through the straw until she found its tail.

They buried the kittens alongside the muck pile and sang *Amazing Grace*. Debbie Dakin was crying bitterly.

'I wish your horse was dead,' she said. 'The Savager should come down here and kill him. Cut him up.'

'You shouldn't think like that.' Jenny felt very culpable. 'You know it's not his fault.'

'Then whose is it?' countered the twelve year old, throwing a stink bomb towards Brown's stable. 'The kittens were my friends.'

'I'm sorry Debbie. I don't know what to say.'

Jenny wished she'd pretended to have taken them to the pet shop, or found some other cats that looked the same. If something looks like the thing you want it to, then you can fool yourself. She wished that Roger hadn't looked like Simon. Or maybe it was the other way around.

The Savager had claimed another victim. Jenny saw it on the news on her mother's television. The horse wasn't dead, thank God, just needed lots of stitches. They gave a description of the injuries but Jenny put her fingers in her ears.

The photo on the screen looked just like Mister. Her heart raced faster as she turned the sound up with the remote.

'This is the fourth local attack in the last two months.' The newscaster looked stern. 'Police are launching a fresh appeal for information. Because of the nature of the injuries, and the way animals have been sedated in some cases....'

Jenny started to dial the phone.

'...police believe that the person they are looking for, known in the press as the Savager....'

Come on. Answer. Pick it up.

'...is someone who once worked with horses, so has an insider's knowledge as to how to handle them.'

A clunk. 'Hello?' His voice.

'Roger? It's Jenny. Are you watching the TV? The local news?' A dim noise in the distance. Static electricity. 'Roger? Are you there?'

'Yes. I see it.'

'That horse, it looked like Mister. Is he okay? I need to see him.' Silence at the other end. 'Please, Roger! I need to check that he's alright.'

Roger came and picked her up. She hadn't wanted to tell him where she was, but he insisted. He wouldn't take her to the horse unless she had agreed. A secret, he said. She mustn't see where he kept Mister. He wouldn't put it past her to try to steal him back.

'Let me see him. Please.' Jenny ran hot palms along the horse's coat. It smelt like Mister. He licked the top of her hand, nuzzled against her.

'Please, Roger.'

He took off Jenny's blindfold, the light stinging her eyes. Tears welled up as she hugged her horse's neck. She glanced round the field to see if she could place it, but the landscape was too strange. Horses were grazing, nonchalant.

Roger's face was full of torment. Jenny ached on his behalf. She wished she hadn't hurt him quite so much.

'It was all just for your horse, wasn't it? Or for somewhere else to stay.' He looked into her eyes, seeing pupils dilating as her muscles tensed. 'You never really loved me, did you?'

'I'm sorry. I thought I did. I tried to.'

Roger shook his head. 'Aren't I worth more than an animal? Shit, how can you justify what you did? What you put me though?'

Jenny quivered, becoming nearly as angry as she was upset. 'I'm not the only one to blame here! You knew what you were doing, and I don't know that I did. I was really grateful.'

'I got your horse back.'

'I know,' Mister pushed against her. 'I can't thank you enough for that.'

'You could have stayed with me. Got married.'

Jenny started to back away. 'It's too much, Roger! You and... Anne.' She fumbled for an excuse. 'I can't deal with it, the pressure.'

Roger softened. 'I've gone too fast, I see that. But what if we slow down a bit. Take it gently for a time?'

Jenny patted Mister's neck, distracted. 'I loved Simon and he's dead. I can't love anybody else.'

'Bullshit.' Scorn spread across his face.

'If you're not going to be civil then I'll leave.' Jenny paced off through the field, no idea where she was going. Cars humming in the distance. Mister following behind.

Roger chased after Jenny and caught hold of her arm.

'Friends? Please, Jenny. Anne she's....' Roger's eyelids fluttered, tense. 'You're the only person I can talk to. You're all that I've got left.' His body sagged with doubt. 'I love you.'

Jenny wished that she could trust him. She saw his pain, and knew she had to help. She kissed his cheek and walked back to the car, with Mister watching at the gate. A white pawn in their big game.

Roger tied the blindfold tight round Jenny's face and drove away.

Possession

That night she dreamt of wedding days. Of walking down the aisle in an immaculate white dress, feet tapping in a pair of ruby slippers. Echoes floating down the long inviting path between bare pews. Her future husband waiting by the altar, broad shoulders beckoning. Jenny walking closer, hopeful, seeing the back of his neck, his nape. Heart beating, praying it was Simon. He twisted round, wearing Roger's smiling face. His pale ivory shirt slowly filling up with red. Blood oozing to the floor, a dark raspberry puddle reaching out for Jenny's toes.

When she woke up she screamed.

Jenny stretched across the bed, disoriented. There was a dint beside her, still quite warm. Her stinging eyes focused on the now familiar room, a vodka headache dulling the morning light.

She heard Roger's Landrover revving up outside ready to leave, and remembered everything. Sank back into the pillow, beads of sweat nestling against her hair, gluing it to tired skin. Since she had got involved with Roger she'd aged a year for every week.

The insides of her legs felt strangely numb and wouldn't move. She tried to raise them off the sheets but they stuck fast. A gnawing in her stomach made her need to roll into a ball, become a safe small armadillo.

As Jenny lifted the covers she knew something was wrong. Saw a fist size stain upon the bottom sheet, with specks of scarlet mucous. Her inner thighs were suctioned together by a seal of drying blood. Jenny forced herself to take a closer look. The bloodstain was in the shape of a squashed face, a child's finger painting of a person. A baby person.

Jenny showered, scrubbing hard. She squatted in the corner, leaning against blue patterned tiles, letting hot spikes of water batter her cold back.

She found her clothes downstairs, tossed on the sofa. Got dressed, made a makeshift panty pad out of layers of kitchen roll and drank a cup of tea.

She couldn't think what else to do.

Baby, gone.

Her here, stuck in the middle of nowhere. Jenny wrestled with the front door. Locked. The back door. Locked. She checked around half hoping to find spare keys, but there was nothing, just old magazines, blunt scissors and sharp hypodermic needles from the vets'. She found a drawer with shotgun bullets, rolling over Roger's photo, sporting dead pheasants and a hare. Damn. Why was she always so stupid? What possessed her to let him bring her here? So stupid.

Maybe she should call the police, get them to break her out, tell them Roger was scaring her? That he's a bad man. He does bad things. No. She couldn't. He still had Mister. She couldn't risk her horse.

The fire brigade, they'd help. They rescued cats from trees.

Jenny went to use the phone, but could only find the gaping socket, left redundant in the wall. Why hadn't she brought her mobile? Why? So, so stupid.

The windows were locked and their metal keys had vanished. Jenny rested her head in her hands, tired from the stress of thinking. She sat in a chair by the front window and stared out through the glass, contemplating the best way to escape.

'Help me! Please!'

A woman walked by with a small dog. Jenny battered the window.

'Wait!'

The woman waved and walked away, a look on her face trying to hide the lack of recognition, thinking she should be more friendly with her neighbours.

'Bitch!'

Jenny sank into the chair, stomach pulling.

Gone, baby.

A man with fishing rods. Jenny hammered on the glass.

'Hello! Help me, I can't get out!'

The man glanced at her whitened, gurning face and looked away.

'Bastard!'

Rods bouncing against his back as his pace increased.

'You bastard!'

Jenny picked up the chair and hurled it at the window pane. Stood still in surprise as glass shattered, shards spilling out onto the lawn. Chair landing near a bucket full of pansies.

She looked around to see if anyone had noticed, dragged another chair towards the sill and climbed through the fractured gap. Her shoes crunching on glass crisps. She walked across the grass towards the road. Headed down the lane towards the lake full of swooping, paddling birds. Kept on walking for three miles until she reached a busy road. Crouched down beside a bus stop and watched the traffic blurring past.

Jenny arrived at her mother's house, her right hand shaking so much she couldn't fit her key into the lock.

'What's the matter?' Mary Barker answered the doorbell, found Jenny quaking on the step.

'I don't want him to find me. Please. Don't tell him.' Jenny's heart pulsed fast. What if Roger was here already? If he had come to get her?

There was a need in Jenny's face that Mary hadn't seen before.

'Shush, love. Let's get you inside. You're going to be fine.'

Mary hugged her daughter to her, caressing tired, lifeless hair.

Jenny stopped answering the phone, in case Roger rang her up. She knew he'd got the number, done 1471 after she phoned him about Mister. He sometimes made calls late at night, no voices, but she knew that it was him. He'd park out in the road and watch her at the window. He tried to disguise himself sometimes, using that shit brown car, but she knew he was still there. He'd stand on the front step and ring the bell, then disappear when she answered the door. It was him. She knew. Sometimes she felt he was inside the house. She'd jerk awake at night, feeling fingers on her flesh. But there was no one.

She shouldn't think about him so much. Hadn't someone told her once that if you think so much about a person it must be because you love them? Never love anyone, never love anything. If only she had stuck close to that motto. If only there weren't so many things she'd done where she'd had to say 'if only'.

If only Simon wasn't dead.

She'd tried to find information, how he'd died, but she and Nina were not speaking, Wit was God knows where, Sharon was in Sydney and the college office was manned by an answerphone that did not supply the answers. She'd have to wait until next term.

Days dragged. Jenny languished at the stables, watching her horse for an increase in weight and watching the gate for any familiar cars. The noise of engines made her nervous. She got so paranoid, she could hear a ticking in her old car. A bomb, she thought, and the more she thought about it, the louder it became. She dropped her keys from the ignition and checked the dashboard for clues. A half empty pack of Juicy Fruit, one piece stuck underneath the shelving. That greying globule was as frightening as Semtex. She knew it wasn't hers. She'd never eaten chewing gum since that day in junior school when she bit off half her mouth.

Roger had been inside her car. She peeled the gum off, trying to guess how old it was like trackers do when they smell elephant turds. She caught sight of something in the rear-view mirror. Backwards letters, scratched in the dust on the outside of the back window. Jenny focused, twisted them round.

DIE HORE

Jenny didn't think that it was German. That was not how

you spelt whore. Tick. Tick. She clambered from the car, looked underneath the engine. Tick. Tick. And the boot. Tick. Tick. Only when she caught a bus back home, took off her clothes to check for booby traps and lay naked in the bath, submerged under the water, did she fully understand that the ticking was inside her, in her heart, her veins. If she lay there still enough she could feel her body living. She held her breath and stayed underwater until bubbles filled her nose and popped her ears. The ceiling looked misty through her eyes, and they began to itch and swell and tell her that this wasn't healthy. She wondered how long she'd have to hold her breath before she fainted, or died, or both. She listened to her heartbeat, counting the thuds within her chest, estimating when they would slow and she would feel all right.

While the smallest things were scaring her, the biggest thing was Brown. His glaring eyes, prime steak ribs and sad pot belly, swollen full of air and steroids, like a burnt-out sausage on a stick. She got to the stables late one evening to give him a final feed, and saw him methodically place his lips around the glowing light bulb. Screaming, Jenny ran across to turn the switch off, reaching it a fraction of a second before the horse bit through the glass into the filament.

That was when Jenny realised that her horse wanted to die.

She started to notice the strangest things, the most worrying of which was the sudden appearance of visitors in the top of the hay barn. One of the kids had seen them first, and ran out screaming that mice had grown wings and were hanging from the roof. There was a simple explanation. Bats. Perhaps they'd sent a scout out looking for new housing and had seen rubber toy relatives dangling in Brown's stable. Tom Deacon said if they didn't shift themselves he would get the pest people in. Sunburnt bats hung upside down from beams in the tall barn, rustling like wind chimes.

Jenny was squirting a worming paste down her horse's throat

when she noticed something else. Two teeth at the corners of his mouth had drastically changed shape. They used to be quite flat at the sides, but now they had somehow worn down into points. The back edges were sticking up in little v shaped hooks. She still had her hand in Brown's mouth when he shut it. She punched him in the face until he opened up again, and pulled her fingers away to check the damage. The cuts weren't deep, but they were bleeding. She knew what this meant.

Jenny told the doctor her horse had bitten her, and he gave her an anti-tetanus injection in the backside. She wanted to tell him other things but didn't have the nerve. He probably wouldn't know the answers anyway. She'd have to do this on her own. She should have asked for sleeping tablets, she hadn't managed to get any rest since the day Brown bit her. She had her suspicions about this fact. He'd drawn blood, after all.

'God, Jenny, it stinks in here. What d'you need so much garlic for anyway? It's dreadful.'

Mary Barker wasn't happy with the aromas in the kitchen.

'Can you please take it away and chop it up somewhere else, it's stinking the place out.'

Jenny carried the cloves into the garage. She didn't like the stench much either.

She went to visit Brown. Her suspicions were correct. She mixed some garlic into his feed and he refused to eat it. She stood in the stable with a necklace of cloves smelling strongly round her throat, watching the horse wheeze loudly in annoyance.

She tried another test, just to be sure. Innocent until proven guilty. Instead of fresh chopped garlic she sprinkled some of the powdered form into his tea, anonymous as arsenic. No. He wouldn't eat that either. That was the proof she needed.

Jenny understood now why the horse went so crazy when she let him out of his stable, leaping around the dusty paddock like a pogo stick on drugs. Kicking, bucking, farting, the fierce force wrinkling up layers of loose skin. It wasn't steroids, it was the sunlight on his back. He was a creature of the night and should come out only in the darkness.

She returned later that evening, silver crucifixes pinned to her waxed jacket and garlic cloves draped casually round her neck.

He's a bad horse. He does bad things.

Brown was daydreaming when she went into his stable, and he whickered in recognition. For a moment Jenny felt quite pleased to see him. He blew warm air from his nose and walked towards her, resting his chin on her exhausted shoulder.

Jenny led the big horse into the paddock and they walked under the moonlight, watching stars, hearing the fluttering of bats as they flew around the barn. Jenny saw some hanging from one of the fruit trees before they took off across the sky, wings flapping, forming letters. She thought how peaceful the world was in this spot, how different it seemed. Her horse was another animal under the moon, a tormented soul finding his peace at last. She understood why people fell in love with vampires. In the glow of night they were so calm and friendly, but once the sun has risen they were bastards once again. Two sides of the selfsame coin.

She let Brown loose for a run, but all he did was walk. She lay down on the ground and tried to sleep, counting the stars above her, pinpricks of light, more than a million sheep. Too many stars for one person to count. She needed Wit to help her.

As the sun began to rise Jenny caught her horse and put him in his stable before the rays could touch his back. Birds started to sing, and behind their chirping lay the distant hum of a far off lonely milk float. Jenny covered up her ears, but the sound was stuck inside.

That Sunday Jenny stood opposite her local church. She watched a hoard of worshippers trickle out from midday mass, smug smiles set on their satisfied faces. All neatly cleansed of sin. As the church car park emptied Jenny crunched along the gravel, getting as far as the front porch before crouching over, dizzy. Blood rushed to her brain, yelling, telling her to get out of there as quickly as she could.

An old lady with some flowers peered out of the church doorway.

'Hello? Are you poorly, love?'

Jenny couldn't speak.

'D'you want to come inside? Sit down? Are you here for Father Matthews?'

Jenny knew she could never set foot inside that place, no matter how much she needed help. She wanted to ask for some holy water, but dared not in case the priest brought some out and it burnt right through her skin.

As she walked back home Jenny took the silver crucifix from round her neck and put it in a trash bin. She immediately felt better.

Jenny stared at herself in the bathroom mirror, wondering how long it would take before her reflection disappeared. If she felt it was worth it she'd have put some make-up on, tried to hide those bags of greyness that hung limply round her eyes.

She looked through papers and personal columns but could not find what she wanted. Hit men didn't seem to advertise. She rang up one guy who said he was a spiritual healer, but when she asked if he could do a killing he hung up.

Jenny went to the library to see what she could find, but they only had stories by Bram Stoker and a reference book with pictures of old actors in hammy horror movies. She read about the original Dracula being transported in a crate from Transylvania to Whitby, and decided to drive over and feel the vibes.

Whitby smelt of fish. Pale pastel huts stood in lines along the beach, facing the long grey sea. Jenny parked her car where the tourists gathered, and walked towards the shore. Scraping bare feet on sand and shale, listening to the squawks of angry seagulls angling for fresh fish. Jenny skimmed a stone into the water and it sank. She remembered a visit to this spot some years before, when Ray was still her dad.

Jenny stared out at the big sea, imagining what would happen if she walked right in, holding her breath for ages while soft saltwater swept over her body. She put her shoes back on and hiked towards the crumbling abbey, past the dark skeleton of the building to the landscape of old graves. A group of squabbling pensioners gloated over salt-bitten tombstones, proclaiming themselves older than most of the inhabitants had been before they'd died. They flapped thick coats in unison, like a flock of scheming rooks.

Jenny wandered round the graveyard, inspecting names, deciphering words on weathered stones. The graves nearest the sea were worn with wind and acrid rain. The names had been erased, thick stones filed down to little jagged teeth. The wind had carved old graves to bubbles, strange moon rocks and beaten shapes. Lichen clung around the bases, damp moss breathed green onto grey stone.

Jenny wondered if Bernard Sykes had been buried or cremated. She would have really liked to know. What words were engraved on his tombstone? Beloved husband and father... was there any mention of her?

As Jenny walked down towards the shops she felt her stomach rumble, which was strange as she'd only recently had food. It was fitting into place. Vampires could not survive as vegetarians. Perhaps if she had put ham in that cheese sandwich she would have felt a little better.

Jenny bought a book on vampirism and some rock from a gift shop, then sat down to read. By page twenty-three she realised one important fact. She hadn't killed yet. Sure, Brown had bitten her and sucked some blood, but she hadn't actually done the deed herself. Yes, she'd killed the milkman, her dad, but that was an accident so it shouldn't really count. She could only be a true vampire when she sucked blood into her body. She was glad she'd not been tempted into eating a rare steak or Cornish pasty, like several German tourists were munching on in the seafront cafe. If she had ordered sausages instead of mushroom quiche then it would all be over.

Some of the blood that Brown drank from the abattoir must have been contaminated previously by a carrier, or else one of the bats must have swum around in it until it was. That's how it started. After this initial taste the horse had needed more blood to survive. The bats weren't a coincidence. The way his teeth were forming little fangs wasn't either. The most damning thing was the fact that Brown had killed. Twice. And there were other things, like when he smashed the window. He knew it wouldn't kill him, though any sensible horse was bound to realise that glass can sever arteries. It was the same with the light bulb, when he tried to electrocute himself. He knew he couldn't die.

There was only one way to do it, and it had to be done. Jenny couldn't carry on like this, no matter how much she cared for the woeful animal. It was him or her. No other choice.

She could ask Mad Mac to put him down... but would the curse be lifted if someone else took charge? What if she rang the vet's and Roger came? What if he came and got her?

Jenny had to sort this out. She reminded herself that Brown wasn't like a horse anymore, that he'd probably be grateful. His soul would be released and then perhaps he'd find some peace.

Dear Agony Aunt,
This may sound deluded, but the brown horse is a vampire. Since he arrived my whole life has gone wrong. Since he bit me, I've not managed to sleep. He's sucked out all my energy and I don't know what to do.
Jenny B from Leeds

Dear Jenny,
Kill it. Kill it. Kill it!

The moon's smug face gloated down as Jenny's footsteps ricocheted around the yard. Cold metal bars threw shadows on the concrete of Brown's stable, white moonshine emulsion on the walls.

Jenny stood in the doorway, motionless. Tick. Tick. She had to go back outside, tick, she couldn't bear to see her horse's face. Tick. She sat on a bale of straw, tears welling. Hayfever, she lied to herself, pulling out a bottle of Southern Comfort that she'd smuggled in underneath her jacket along with the wooden stake. She'd made this from a broom, sat for hours in the garage, whittling away with a knife until one end was sharp. The handle was too long, so she chopped it in half with an axe and put the evidence in a bin. If she did this killing to her personal property, would it be looked on as a crime?

Half a bottle of spirits later she went inside and took off her sweaty coat. She'd hung a wreath of garlic round her neck, even though the stench made her feel sicker. She pulled a rosary from her pocket and dipped it in a water bucket, making the sign of the cross and praying that what she was going to do was right.

Father, Son and Holy Ghost...

She opened the stable door, flicking water towards the horse.

I baptise the thing I love the most...

A splash, crucifix shaped, on his head. Brown snorted, screwing his nose up, shaking his face and body.

So God will keep you safe and well...

Jenny clenched the stake hard in her palms, sweat sticking, a set adhesive on the wood. Moving forwards, eyes focused on the animal's beating chest.

Then you'll go to Heaven, not to Hell.

She lined up her mallet against the stake and aimed towards his heart.

Confession

He's a bad horse. He does bad things.

Hard hooves punched the air in front of Jenny's face. She ducked backwards, Brown knocking her to the floor with his forelegs as he bounded round the straw. Whites of his eyes flashing in panic as he bumped into the wall.

'Shit.'

Jenny tried feeling through piss-stained bedding to find her wooden stake. She'd heard it fall somewhere.

'Owwwch! Fuck!'

Brown stood on her left hand, not leaving his weight on long as the softness frightened him. He snorted and darted up and down the stable, keeping as far away from Jenny as he could. Yellow foam started rising from his neck, his coat heating with worry. Veins swelling like rippling snakes under his skin.

Jenny grabbed the handle of her weapon, left hand shaking with a mix of fear and pain. Brown quivered as she moved closer, aiming the stake directly at his chest, the mallet drooping a couple of inches behind, limp in her hurt hand. The horse leapt forward in an inspired burst of energy, back hoof brushing hard against Jenny's leg. Brown belted at the door, his weight bending the bolt into a Uri Geller twisted spoon, opening the way for his escape. Cantering on the cluttered concrete, avoiding the sharp arms of a neglected wheelbarrow, aiming for the comfort of the feed bins inside the enclosed building. He stood, spraying hot froth from his nose, back arched and ready for attack, head raised high on his elastic neck. Standing proudly for a moment, until the realisation sunk in that he was still not free and clear. Merely absconded from one prison to another, with no escape through the closed outer door.

Jenny took a deep breath and went after the horse again, dragging the spikes of a pitchfork behind her.

The blue flashing lights of a panda car made the ponies

snort and stomp, fear hanging in the air like a bad smell. Car doors slammed as the siren stopped. Riotous scrambling noises echoed from the isolation block. Two policemen crept up, truncheons poised, keen for a piece of conflict on what had been a rather boring evening. A nearby resident had reported a disturbance at the yard, thinking it was burglars. Their radio crackled, waiting for more news.

The smaller officer puffed his face with air to shout a warning through the doorway. 'It's the police. Come out. Right now.'

There was no reply.

His partner pushed the door open, leaping back as a large brown horse jumped briskly through the gap, trotting in the direction of the paddock.

'We've a loose horse here, not robbers.' The man chuckled into his two-way radio. 'No sign of forced entry.' As he pulled a notebook from his pocket he noticed a fresh stain on his sleeve. 'I hope that's not frigging horse shit.'

Too red for that. His humour quickly subsided when he saw that it was blood.

A figure in the doorway, lit from behind by a bright fluorescent bulb. Bleaching out her hair and face so she became a ghost. An object, like a small crucifix, in her hand.

'I couldn't kill him.'

Jenny gasped for breath, her life force sucked out as she collapsed, unconscious on the ground.

Jenny wasn't able to remember much about her time in hospital. She had a blurred memory of a vase of flowers and an orange bedspread. A smell of horrible violet perfume which old ladies always wear. There was some misty recollection of a white-haired woman telling her that Frankenstein was her cousin, and asking if she'd like to play a game of Scrabble.

She had this stronger image of a wide man with a beard who sat on a swivel chair and asked questions she could not remember answers to. She could hear the soft lilts of his Welsh tones in her head, despite the fact that she wasn't sure if he existed.

They told her she'd had a breakdown.

Jenny remembered fragments. Flashes of things, like pieces of a picture she'd once seen, in a movie or the news. Moments with black pauses in between. That man's smiling face coming towards her, a horse's mouth, something sharp, a knife, maybe a pitchfork. She tried to think of what had happened, and who the suspects were. The only piece of evidence she came up with was a scratchy, fresh drawn artist's impression, a portrait of herself.

She lay in her tight fitting bed, puzzled and intense. The thing that worried Jenny most about this recent series of events wasn't the fact that she was going to be sent for therapy every week, or that her horse had needed stitches, but that she didn't know what they'd been feeding her in hospital. She wondered if her vegetarian principles were mortally wounded by the fact she may have unconsciously eaten meat. And she wondered why the police were here to see her, why they were making her get dressed.

Cold grey walls, a table, a cassette tape spinning round. A portly male detective with grey hair and greying skin sat opposite Jenny, who hid politely behind her tired fringe.

'What happened to your hand?'

'He stood on it. It was an accident.' Jenny stared him in the eyes, trying her hardest not to blink, leaning across the table as she waited for the next part of the quiz. Her eyes began to leak, a teardrop surfing down her cheek. The young woman constable who was wavering in the background promptly handed her a tissue.

'Why are you crying?' Inspector Redmond fiddled with his pen, scribbling circles on a notepad. 'Is it because you hurt the horse? It's going to be okay, you know. We got the vet out to it.'

'It's not it, he's a he.' Another tear on Jenny's face. 'I'm not allowed to blink.'

Redmond straightened his plump arm. 'Why not?'

'I don't remember.' If you blinked, they won.

'You don't remember?' A slyly helpful smile. 'You seem to be doing a lot of that recently. Not remembering.'

'Can I go home now? Please?'

'That all depends on you, and what you have to tell us.' Redmond leant back in his chair, tapping jaundiced fingernails on the table. 'Explain everything you can think of and we'll see what we can do. The more you help us, the more we can help you.'

Jenny pulled in a long deep breath as she began to speak.

'I didn't want to hurt my horse, but if I didn't kill him then he wouldn't go to Heaven and I think I'd probably die. He's living off my blood, you see.'

A worried look. 'Your blood?'

'His got infected.' Jenny's enthusiasm was building, she felt better as she spoke. 'I was trying to save him. I didn't want to hurt him. I was helping him.'

'You like horses?'

'Yes.' Jenny started to relax.

'You like to help? You want to save a lot of them?'

'Yes. I love horses. I always have.'

Redmond drew a puff on his cigarette and glanced down at Jenny's file. 'You had another horse, didn't you? You came in to report him stolen.'

'Yes. Last year. In May...'

He made a quick note in the margin. 'Never turned up, I see. You don't suppose he could be dead?' He looked into Jenny's eyes for a reaction. Her mouth set hard against him, never uttering a sound. 'Maybe he was in an accident, you know, he made someone get angry? Perhaps he stood on her foot, or her hand, or maybe kicked her. He could be buried in a ditch.'

'Mister isn't dead. I've seen him. He's in a field.' She'd tell the

204

smug man where the field was, but she didn't know herself.

Redmond shook his head. 'It doesn't say that here. No one came in to tell us he'd been found. Why's that then, d'you think?'

Jenny reddened. 'I'm not stupid.'

'I never said you were.' Redmond skimmed through some more notes. 'You've been here a lot, haven't you, Jenny? Asking about your horse. Phoning up. Maybe you were trying to tell us something.'

'I was telling you to find my bloody horse.'

'Really?' He pushed the cuticle of his nicotine stained nail down with his thumb. 'Are you sure it wasn't just a cry for help?'

'I needed your help. That's why I kept coming in.'

'And we let you down?' He lit another cigarette and took a long, dry drag. 'I bet that made you very angry.'

'Too fucking right it did.'

'Remember the stone lions, Jenny? You and two policemen outside of Leeds town hall? Talking to the lions, you were.'

He stared into her face, and could see that she was thinking. Silent. Building a wall around herself.

'Remember that?'

In a little lost world of her own.

'Mad as a bag of cats,' he mumbled. 'Wired to the stars.'

It wasn't like this on the telly. They didn't keep you waiting around as long as she was now. Jenny paced back and forth, counting numbers in her mind, trying to remember blocks of time that she'd lost track of. She wished she'd asked more questions about Brown. Maybe he was dead, she'd killed him. Why else was she in here? That Inspector seemed to think that he knew something.

More questions, but no more signs of coffee.

'You've been around lots of stables, snooping? Remember Tracy Reams? Near Manchester? You visited her yard.'

Redmond had a map stuck on the wall, little red and white

pins speared in towns and cities in the shape of a slipped smile.

'Yes, so....'

The Savager.

'And you went back there? On your own?'

'No! I don't....' Jenny winced. She didn't think so.

Redmond smiled. 'Let me guess, you can't remember?' He pulled out a photograph, black and white, and put it close under her nose. 'Have you seen this horse before, is it at all familiar?'

She looked up at his face, then back down at the picture. A felled horse in a field, stomach cut, head twisted, tongue lolling out like a dog begging for treats. Jenny's stomach heaved.

'I thought you'd like that, being an admirer of photography.' He reached across the table for a large manila envelope.

'That's sick.' She pushed the photo well away.

'I know, I know. It's very sick. There's a very sick person out there doing this. Someone that needs help.'

'It's horrible.' Jenny wished she hadn't seen it.

He put another photograph in front of her.

'This horse was stabbed, six miles away from York. They couldn't save her. She was going to have a foal. That's terrible, don't you think? It makes me very angry, I mean, I'm not even a horse lover and this stuff makes me want to puke. It gets me in the guts. You too, I suppose?'

'Yes.' Jenny was feeling dizzy.

'You tried to stab your horse, didn't you?'

'Yes.'

'You made a dagger. Why was that? So you could hide it afterwards, maybe burn it or something?'

'Yes.' Jenny's mouth was tingling.

'When you couldn't kill him with it, you chased him with a pitchfork?'

'I don't remember.'

'He had a slash along his shoulder when we found him.'

Jenny hunched over the desk. 'I think he knocked himself. I think he might have run into a pitchfork.'

'Your pitchfork?'

'Yes.'

Redmond looked across at his assistant, making a mental note. 'Jenny, I want you to be completely honest with me. I'm not judging you, or saying what you've done is wrong. D'you understand?'

'I think so.'

Redmond tipped fresh photos out of the envelope. Spread an assortment of Jenny's paper cuttings across the desk. 'You know a lot about the Savager, don't you? All these clippings, looks like you're really interested?'

'Yes.'

'I saw the chart in your bedroom. Details of each known Savager attack, your map, with marker pins. Very efficient.'

'Thank you.'

He watched her, sombre. Listened to her humming.

'Have you ever killed anything, Jenny? You know, killed something? Maybe in an accident? It might not have been your fault.'

'Yes.'

Jenny started crying, her mouth gaped wide before she spoke.

'I killed my dad. I didn't mean to.'

A scrape of the policewoman's chair as she stood up. 'Do you want a lawyer, Jenny? It's in your own best interest.'

A bitter flow of tears. 'No. I don't want a lawyer. I want my dad back. I don't want him to be dead.'

Redmond signalled to his colleague to get help.

'I kill everything,' Jenny sobbed. 'But I never mean too, really. The cat got squashed, it wasn't me. The dog, well... They all die! My grandad smelled of petrol. Simon... Simon! It's not fair, you can't be dead!'

'Did you kill the horses, Jenny?'

'They all die, everything!' She was rocking on her chair, gazing at the wall, seeing the beige paint change into different colours. Spots of orange jumping around her eyes.

'So, you killed some, and hurt the others?' Redmond's brow filled up with sweat. 'And you killed your father too?'

'Yes. I think I need a lawyer, don't I?'

'Yes indeed,' nodded Redmond. 'I really think you do.'

Revelation

Inspector Redmond was surprised to meet Jenny's father. He'd seen her mother at the house, but thought this guy was in a grave.

'You're Raymond Barker?'

'Yes.' Ray didn't appreciate being interrupted from his new job. It made him feel less professional.

'Jennifer Barker's dad?' Redmond scrutinised the man's passport photo, linking the picture with the name.

'What exactly are you after?' Ray hadn't liked the police since they made him trim his rose bush, saying that it obstructed traffic. It had those wondrous red blooms on it as well. Ruined.

'Your daughter just admitted that she'd killed you.' Redmond was starting to look embarrassed. 'Any idea why she'd say that?'

'Must be meaning some other father.' Ray smirked, now enjoying the line of intrigue.

'What are you trying to say?'

Ray sucked in a breath, puffing up his cheeks.

'I'm trying to tell you, Mister Detective, that she's gone bloody crazy. She should change her name to Jenny Barking Mad.'

Ray's face reddened a shade as the policeman walked away. He shouldn't have spoken like that. It wasn't her fault she'd been ill. He looked at the framed photo on his desk, with toddler Jenny grinning on a swing, pushed by her proud young mother. In those days of puppy fat and promises, before glimpses of the milkman's face grew into her visage.

He'd ring his daughter up this evening. Check she was okay.

The police released prisoner 8543009 at 5.22pm, lacking enough evidence to press charges. Circumstantial musings only. Doctors ruled that Jennifer Barker had been in no fit state to answer questions, so the lawyer slapped on a threat of improper interview procedure. They wouldn't be able to use her confession in a court of law. Maybe they'd find some incriminating evidence further on, linking the Savager attacks perhaps, but for now the girl was safe. Let out on her own recognisance, willing to answer more questions in the future. Until then her new lawyer hoped the psychiatrist would help. He wondered why she kept talking about milk floats and sausage rolls.

Mary Barker drove her sedated daughter home. She didn't notice that they were being followed by a familiar car.

Dear Agony Aunt,

I've not been very well. I tried to kill my horse, I'm not even sure why. The police thought I was the Savager, but that's insane, isn't it? I would remember if I was. I can't be. I've just been trying to help.

Jenny B from Leeds

Dear Jenny,

Of course you have. You've been under a lot of stress, what with killing your milkman father, Simon being dead, Mister being missing and the brown horse being sick. What you need is some fresh air. And probably more lithium.

Jenny went up to the stables. She walked towards the isolation block, worried what she would find. How badly had she hurt Brown? Was he scarred? Would he be scared of her, hate her? Jenny's pulse moved faster than her weary body.

The outer doorway was open, flies buzzing inside. As Jenny scraped her feet along the concrete she heard the big horse snorting. She raised her head to look over his stable door.

'Hiya Brown. How are you?'

The horse peered at her questioningly. Tilted his long head to one side, ears jutting out like bicycle handlebars. Pink muscle flashed inside his nose as he drew breath. Then whickered, walked towards her.

Jenny slunk into his box, relieved. The vampire horse was

gone. Here stood a gentler animal with a tick shaped scar on the right side of his chest, as if a teacher had been busy marking homework. Thin stitches sprung from the healing wound, like a pattern on a quilt.

A small shape appeared beside her, face hidden inside a pert green parka hood, Yorkshire's own Kenny from *South Park*.

'They stopped the drugs and he calmed down. Them stitches will come out. Nice vet's coming back tomorrow.' Debbie Dakin stroked the horse. 'He was here earlier, but had to go. An emergency.' The small girl looked up at Jenny, chewing beige hair in her mouth. 'I'm sorry about Brown, it were my fault. I wanted him to die. It were the baby cats, he killed 'em.'

'What?' Jenny didn't follow.

'When he killed them cats. I wished that he were dead. I made a spell. Wi' worms an' that.'

'You what?'

'I dun't think that it worked.' She tightened up her hood, face burning.

The ticking car. Words on the window. *DIE HORE*. Not her, but him, the horse.

'You missed the letter *S* out,' Jenny grinned.

'Sorry.'

'That's alright.' Brown nuzzled Jenny's shoulder. Debbie reached out and took her hand.

'I've got to show you summat.'

'What?' Jenny followed the small girl, bolting the door behind her. They crossed the yard and walked along the row of breeze block stables.

'Debbie, come on. What is it?'

The girl led her to the end stable. Jenny's pace increased, an anxious feeling returning from this spot some time before. With the bird pulling at straw, and Mister being... there. Standing in his old stable, half asleep, relaxing in the heat.

'Mister? Mister!'

He whinnied, surged towards her, crunching through fresh

bedding. Flopped his face over the door, flapping his lips.

'When did he... how did... when?'

Jenny spotted a scrawled note addressed to her, stuck by a drawing pin onto the stable door. She opened it.

No strings attached. You owe me nothing. He's yours. I'm sorry.

Roger had drawn a kiss under his name.

Jenny sat with her horse all afternoon, as if the act of leaving his stable would make him disappear. She stared at him until her eyes grew tired, and when she closed them she could still see him glowing on her lids.

A grey shadow slipped over the door.

'I heard that you'd been ill.'

Jenny looked up. Saw Nina.

'Your mum said that you'd be here. She rang me.' Nina was puffing, awkward. 'Sorry I didn't visit you in hospital.'

'It's okay.' Jenny got up out of the straw, legs itching. 'I can't remember much about it anyway. I wouldn't have known you'd been. We're talking crazy paving.'

Nina's eyes settled on the horse. Then focused. She took a sudden breath.

'It's him! I don't believe it. Shit! You got him back!'

Jenny picked straw flecks off her socks. 'Yes, well, Roger....'

'Good bloke!' Nina laughed as Mister paced towards her, plonking his neck over the door, eager to be reacquainted. 'Hello, my old mate. I missed you.'

Nina looked at Jenny, said nothing. Offered a weak smile.

The horse banged his chin against the door, seeking attention, breaking the silent pause.

'Simon isn't dead. He's down in London.'

'What?' Jenny's heart banged at her chest.

'Marcus saw him, bumped into him at the Tate. Near the chopped up cows.'

'What?' Jenny couldn't follow.

'Mother and Child Divided, Damien Hirst.' Nina stared at

her friend. 'And yes, it was after we saw the psycho lady. Don't worry. He isn't dead.'

Jenny couldn't speak. Her arms punched into air.

Nina cleared her throat. 'I found out last month but I... I didn't tell you. Sorry. I hope that didn't, that it.... Well.' That it wasn't this that drove her mad. 'I was angry at you, how you reacted about Simon. He was my boyfriend, you know. I was the one to get upset.'

Jenny started shaking, excited. Ears buzzing with relief.

Simon Marles isn't dead.

She pushed open the stable door, was about to give Nina a hug when she noticed her friend's size.

'Four months now.' Nina patted her swollen stomach. 'It's really started showing.'

'You're?' Jenny couldn't say it.

'Yes.'

'And it's?'

'Simon's. Yes.'

Nina was getting tired. She leaned against the stable door, shifting her weight from foot to foot.

'What are you going to do?' Heat rushed to Jenny's brow. She couldn't take this in. Couldn't understand the mixed feelings in her gut, a cocktail of jealousy, annoyance, worry and relief.

'Dunno. Have a baby, change nappies, make a life. I'll manage.'

'But what about Simon?' His perfect face, his smile.

Anger spat from Nina's lips. 'This is nothing to do with him, the bastard. Going off like that, not even bothering to leave a note? Shows how much he cares, doesn't it? Bastard.'

'But he...' Jenny panicked, stopped herself.

'He doesn't know, and I don't want to talk about it, okay?'

'Okay.'

Nina reached out and hugged Jenny close to her. Jenny sucked her stomach in, not wanting to squash into the baby. Simon's son or little daughter. She clung onto Nina, thinking how happy she should be to have her friend back, Mister back, and Simon back from the dead. But instead she felt more anxious.

Jenny returned home, elation growing, but also a gnawing sense that there was a problem here to solve. She passed her mother on the stairs.

'What are you looking so jolly about?' Mary Barker's hair pulled tight in pink spiked plastic rollers.

Jenny gushed, purple prose flowing like Ribena. 'Simon isn't dead! I thought he must be, because when we visited the clairvoyant, the psychic Brummie, he got through with a message.'

'What? A Simon?' Her mother's eyes narrowed.

'Yes, my Simon, so I thought, we both did, that this meant he was dead, which he isn't, so it's great! But he's going to be a daddy, that's the thing. He's going to have a little sprog.'

Mary Barker thudded down to the lower landing. 'And what did Simon say, at this, what... seance? Was there a message? Was he trying to get through?'

'I dunno. I can't remember. Anyway, it's not important.' Jenny spun around to go upstairs. She caught her mother's glare.

'Jenny Barker, you're so selfish!' The woman choked, emotional. 'Didn't it even cross your mind that your grandad's name was Simon?'

Jenny held the phone to her ear, pleading for an answer. Wit had to be there, he must have gone back home by now. Surely. She needed him, needed his advice on Nina and Simon. He would know what she should do.

A crackle down the line. A soft voice, furtive.

'Mrs Stanton? It's Annabel.' Jenny the impostor. 'Has Wit... William come home yet please? I need to talk to him.'

A stifled coughing sound, a lull.

'Hello? Mrs Stanton?'

'Yes, mmm, Annabel, dear.' The voice was tense. 'I'm glad

you called. I've been wanting to have a talk with you.'

'Oh, right.' Jenny was surprised.

'It's about William,' the woman started to explain. 'But I can't do this on the phone. Could you come down? I'll pay your fare if you're short of cash. I'm afraid I've got bad news.'

'Is he alright? He's not..?' Jenny's palms began to sweat. Something was seriously wrong. She thought she was going to faint.

'Can you come down tomorrow and I'll tell you everything? I'll be in the house all day. I can't chat now.'

'Yes, fine, but... hello?'

The line was dead. Jenny prayed that her Wit wasn't.

The three biggest regrets in Jenny Barker's life:
1. Killing her father, the milkman.
2. Losing her virginity to Roger and not Simon.
3. The death of dear friend Wit.

Jenny sat alone on the fast train, desperately trying to remember what Wit had taught her about being Annabel, what food she liked, what places they had been to. How they had wandered round romantic Paris speaking French and falling hopelessly in love.

She couldn't lose him. Not Wit. Not after all this.

The green Mercedes was waiting at the station, pensive. Ready to whisk her off to the Stanton inquisition.

'What type of vegetables do you like best?'

'Peas and carrots.'

Wrong answer. Asparagus and aubergines were much more suitable.

'Where do you buy your clothes?'

'Banana Republic and The Gap. Oh, and of course, Harvey Nicks.' Not a bargain market stall in Leeds.

'When did you and William have your first orgasmic sex?'

The long car coasted up the driveway. Mrs Stanton was

pacing in the hall, looking older than before, darker make-up covering the lines. She kissed the air on each side of Jenny's face and begged Annabel to come in, leading her, limp wristed, to the lounge, squeaking down into a creaking, leather sofa.

'You're looking poorly, dear. I hope you've not been unwell. Your pallor, it's quite dreadful.' Mrs Stanton signalled to her maid to fetch a fresh pot of Earl Grey tea. 'I needed to talk to you in person.' Tension croaked through her soft voice. 'To see if you knew what had happened to my William.'

Jenny's stomach lurched, pushing air back through her throat.

Please, Wit. Don't be dead.

'Sorry to drag you down like this, but it wouldn't have been fair to tell you on the phone.' Mrs Stanton gazed dreamily at a photograph of her favourite son on the varnished mantelpiece. Jenny followed the sad stare to the sight of Wit's grinning bright face, somewhat incongruous with subdued brown hair around it. He even wore a tie. This Wit was not the one she had come to know and care about. In that moment she fully understood that parents never know their children, not as individual people whom their friends attach themselves to with such passionate aplomb. Like her own parents didn't know her either, and she was mystified by them.

Mrs Stanton cleared her throat. 'He's vanished,' she mumbled, eyes cast to the floor. 'I need to find out if you know where he's gone.'

Relief. 'I thought he went to Europe. On a train.'

'He sent us a strange postcard from Florence which only said goodbye.' She looked at Jenny's kneecaps beneath cheap sheer cream tights that had been worn for best. 'We're so worried that something might have happened.' Mrs Stanton leaned closer, eyes glistening with her words. 'I don't think he's ever coming home, I think he left. There was a huge row with his father. He'd lied to us for years, telling us he was in Leeds to do accountancy. I've never seen my husband so furious.' She sniffed again, glancing furtively round the room. 'William showed me some of his pictures, and they were really quite good. Not like Constables or Rembrandts, I mean, they were rather odd, but I could tell that they were art. I don't know why he couldn't show me them before.'

Jenny nodded, understanding the family conflicts, lies and secrets.

'My husband threw him out. I don't think he really meant to, but he's too proud to own up now. William upset him, he really did. He said he voted Labour, that we were capitalists! You don't say that to your parents, do you?'

Jenny shrugged, beaming, happy that Wit was safe.

'Do you know what he did?' Mrs Stanton's eyes had widened. 'He took his sweater off, and he was covered in tattoos.'

Jenny tried to hide her smile.

'It was awful,' shuddered the woman. 'Things drawn all over him, on his skin. And you can never get them off.'

Mrs Stanton shuffled herself straight, uncomfortable that her guest remained polite and not surprised. 'He conned us, dear, you too.' She took hold of Jenny's hand. 'I don't know how to tell you this, Annabel... but the whole time he was going out with you he was seeing someone else. I'm sorry. I feel so sick at his deception.'

Jenny sat there, numb with cold. Leather sticking to her bum. The swine. How could he two-time her like that? How could he two-time her without them going out in the first place? Why had this woman needed to impart such potentially hurtful information in person, if not to get some huge soap opera reaction? And what was even more confusing, why did it make Jenny feel betrayed?

Mrs Stanton sipped from her bone china teacup, quite relishing the news. 'I knew it would be a shock, dear. Too much for on the phone. I could see how you cared for him, that time you came to stay.'

'Who is she?' Jenny surprised herself with a heated sense of jealousy. If it was Nina again she'd....

'She's some Joanne girl, lower class. Probably from a council house, I expect. He's picked the dregs just to annoy us. Of course, we've never met her.' Mrs Stanton looked closely at her guest, gauging a reaction. 'No, her name is Jenny, that was it. She won't be good enough for him.' A sharp look at Jenny's face. 'But then, they never are.'

Jenny couldn't think what to say. Her host poured out a cognac.

'Can I, umm, use the loo?' Jenny needed to get away.

'Of course, dear.' A patronising look. 'I expect you need to be alone.'

Jenny could feel the woman's stare burn through her back as she departed from the room, eyes stinging with annoyance. She locked herself in the upper bathroom, part of her wanting to piss in the bidet just to annoy the snooty bitch. She dried her wet hands on the curtains.

Jenny walked past Wit's deserted bedroom, the door wide open, begging her to come inside. She walked softly into the centre and looked round. Everything was neat and tidy, any sign of his personality packed away. She wanted to hunt through his things and find notebooks and diaries and then pick out days to read to see if she was mentioned, good or bad, as even her name written down was some proof she was important.

Wit had a collection of brown shoes, a five book stamp collection with two penny blacks and some Elvis memorabilia. A Leeds United scarf hidden in his closet, along with three dirty football boots.

There were pictures in his drawer. Not just miscellaneous photographs of people's dogs and houses, but photographs of her. Some of her smiling on a hill in Ilkley Moor baht 'at, the wind splattering her face and making her teeth whistle. The pair of them at work behind their desks, in one of those poses where you know the person isn't really working, as they are holding the pen too tight or the brush too low and anyway, it's fake.

All those photographs of her.

She pulled out a large art folder that was hidden behind a cupboard, and carefully laid Wit's pictures on the floor. Portraits of Jenny, sketches, pencil studies, sitting at her college desk. One where she looked almost angelic, the sunlight streaking her hair with different coloured stripes. They looked more like her than she did.

She knew now that Wit had loved her.

'Let's make Chris Isaak happy.' Jenny smiled, remembering. She hunted for a scrap of paper, a decent envelope, and wrote her friend a note.

Come find me, Wit. I need you.

She taped her message onto his looking glass, hoping he would return soon from his travels, plonk himself down at the dressing table and have her writing catch his eye. Unless, of course, that snobby witch downstairs dropped the missive in the bin.

Jenny rolled one of the precious portraits up and put it underneath her dress. She perched on the end of Wit's king-size bed, and wished that he was there. She imagined where he was now, what he was thinking, what he was drawing. She pictured him floating down the Nile on a wooden raft, tattoos exposed for everyone to see, slowly browning in the sun until the blue baked into purple.

Jenny went downstairs and said goodbye to Mrs Stanton. The woman didn't offer to reimburse the train fare. She shook the pale girl's hand and said goodbye, then promptly closed the door.

Suspicion

Jenny had a plan. Go into college, sort the Simon problem out. She ascended in the freshly painted lift, last year's graffiti emulsioned over. The doors sprang open at the top and Jenny walked along, tip tapping on the cold linoleum floor. A worried anticipation.

New students glanced at her as if she did not belong, like she wasn't part of things, their world, which Jenny knew was true. Strange that a room where she'd spent three years of her past life could feel so uninviting. A girl with curly hair and glasses was sitting at her desk.

'Excuse me,' Jenny stood in front of her. 'Have you seen Simon Marles?'

The student shrugged, unhelpful, glanced around for her peers' support. Nobody had an answer.

Jenny retreated to the corridor, feeling strangely taller than when she was here before. Like when returning to her old junior school, finding that her bottom was now too big for the small chairs.

She knocked on the door of Marvin and Tex's office but they were not in, only a middle-aged woman she'd never seen before, pulsing words onto a glum computer keyboard.

'Can I help you?' The woman nearly smiled, glasses resting on her nose, held firm by a bump of bone she'd wanted fixing as a youngster but which now came in very handy for her slickly framed bifocals.

Jenny glanced about, eyes skimming across large photocopied pictures of students on the wall, displayed in years, immortalised for three until they were pulled down and placed in the waste bin of past graduates. A thick black line was crossed through Simon's face.

'He isn't coming back?' Jenny knew the answer before she even asked.

'Who?' The secretary swirled round and took a peek.

'Simon Marles.' Jenny pointed. 'It's important that I speak to him, urgently.' She walked closer to the desk, throat drying with the tension. 'I need his address, his home address. I'm sure he'll be on file. Please?'

The woman chewed toffee-tinted lips, wanting the act of appearing to be thinking to look honest and concerned.

'Privileged information, new rules. If you were one of our students then I could, but as you're not...' She peered over her glasses, noting no recollection. 'I can't. They gave out an address last term and some creep parked outside this girl's house until the police took him away. It was rather embarrassing.'

'But I was a student,' Jenny pressed. 'I only finished before the summer.' That had to count for something.

'So now you're a member of the public, and we can't give out personal information to members of the public. Sorry. It's a rule.' She softened a moment, registering Jenny's disappointment. 'You could ask one of your former tutors if you like. They might be able to help.'

Jenny beamed, exultant. 'Great! I'll see Marvin. D'you know where he is?'

'Malham, he took a trip. Gone painting sheep with the second years.' The woman pulled a face, not thrilled by the delights of nature.

'Well, Tex then. Is he around?'

The woman spluttered, instantly distressed. 'You haven't heard?' Her set stone face relented. 'You'd better sit down. I'm afraid it's not good news.'

Jenny sat and listened, thinking how ironic it was that this woman could tell her this and yet not be able to impart a simple phone number or address. She grew anaesthetised listening to the words. For a while she sat in silence, feeling guilty that this was probably her fault. She had scribbled over Tex's picture with coloured pens, sliced his hand off while wishing voodoo badness on him. And now he was taking enforced leave in the hospice down the road.

The hospice reminded Jenny of her late grandad's care home. Trimmed lawns and bending flowers. A long expanding building with clustered blocks of rooms. For some reason the outer bricks were painted red.

She found Tex in a corridor near the entrance, sitting by a lengthy wall, surface coated with subtle creams and mauves. Childish black marks drawn on the top where future parts would be. He was surprised to see her.

'Hello, young Horse. Didn't think I'd run into you again.'

Jenny looked with caution on his glowing cigarette. 'Should you be smoking in here? Isn't it like a hospital?'

Tex let out a bitter laugh. 'Not one that you come home from.'

Jenny was rather flustered. Tex picked up on her embarrassment.

'I draw the outline,' he explained, spotting her evasive looks towards the mural wall. 'Residents will fill it in. Flat colours, nice and bright. Reckon it's just your kind of thing.'

Thin patients passed them, smiling. Tex felt Jenny looking at his right hand, put it behind his back, self-conscious, then held it out for her to see.

'Touch it if you like, it won't bite you.'

'Is it heavy?' Jenny always thought false hands were made of metal, with sharpened golden claws. This prosthetic limb was toughened plastic, a Barbie doll skin colour to make it appear real, with four fingers accounted for, even a proper right hand thumb.

'How did it... how did you?'

'Lose it?' Tex shrunk down, defeated. 'It was that business with Sharon. Big mistake.' He glanced at Jenny for a reaction, to see how much she knew.

'Sharon? What! You mean she cut it off?'

'No!' Tex scratched at his new hand, half hoping for some feeling. 'But she'd have loved that, wouldn't she? A right proper revenge. No, I had a do with Marvin, at the degree show, after...'

Sharon's blood, dripping on the toilet floor. White faced.

'... that suicide business. Marvin twigged and... well, we had a fight.'

Jenny recalled the shouting. Tex's scream.

'He slammed the car door on my hand, it got infected. I didn't bother going to the doctors.' He sighed, this could have been prevented. 'I got gangrene, can you believe that? Gangrene, nowadays. I thought it was extinct.'

Tex gave her a tour around the hospice, making light of the fact that he was the only person who was getting out alive. He'd become involved after meeting a man at St James Hospital, while having surgery on his hand. They'd become friends, avoiding the cliché illness topics until the man told him he had AIDS. Just said it, out loud, like that. He'd asked Tex to help out at the hospice. He still didn't know why he'd said yes.

'Anyway, Horsey, that's enough emotional crap. What can I do for you? I presume there's an agenda for this visit? It's not about my health.'

Jenny cleared her throat, passed Tex a piece of paper. 'I need Simon Marles' address. This is mine, I've moved. If you could post me his?' A shiver. Tex was standing far too close. 'It's extremely important.'

'What's it worth, hey Horse?' Tex flashed his old style smile. Any sympathy Jenny had felt for him rapidly departed.

'I need it, Tex, just like you need your job back.' She hardened, tense. 'So if you can let me have it, soon, then maybe I won't tell about your proposition, that time in your office.' In case he needed a reminder. Jenny didn't. Her skin stung, painful, stretched. 'I'm sure that you remember? And my name is Jenny, it isn't Horse.'

Tex's nostrils flared, distracted. 'Okay, okay. I'll sort it.'

'Promise?' Jenny's throat pulled tight, not believing she could say this.

'I'll find you his address, okay.' Tex tapped the artificial hand against his leg. 'And I'll send it on to you.'

'Thank you.'

'You're welcome.' Tex's top lip curled at the corner.

Jenny took a big breath.

'And in case you're wondering,' she looked at him, musing how such an individual could have made her feel so scared. 'Sharon's fine. She's gone out to Australia to spend time with her folks. Thanks for asking.'

Tex weakened, scolded. Watched as the young woman walked away.

Jenny let her breath out as she left, heart racing. She stood waiting at the nearest bus stop, jangling through her battered purse for change. Alongside a dull fifty pence piece was that sacred cocktail stick with a long lingering smell. She raised it to her nose and sensed the scent of margarita, hearing the rumblings of the Dry Dock, the soft words spoken with Simon.

A sharp wind snatched the paper umbrella from her fingers and whisked it along the pavement, racing off on the fresh breeze. Jenny ran to pick it up. She missed her bus.

Jenny had a visitor. She pretended not to be surprised to see him, lounging in the front room, getting friendly with her mother.

'Hello Roger.' Her stomach jittered. Mum should not have let him in, she thought. He'll try to lock me up.

'I went to check on Brown, took out those stitches. With any luck there won't even be a scar.' Roger was looking drawn and tired. 'He seems much better, anyway. He's put on a bit of weight.'

Mary Barker smiled and skulked away. Roger reached for Jenny's arm.

'Your mother told me you'd been ill. I hope I'm not to blame?' He took hold of her hand, concerned at the thinness of her wrist, how he could wrap his fingers around the bone and still have whole fingertips left. 'I know, I acted like a bastard. I put you under too much pressure. I'm sorry, I haven't been myself.' He tried to catch her eye. 'Anne, she was hounding me, she wants to give our marriage another chance. Loves me too much to lose me, so she says. She's so possessive. I guess some of it rubbed off.'

'What are you going to do?' Jenny threw him a quick glance.

'I don't know. I just don't know.'

They sat quietly, staring at flock wallpaper. Jenny more uncomfortable in the silence.

'I'm really grateful, you know. For Mister.'

'Don't mention it. He's your horse, isn't he?' Roger shrugged, disconcerted. 'Sorry about the kidnap thing, hiding him in that field. God knows what I was thinking. Bloody stupid.'

'Well, thank you. I'll pay you back one day. I'll get a job or something.'

'Ah-ha!' Roger sprang up off the sofa. 'I nearly forgot. This came for you last week. It looks pretty official.'

Jenny's eyes lit up as he pulled an envelope from his pocket. She peeled open the back, saw the Yorkshire Post logo inside. Flipped it shut again, not daring to read it.

'Go on.' He smiled at her. 'They rang as well. They must be very keen.'

'You what?' Jenny tweaked the letter open and quickly scanned the words. Her photographs, they liked them. Could she come in for a talk? 'Oh God, that's brilliant! They might give me some work. Wow! They like my photos!'

Roger wrapped his arms snugly around her.

'And you'll get some money, you'll be less stressed, and happy.' He softly kissed her forehead. 'Then you'll come back and live with me.'

Jenny's muscles tightened, pulling away.

'No, Roger. I can't.'

'Why not?'

'I just can't. I mean, I won't. I don't want to. Sorry.'

A storm brewed on Roger's face as he struggled to stay

calm. 'What d'you mean, you don't want to? Don't be selfish! Why are you doing this? What I've been through with Anne, what I sacrificed... it's all because of you. Because I love you! You know I do. God, Jenny, please!'

Roger stopped abruptly when Jenny's smiling mum appeared. He thundered out through the front door.

Mary Barker raised an eyebrow. 'Guess he's not stopping for his tea then.'

There was a Savager report on the local news the following day. A horse had been attacked in Pontefract, suffered a knife wound in the rump. Jenny sat transfixed in front of the television, worried. Even nearer than the others, that one. Six miles from Deacon's yard.

That would serve the police right for suspecting it was her. How could they even think she was the Savager, just because she'd tried to kill her horse, and happened to visit places where attacks had then occurred? She had an alibi for last night, involving her mother and a plate of fish and chips.

A dark thought wafted over. Attacks, where she had been. Where she and Roger were... The police always said the Savager was experienced. A vet's knowledge, Jenny thought, trembling at the recollection.

But the police had already spoken to him, after Tracy was attacked. He said so. What if he lied? What if he'd made that up? If he knew the girl had been attacked because he'd done it?

Jenny parked her car behind a wall near Roger's cottage and waited for dusk to fall. Lights flicked on and off inside his rooms as he wandered about inside. Jenny had just decided to go home when he emerged from the front door, stepped up into his beaten Landrover and revved out of the drive.

Jenny followed at a distance, driving miles down unlit lanes, past darkened fields and ink spiked woods. She thought they were near Selby.

Roger turned off onto a track leading to an unfamiliar farm. Jenny started following, but felt conspicuous and reversed back up the road. She waited at the top, distracted, suddenly aware of the swelling sky dripping shadows on her view, turning the most innocuous shrub into a slavering, rabid monster. The black fingers of trees shook fists against the wind as the cold wood crept closer to the fields. Night owls shrieked and Jenny grew more unsettled.

She pulled her mobile from her rucksack and tried dialling Mr Blonde, but the battery was dead from lack of charging. Why hadn't she thought of this before? Two people were always safer for midnight surveillance jobs, and that was just with stolen horses, not for him. The Savager. Her nemesis.

Jenny's right hand started to shake. She needed tranquillizers. She scratched around inside her bag and found some chocolate. Broke off a satisfying rectangle and popped it in her mouth, immediately feeling better. She glanced across at the long farm. There were lights on. Movements. She checked through her binoculars and traced silhouettes of people. Someone tall, could be Roger, and the shape of a wide cow. Smaller shapes scuttled nearby.

Jenny let out a night chilled breath. Ridiculous. Not the Savager, but a keen vet out on call.

She'd have to tell her therapist. Delusional, he called her. Paranoid. She preferred the word 'mistaken'. Jenny chomped another chocolate chunk, starting to feel relieved. She might as well go home, work over.

Headlights flashed in the rear-view mirror. She bolted upright in surprise, almost laughing at the shock.

'Go on, then, pass me. The road's wide enough.'

The headlights didn't move, full beam into the glass. Their glare made Jenny blink. She craned her neck around to look, but the lights were so bright she couldn't make out the vehicle's shape. A space ship, Jenny thought, half panicked. Bloody aliens again.

The invader's engine revved, pushing towards her.

'Okay, okay.' Jenny wasn't sure what was going on. She turned the key in the ignition. Stalled.

The head lamps lumbered closer. They bumped hard into her car.

'I'm moving!' Jenny's heart pulsed, frightened, trying to convince herself that this was country road rage, but knowing it was more.

She fumbled with the ignition key, which fell onto the floor. The aggressor shunted into her as she scrambled in the footwell. She couldn't reach the key, and banged her head against the dashboard as the car took another jolt.

Jenny grabbed her bag and scrambled out, shielding her eyes as she looked towards the lights.

A Landrover or a car?

She didn't have time to check before it roared towards her. Jenny raced along the quiet lane, not wasting time by looking back, feeling the engine's heat burning behind. Getting closer.

Adrenaline kicked in and Jenny pulsed along, skidding off the road and through a hedge. Sharp thorns scratched as she broke through the shrubs, hands bleeding as she ran. Swimming through the air across a field, cut corn bristling at her feet, hard spikes biting her shoes.

She was choking as she ran towards the wood, into the shadows that had scared her with their shapes. She sat quaking under a quiet oak, sucking in lost breaths, hoping that her blood would soon calm down. That her body would stop shaking. That the person who was after her would not think to look in here.

Expectation

Sun rose over cold fields, warming the earth and blades of dew tipped grass. Mushrooms of grey cloud blew overhead, streaking the coloured land with darker stripes. Jenny watched as a fox broke cover and ran towards the corn, a yapping orange dog demanding food.

She pushed ferns off her legs and levered herself up against the bark of a stout tree. Arms koala tight around it, clinging on. Her feet were fizzing, her eyes as heavy as cricket balls as she adjusted to the light. The woods were full of sounds, buzzes, snaps, sharp insects clicking wings. Shy birds started to sing.

Jenny forced her legs to move and waded out of the dark wood, her shape a sultana spot against cut corn. She walked in a straight line towards her car, affixed to the horizon, waiting abandoned on the long deserted road. With every step she saw a shadow, a cloaked fiend in the driver's seat, a hand protruding from the boot, a body in the back.

She reached the car and there was no one. She pumped the ignition and drove home.

Jenny hovered by the phone in her mother's hall. What would the police think if she rang them? Redmond would probably say that she was attention seeking, mad, that nobody tried to ram her, that dark forces were not at work in the Yorkshire countryside.

Who was it in that car? The Savager? Roger? She flicked quickly through the paper, searching for any overnight attacks. Nothing. Just more adverts for the never-ending Northern Upholstery sale.

Maybe she should phone up to check Roger wasn't lying, that he had been interviewed previously and then sent home blemish free.

Jenny reached for the receiver. The phone rang as she approached.

'Hello?' Heart pumping.

'Jenny, it's Roger. I wanted to make sure you're okay. I thought I saw your car last night, out in the middle of nowhere.' A pause. 'You're not following me are you?'

'Sorry, I've got to go.' Jenny promptly cut the call off and stepped back. She glared at the receiver, daring it to ring again. It didn't.

There was a letter addressed to Jenny in the kitchen, the writing so appalling it was a miracle it arrived. Scribbled in useless left-handed letters, wobbling angry capitals like a disguised ransom demand. Tex had sent Simon's details.

Jenny waited two hours before she rang him, practising scenarios, making her voice sound more grown-up. She didn't know what she should say. She pulled a chair up by the phone and started writing helpful lists. Topics of conversation. Nina's name.

Eventually she dialled the number. It rang, unanswered.

She tried fifty minutes later. Simon's voice.

'Ummm, Simon, it's... it's Jenny. Jenny Barker. From the...'

'Jenny! Hi! How are you? How's Nina?'

'Fine, yeah. Thanks. We're great.'

'Great!'

'Yeah.' Jenny imagined him by the phone, wondered what kind of shape it was, how near he held it to his mouth.

The line went quiet. Jenny could hear the radio in the background as Simon cleared his throat.

'So, Jenny, what can I do for you? What's new?'

Jenny glanced at her nearest list.

Ask him how he is.

'I just wondered how you were. What you'd been up to.'

A chuckle. 'Long story, better for after six o'clock.'

What is he doing now?

'What are you up to then? Anything?' Her hand was shaking.

'Actually, Jenny, I'm off out to the gym. I've got to rush. But if you're ever down in London, give me a call. We could meet.'

Jenny gulped. 'Tomorrow? I'm in London tomorrow.' She thought quickly on her feet. 'That's why I... I called. Because I'll be in London.'

Simon appeared to cover his surprise. 'Right. Tomorrow then. What, say one o'clock? There's a cafe near the Hippodrome. The Paradiso?'

'Yeah, fine.'

'One o'clock then.'

The phone went dead before Jenny could ask about the Hippodrome, if it was an annex in London zoo. She glanced at her next question.

Does he know Nina is pregnant?

Then she screwed the paper up.

Dear Agony Aunt,

Why can't it be me having Simon's child? I don't think Nina likes him as much as I did. Do. The thought of this little person growing inside her, wearing Simon's smile... When my mother found out she was pregnant, to the milkman Ernie Bernie, do you think that she was scared?

Jenny B from Leeds

Dear Jenny,

What are you rattling on about? Remember to get off the tube at Leicester Square.

Jenny set her feet firm on the escalators that rose from the depths of the Underground. She couldn't stop herself from smiling, a mad grin stuck on her face. Simon. Simon Marles. She was going to meet Simon.

She found some stairs near the top kiosks and walked out into the street. Impatient people pushed beside her as she stood in front of Wyndhams Theatre, opposite the black fronted Hippodrome. She crossed the busy road, passing morose foreigners who thrust leaflets at bewildered passers-by, encouraging them to take a course in speaking English. Jenny clutched her A to Z and walked up Charing Cross Road, past bookshops boasting millions of words, Chinese restaurants with lunchtime special offers and billboards for the long-running musical *Blood Brothers*.

A thought crossed Jenny's mind. She'd once wished that Wit was her brother, but now she had a real one somewhere. And a sister. Did they know that she existed? When her mother was plodding the streets with a maternal bump, did the kids from round the corner know their baby sister was inside?

Jenny reached Shaftesbury Avenue, then checked her map again. She doubled back and took a side street, walking along until she found the meeting place. The Cafe Paradiso, one o'clock, on a street behind the theatre with the Miserables. As Jenny walked through the chiming door the diners seemed to look up in choreographed unison, regard her for a moment, then return to their pesto and conversation. She sat in a corner of the quiet cafe, next to a wall splashed with flecks of cappuccino, conspicuously female amongst tables populated by swarthy men in shiny suits. Deep coloured eyes glancing out from glowing tans, sitting in low voiced cliques, briefcases clamped underneath their chairs. Jenny watched with interest through a gap between her fingers, imagining they were the London branch of the Mafia. That would explain why no other customers seemed to bring their business here, and as the cakes she'd seen underneath the glass by the cash register looked edible enough, she hoped it wasn't a lack of quality in the food that kept people away.

Jenny ordered an espresso from a squat dark-haired woman with heavy eyelids hanging below a furrowed brow that hinted at despair. As the hot liquid tinged her lip Jenny caught a memory of Italy, of Roman stallholders, the Pantheon with its centuries of ghosts. Seeing Simon's shape there in the distance, with Roger tight against her side.

I love him. I love him not.

Simon was eleven minutes late when the door chimed open

and he walked back into Jenny's life. She wanted to cry out where she was, make him notice her immediately, come running over open-armed. Instead she sat in silence, peeping through a latitude of eyelashes, waiting for that moment when he would turn and see her, and he'd respond with that slow smile.

'Jenny. Hi! Sorry, am I late?' He glanced briefly at his watch. 'You're looking well.'

'Thanks. You too.'

She had been hoping for a kiss. Even a peck on the cheek would be a pleasant start. Instead he put out his long fingers to shake, as if forging a deal. Jenny dropped her hot hand back into her lap, feeling awkward.

Simon sunk his head into the menu. 'I'm starving. Didn't have any breakfast. So, what are you down the Smoke for? Work?'

'Um, yes.' She blushed, shading her face with a menu. 'You know, sorting things out. Getting started.'

'I've had it with college,' Simon yawned. 'I thought I might go back, but I've had a change of plan, a new direction.' His eyes sparkled. 'I was in Florence, and I realised... it's old art that I like. The masters, the age of things.' He clicked his fingers for the waitress. 'I've got a part-time job at Sotheby's. I'm learning about the trade, valuations, authentication. You know, if things are real or not.'

The waitress perched a biro on her notepad. Jenny wanted to tell Simon how she'd missed him, how he had hurt both her and Nina by absconding like that. Instead she ordered mushroom pizza with a salad on the side. She started running her fingers through the lumps of crystalline objects in a shell-shaped blue china dish. She wondered if they were there to clean your hands on, to take away lingering odours of cheesy garlic bread.

Simon smiled as the waitress brought fresh coffee, along with ciabatta. Jenny reddened as Simon spooned some of the crystals into his drink, realising she'd been cleaning her fingers

233

in coarse cut rocks of sugar cane. She hoped he hadn't noticed. He didn't seem to, and if she was quite honest, a lot of things went unnoticed in front of Simon's gaze.

'So why did you run off?' Jenny grew more confident. 'You disappeared without a word. We didn't know what had happened.'

'I left Nina a letter. Didn't she say?'

Jenny sunk her head over her coffee.

'I went to Italy. Just did it, got on a plane and went.'

'I saw you,' Jenny's food arrived. 'I spotted you in Rome. The Pantheon.'

'You went to Rome? With Wit?' Simon plunged a fork into his pasta.

'No, um... a friend.' She didn't want to tell him about Roger. He might see her as tarnished goods. Or was that being weird?

'Well, I must have a handsome twin!' shrugged Simon. 'I didn't get there this time. Just Florence and Venice.'

'You weren't in Rome?'

'No. Sorry.'

Jenny felt strangely worried. How could she have been mistaken? She was sure that it was him. Seeing him like that, it made things with Roger wrong. An illusion, or delusion? She picked angrily at her pizza.

'But now you're back,' she stabbed the doughy base. 'You should ring Nina. She's...' The oven crust was very hard. Jenny yanked at it. 'You should really go and see her.'

Simon twirled spiralling pasta round his fork. 'But she wouldn't want to see me, would she? I explained things in my note.' He locked onto Jenny's eyes. 'I hope she wasn't too upset? I didn't mean to hurt her.'

The letter in the washing machine. His goodbyes flushed away.

'She didn't say anything.' Jenny rubbed her throat, uneasy. Hid her mouth behind her hand.

Simon smiled. 'See, everything's turned out perfect! And I've you to thank for this, Jenny. I mean, it's down to you.'

Jenny didn't follow.

'When we went out, you know, in Leeds. When we were talking....'

'Yes?' Jenny's heart lifted. She saw him sitting next to her in the cinema, the rise and fall of his strong chest, the shape of him beside her.

'... in the Dry Dock, about that actress and James Dean?'

Please let him have fallen in love with her.

'And you were saying, how he should have been with her, and not that other bloke?'

'Right. Pier Angeli, Vic Damone.'

'Well,' Simon grew an eager smile. 'I took your advice.'

Jenny dropped her fork into the radicchio and lettuce. 'What advice?'

'That if you love someone, you should be with them.' Simon beamed. 'See, Ornella wrote to me, but I couldn't read her letter, I left it unopened. Nearly threw it away, in fact. I thought she'd betrayed me, married him. But that night, after we'd been out, I read it.' His face was glowing. 'She said she loved me. She really loved me!'

Jenny started to feel sick. Espresso bitter in her mouth. She signalled for some water.

Simon was gushing, proud. 'And if you love someone, you should be with them. Right? It was that simple, I couldn't see it. So thanks for that. Do you fancy any pudding? They do some nice ice creams.'

'No. Thanks. I need the....' Jenny scratched her chair along the floor and ran for the toilet. She crouched down on the seat, pulling reams of paper off the roll even though she needed none. She blew her nose on seven sheets, splashed tap water on her face. She checked her hair in the mirror. Crap.

Jenny made her way back to the table, surprised to see another person sitting there. The young woman stood as she approached, greeting Jenny with a wide elastic smile. Simon gestured across the food.

'Jenny, meet Ornella. My new wife.'

Jenny collapsed onto her seat, buttocks banging on the wood. She stared at Simon to check if he was joking, saw him fiddling with his new golden ring. A matching one on his bride's eager finger. They held hands over the table. Jenny felt sick. She wasn't even pretty.

'Jenny? I have to thank you a lot for. For sending him to me. I like you very much.' Ornella kissed both of Jenny's cheeks on her white face.

'This calls for a celebration!' Simon snapped his fingers, laughing, and ordered a bottle of house red wine. 'It wasn't a massive wedding, because I'm not a Catholic yet... but I am converting. Then we'll have our vows blessed in a church.' Simon looked lovingly at his coy wife. 'The family are pleased, we'll bring our kids up in the faith. It's my First Communion next month.'

Jenny remembered hers, how she stuck Jesus up on the roof of her mouth and let him stay there until he melted.

God, you little bastard, giving Simon back to her.

Jenny inspected the soft cooing Ornella, sunk into Simon's shoulder like a sweet malignant lump. She was slightly built, quite leggy, with a raven stream of stiff straight hair. Her eyebrows joined up in the middle, like someone had drawn a line across her forehead in thick black marker pen. Her nose was quite lopsided, slightly bent, and much bigger than Jenny's own.

Nina's theory was fucked. This woman was not attractive.

Jenny stayed quiet for a while, listening to the sing-song of Simon's radiant voice, hearing happiness roll off every syllable. Ornella's childish chuckles, little sighs. Jenny gulped red wine, even though she didn't like it. She scrutinised the condensation on the outside of her glass before wiping a mark along it with her finger.

'I'd better go now. I've got to be somewhere.' Anywhere but

there. Jenny pushed herself up from the chair, leaving the lovebirds canoodling in theirs. She placed some money on the table.

'No, I'll get this.' Simon forced the notes back in Jenny's hand. 'My treat. A sort of thank you.'

'Thanks.' It hurt Jenny to look at him, but she still had to. 'Well, 'bye then. Take care.'

Simon and Ornella gave her a quick wave and returned to their whispered language, pouring more wine into their glasses, touching mouths. There was a piece of spinach wedged between Simon's front teeth. She so wanted to slap him.

Jenny rushed out into the street, eyes stinging with wind and pain as she stomped up to the main road. She walked half a mile in an unfamiliar direction before she realised she'd gone wrong.

She should have told him about Nina.

She should have told him about the baby.

He should be with Nina, not Ornella.

Jenny reached Leicester Square tube station, then decided to go back. She swelled, determined, retracing her shrill steps up Charing Cross. Jenny paced along, arms flapping, weaving through the oncoming tourist flow.

She had to tell Simon about the baby. She wasn't sure on the trip down, as she sat, bored on the coach. She'd had vague hopes of future happiness, thinking he would fall for her. But she was doing this for Nina. Nina's child.

Jenny took a giant gulp of air, entered the Cafe Paradiso. The waitress did a double take, gave a nod in her direction. Jenny rounded the corner to the table. Their places had been cleared.

Simon gone. Gone, Simon.

Jenny sank down into a chair. Ordered a cappuccino.

The National Express coach arrived in Leeds, snaking its way past the towering Armouries and the prospects of The Calls. Jenny levered herself up and got her coat. Hitched a rucksack on her back and joined the queue of huffing passengers in the central aisle, bumping into each other in their eagerness to depart, as if standing and pushing would speed the journey up at last. Huddles of people were waiting, bored, inside the coach station, polystyrene drink cups in their hands. Each face made brighter by the recognition of arrivals.

There was no one to meet Jenny. She hurried past the swell of travellers retrieving cases and stepped into the quiet bus station. Craned her neck up at the information board to work out where to go.

'Do you believe in justice in today's society?'

'What?' Jenny twisted round to catch sight of who had spoken. She glanced down on bare feet in Jesus sandals, blue nail varnish daubed on thick nails of stubby toes. Above those, some black silk trousers and a coat.

'Do we have the right to what we want and what we need?'

A clipboard at the ready. Iron filings of stubble popping through his bald pink pate.

'Do you believe we are responsible for our own actions?'

'Yes.' Jenny stared hard into his face. He did not remember her. 'We are responsible. Completely. Every single thing we do has an effect.' If you do a bad deed, bad deeds are done to you. 'Like with me, the milkman. Tex and Sharon. I'm not sure about Simon and Nina.'

The bald man started backing off as Jenny's passion rose.

'And what you want, well, it's not yours to have. But if you try to do what's right... maybe you'll make up for all that wrong.'

She'd tell Nina about destroying Simon's letter, own up to everything. Give her friend his home address, let her decide herself what she should do.

The bald man pushed a home shopping leaflet in Jenny's hand then sped away, glancing back over his shoulder. Jenny sank, deflated into a waiting chair and sat in vigil for a bus.

Culmination

Energetic traffic roared along the adjacent road as Jenny walked up the sombre slope of Killingbeck cemetery. A sprinkling of cars were parked around the chapel, their owners on a Sunday morning ritual to pine for their lost loves.

Jenny gripped crisp flowers in her hand, wind blowing sharply at the yellow and crimson petals. Her mother should have drawn a treasure map to find the grave. Her eyes scanned the horizon, different paths shooting off in various directions like a swell of busy veins. Jenny tapped her shoes together, feeling chilled. Drew a memory to her mind, a not too distant rainy day, with tears and stiff black suits and sad recriminations.

Grandad was buried in a plot at the hill's brow, a diminutive black headstone with his name carved in silver letters. *Simon Reginald Butler, rest in peace. With his beloved wife at last.*

'Happy birthday, Grandad. Hope you like it.'

Jenny placed a tiny wooden tortoise at the base of the stone, a metal flower holder shielding the trinket from the wind. She pulled the deadheads out on wilted stems, and replaced them with some fresh blossoms from her bunch.

Grandad used to collect ornamental tortoises, before he forgot that they were something he liked. Jenny read in a book that one lived a hundred years. No one knew what it was called as nobody was alive who could remember the creature's name. Jenny had a tortoise once. Raphael, she called him. She put him in a box to hibernate, and buried him in the garden, under the soil. Only when the spring came she couldn't remember where she'd put him, and her dad wouldn't let her dig up the lawn to check. He was probably still there.

She gazed about her, along the expanse of silent graves. How would she find Bernard Sykes amongst all these? Unending rows of graves, sharp teeth cutting through the gums of grass. Stumpy headstones alongside palatial statues, rain battered angels and gigantic concrete scrolls.

Jenny walked by a wave of stones, well weathered by the years. She read off lists of Polish names, unending, unpronounceable, the stonemasons must have relished the expense of each extra letter charged.

All that history. All those lives. Some ended in their eighties, with creaking bones and raspy sighs, others dragged screaming from life decades before their time. Jenny's eyes stung as she passed the elaborate graves of stolen children, the breeze snapping at bright coloured seaside windmills. Spinning, clattering, revolving briskly on the top of sunken sticks within the plots. Scatterings of rain dampened toys sitting quietly by the graves, weighed down by chunky pebbles and coloured stones. Fading cushions with hurt words embroidered on. To my son Glenn. To Alice, with Mister Blobby keeping guard.

Jenny left a flower on a sad grave and walked along the ridge, passing a young man and woman in their late twenties. They nodded and gave her a supportive, hard-work smile. Jenny looked back at them trailing down the hill, feeling a sense of recollection, a familiarity, as if they were two forgotten friends from school. This place united them somehow. Gave them a common purpose.

A white shape caught Jenny's eye, pleading for attention. Her strides lengthened as she took a path down to the left. Feet faster, pace set. He had wanted her to find him.

Bernard Sykes' grave wasn't notable in stature, a simple dull grey stone with basic letters and neat surround. What made it his was that pint of milk propped by the headstone, the shiny silver top still left unpecked by nosy birds. Jenny touched it, surprised by the cold glass. She took the bottle in her hand, holding it to the light to check inside for signs of bacteria and growing cheese. No, it was fresh. Only recently put there.

Someone had just been here, left the milk and an impressive spray of flowers. Jenny glanced around, distracted, feeling as though she herself was being watched. Nobody was visible above the sleepy graves.

'I'm sorry, Ernie... Bernard. Dad.' Jenny reached out to touch the gravestone. 'It really was an accident. I didn't mean it.'

She covered her mouth with a cupped hand. She hadn't realised that he had been so young. He was only thirty three the day he died. Lived to the age of Jesus. Hot tears burned at her eyes.

Bernard Jeremy Sykes, beloved husband and father.

'I'm so sorry.'

Jenny sank to her knees before the grave, placing her remaining flowers on the ground. They weren't smart enough to slide in with the new bouquet that had already been placed there. They were not as good as that. Those ones were from his proper family.

She shot up from the grass. That couple, the young man and pale faced woman. Was it them who had been here? Could they be her brother and sister?

Jenny ran along the path, racing down the hill towards the cars. Maybe they hadn't left yet, she could ask. Her pace started to slow. What? Say, hello, I'm your long lost bastard half-sister, you know, the one who killed your dad?

She reached the chapel entrance and struggled to catch her breath. Saw a car turning out of the cemetery to the main road, two shapes in the front seats. Driving off in the direction of the town, lost in the flow of human traffic.

Jenny drove to the stables in Pontefract, where the most recent Savager attack occurred. The girl there recognised her from local shows, so Jenny couldn't use her technique of pretending to be enquiring about the price of riding lessons.

'I heard you found your horse,' noted the girl. 'Roger said. You must have been right chuffed. That's what I call a happy ending.'

'Roger the vet?' asked Jenny, though she already knew.

'Yeah, he's treating Maisy, the mare that got cut up.'

The attack had occurred at night, as always, but with one

241

interesting change. Though the event took place in a pasture overlooking the canal, the actual horse was taken from an inside stable, and walked out into the field. There were nine other horses already grazing there, so why would the Savager do that? Take an animal from a stable, risking capture as they walked along the concrete, instead of picking an easier prey?

'Do you think that I could see her?' Jenny had brought her camera. 'I'm not being creepy, honest, only I've been doing some research.'

Karen didn't mind and took Jenny on a tour. Bored, she said she was. Now the little buggers had gone back to school she didn't see anyone for hours.

Jenny's mobile phone interrupted their conversation. She pulled it from her pocket, glancing round. A strange feeling that it was Roger, spying. That he had followed her.

'Hello?' A moment's hesitation.

'Jenny! Hi, it's Wit.' The line was distant, crackling.

'Wit!' Jenny's face flushed in excitement. 'God, how are you? Where are you?' A happy sigh. 'I missed you, I really did.'

'I found the note you left. Are you alright?'

'Yeah, fine.' All the better for hearing you.

'Can we meet up?' Wit echoed. 'It's been far too long.'

'Yes please! Let's get together. Soon!' Jenny was surprisingly elated, her heart thundering inside. She started to feel self-conscious, with Karen scrutinising her keen face, piecing together the two halves of conversation. 'Look, Wit, I'm kind of doing something. Can I call you back?'

'I'm going out at three.'

'Well, you can call me later then. Yeah? Have you got my mobile number?' Jenny pulled a face. Of course he had, he was ringing her right now. Karen giggled. 'I've got to go, I'm sorry, I'm with someone.'

'Him?'

The reception faltered. 'That's over. Finished. It was a big mistake.... Wit? Are you still there?'

'I hear you. I'll ring you later. Promise.' His gentle voice. 'Let's make Chris Isaak happy.'

'Wit? Guess what? I think I love you.'

Jenny said this in her head. It was all that she could manage.

She wore a big banana smile as she put her phone away, walking behind Karen as they went inside the stable.

The horse was tranquil, tranquillised, with painkillers to help the hurting. Daubs of antiseptic purple spray splashed shapes of countries on her body. Coloured continents floating on pallid grey.

Jenny was disconcerted. She'd not seen a Savager victim this close up. Only in photos or on the news.

'Is she going to get better?'

Karen shrugged. 'Fifty-fifty. The outside's healing well, but we don't know about inside. She has good days and bad days, you know?'

Jenny did. 'My new horse, Brown, we were sure that he would die, but in the end he was okay. He's still got a way to go, but we can tell he's getting there.'

'Roger thinks she'll probably be fine.' Karen gave her a sly smile. 'Bit of a hunk him, i'nt he? We get kids skiving off school when they know he's coming by.'

Jenny brushed her hand along the grey horse's soft back, white hairs moulting off onto her coat. A dark thought crossed her mind. Was there a kind of person in the world who could cause distress and injury deliberately, then be a key factor in the cure? A kind of power trip, a way of taking full control.

She stared across the field, counting up horses and ponies. One, a bay. Two, a chestnut. Three and four, both dark bays. Five, a palomino. Six and seven both skewbald. Eight, ebony black. And number nine a strawberry roan.

No grey horses in the meadow. The Savager had wanted to maim only a grey. Not as random a victim as it had initially appeared.

When Jenny got back to the house later that evening she

hunted through her notes. A horse attacked in Chapel Allerton, its stomach on the ground. She'd seen the photograph when the police had questioned her. She cleared her mind out to remember, and then knew that it was grey.

An in-foal mare murdered recently in York, and no points for guessing what colour coat she had. Yes. A blue-flecked-dapple-grey.

Then that horse they'd shown some film of on the telly, white coat blurred in the owner's bad home movies. A fleeting shape of paleness, like a wipe across the screen. She'd thought it looked like Mister. When she phoned Roger up, concerned, he took her blindly to the field.

No white horse was ever safe, especially her own.

Bats twitched across the blue-black sky, wings flicking in the wind. Jenny shivered inside Mister's stable, wishing she'd bought a sleeping bag with a higher insulation factor. This one was fine for a couple of hours, snug and dry and warm, but when the clock struck twelve it reverted into a piece of idle down whose feathers had dried up. Jenny wriggled her toes against each other, like frozen stumps of shrimp. Big decision. Either stay in the bag and fidget until her body heated up, or walk around the yard. She wished she had an illuminated watch so she could see the time, know when another tour was due.

She had been doing this for three nights now, sleeping over, checking the horses were protected. The idea was to get other people involved, have a few kids hang out at the stables doing shifts. Their parents were against it, they felt it wasn't safe, and anyway, there was always homework to consider. Homework. Jenny wished that she still went to college.

The Savager hadn't made an attack since the one in Pontefract. Jenny had been checking the papers, watching local news updates. She'd tracked back to the first reported incident, at the end of May the previous year. She wondered what had sparked it off, which event had spawned the evil. It appeared to

244

have escalated over the last three months, with more attacks reported. Each one signalled more anger, frustration, and the injuries themselves had grown more vicious.

The Yorkshire Ripper was like that, Jenny recalled. There was an initial crime, so shocking no one could believe it happened, but then it simply carried on. Were there more murders at the end, had his actions speeded up? Did the Ripper get more desperate because he knew that he'd be caught, or was it that his urge to kill was growing stronger?

Shadows drew devils on the walls, stretched faces caught in sighs, long-fingered hands reaching out for stick-thin throats. Mister shuffled on the straw, moving his weight from leg to leg. He had his eyes closed, pretending to be asleep, but Jenny knew he wasn't. He made a special noise when sleeping, a gentle nasal rumble, talking to himself or counting carrots to inspire a tasty dream.

She listened hard, watching his windpipe, following the track of air as the horse breathed out and in. A two-tone note, resounding, building to a thought.

As Jenny studied Mister she marvelled at how much the noise increased the longer she looked, like her watching his respiratory functions could increase the volume. Louder, more rumbling, almost an echo in the dark. As the noise got stronger, nearer, Jenny realised it was not in fact her horse, but a slow approaching car.

The way her fingers jumped, pulling up with them her arms, her legs, her sleeping bag attire, Jenny knew the Savager was here. Like in the movies when the hero goes down to the darkest basement for a clue, and the evil baddie is already lurking there. Jenny thought again. That was wrong. The heroes didn't go into the basement, that was where the victims went. And they always got cut up.

Jenny slid out of her blue bag. Don't go in the basement. She took hold of Mister's headcollar, his eyes blinking twice open in surprise. Don't go in the basement. She led him from the stable, across the yard towards the field. There were headlights on the horizon, white-yellow eyes peeping over the hill. Cat's eyes. Evil eyes.

The troll under the bridge.

'Come on, Mister. Hurry!'

She ran, pulling her horse along, him breaking into a canter, excited to be running in the dark. Jenny's mind flashed as she pulled open the gate. Why hadn't she worked out a plan before?

Don't go in the basement.

'Shooo Mister! Run!'

He stood and looked at her.

'Go on! Scoot! Get lost!'

She clapped her hands to chase him off, picked up a stone and threw it at his belly. He trotted off, insulted, shaking his slender head. Jenny backtracked to the stables, glad she'd left a light on in her horse's box so she could work out where to go. The moon was covered by a film of mist, cold dampness hanging in the air.

Jenny heard grumbling tyres stop sharply on gravel. She ducked behind the back wall of the feed room as a car door slammed.

She could hear a pony chewing hay, grinding its teeth with set annoyance, perturbed that it was still awake when all its equine friends had dozed.

Jenny's eyes grew more accustomed to the dark, her pupils widened like golfing holes as they soaked up the lack of light. As she peered around the brick edge she could see his walking shape, with something long beside him as if he'd grown an extra leg. Extended staring showed it was a gun. A long barrelled farmer's weapon, the type men used to shoot rabbits and pheasants.

Jenny shivered while she watched the shadowed figure make his way across the yard. Moving towards the far end of the stables, to where the Brown horse lived.

A tremor bit at Jenny's throat. She pulled open the feed

room door, wincing at the creaking sound, hoping the squeaking would be mistaken for a mouse. She sneaked inside, not daring to put on a light for fear that he might see.

Don't go in the basement.

She felt her way along the feed bins, the coward part of her saying she should hide inside, the hero saying that she had to find a weapon.

Footsteps coming fast towards her. Echoing round the stables as the big boots crossed the yard. She heard a door being pulled open farther up, presumably the tack room. One. Two. Three. Counting the time she estimated for him to turn the light switch on.

Jenny leapt up on a bin and reached for the tubular bulb, knowing vaguely where it was as she always stood underneath it when she mixed her horses' feeds. The third bin along, where the light was always brightest. She reached into the dark. Nothing. Higher. If only she was a fraction taller, maybe another inch. She stretched her arms until her armpits ached. There. She grasped the bulb between her hands and pulled it from the metal socket.

He was on the other side of the door, she could sense him, hear the vibration of his soles. Jenny jumped softly off the bin, cushioning the sound by landing on a bulky New Zealand rug. She hurried to the corner, pulled a pitchfork to her chest, and huddled out of sight behind some thick sacks of crushed oats.

The door opened and she saw him, back-lit by the softly diffused moon. A wash of greying light across his face. Roger had the gun down by his side, tense hand clenching it tightly.

'Jenny? I know you're in there. I've looked everywhere else.' He hit the light switch. Nothing.

She held swallowed air inside her lungs, hoping he hadn't seen cold breath stains in the unsettled atmosphere.

'I know you're hiding, Jenny. I came over here to find you.'

He's a bad man. He does bad things.

The end of the barrel shone bright as silver, a circular rim caught on the end like a sparkling wedding band.

'Jenny!' His voice grew agitated, patience waning. 'Stop messing around. I've got to tell you something. It's really bad.'

If the gun was at his side it would take a moment or two for him to raise it up and fire. Jenny had seen this in the westerns, or at least she hoped she had. Like when Mr Blonde showed her *Wyatt Earp* and Michael Madsen got shot. Bang, in his chest as he walked along. Bang, through his back as he stumbled on. Bang, in his legs as the bullets ripped his flesh. Mr Blonde had screamed, rewound the video tape and watched it over again. He didn't die, Wyatt Earp's older brother, but then it was only movies.

BANG!

The gun went off moments after Jenny made her run, when she raced out of her hole, pitchfork raised, held fast before her, eyes closed tight. The pressure hit her chest, the pitchfork handle pressing deep into her breast. A pain so constant, a low vibrating hum, pushing the air outside her body, making her collapse onto the floor.

Roger stood where he was, door frame arched behind him, a stunned look upon his face. The smell of gunshot in his nose, rising from the gun barrel and its mine hole in the floor. He looked down at his stomach, at the pitchfork prongs embedded in his gut, a couple puncturing his sweatshirt, the others made less intrusive by his coat. Roger glanced over to Jenny. An expression more of surprise than horror, dumbfounded disbelief.

He toppled a moment, like a swimmer in a pool about to take a dive from the high board. If he fell forward he would injure his other organs, become human cheese on a giant cocktail stick.

Roger put his arms out behind him and dropped backwards. He was in too much pain to scream, wanting to save his energy for recovery. He sensed blood seeping from his wound, erupting wells around the metal spikes. He pressed his hands down firm, creating pressure, thankful at least that the weapon was still inside him. He knew from veterinary practice that to extract an intruding object, too far away from medical help, would result in a much quicker bleed to death.

Jenny appeared above him, looking down. He could hear her kick the gun away behind a bin.

'Why Roger? Why did you do it?'

He couldn't answer, his mouth too full of pain.

'Did you know I would be here, or did you just come for Mister?' Jenny was light-headed, sick with shock. She did not want this to be happening.

Roger gurgled, spit collecting in his mouth. 'I tried... your house....Your mum....' His gulping fish mouth, panic racing. 'I came to warn you. She said... I'm here....' Chalk faced, lip trembling. 'I'm here to help.'

'What? To help with Mister?' Jenny recalled Inspector Redmond's suspecting tones.

'Yes.'

'Like you helped the other horses?'

'Yes! Jenny, please... she's coming. She sent... she sent a note.'

The Savager in a pool of blood, thought Jenny, like that grey horse in the field. Stomach pumping out the evil platelets.

'Don't move, Roger. Don't you dare.'

Jenny lurched towards the door, sucking her tears back, and then started to panic. The gun. She had to put it where he couldn't find it or he would crawl out and shoot her. She kept her eyes set on his while she retrieved it, dragging it from the feed room, sliding it between tight bales in the barn.

Devastated, Jenny sank gasping onto the straw, her hands shaking in shock. She scrambled for her mobile, pressed on a green button. The phone started to redial. Her glazed eyes retrieved the number. Wit's. She'd rung him last, now he owed her a call. The phone connected to his number. She cut it off, slow motion.

Dialled 999. Emergency.

'Police, please. Ambulance! I've stabbed... I've stabbed the troll. The Savager! I got him, but can you come and save him, fast.'

A calm voice at the other end demanded details, names, Jenny's phone number as well. She gave the operator directions, her voice stretching into a high pitched helium wheeze. She had this dreadful, gnawing feeling that she had told them to drive over the wrong way.

She walked slowly back to Roger, part of her expecting him to have crept off, maybe be dead already. She was relieved to see him in the same spot as before, still breathing, hanging on. Face blanched white, eyes popping. His thick coat had saved his stomach from instantly fatal prongs. A steady pump of blood spat through his shirt, collecting in a puddle by his buttocks.

Jenny hoped the ambulance was fast. She didn't like to see him hurting, whatever he had done. A question burnt into her mind, trying to shift her guilty feelings.

'You'd have shot me, wouldn't you? If I hadn't got you first?'

Roger didn't want to speak. When he moved his mouth his stomach pulled.

'I guessed that you're the Savager. I figured it out.' A tear rolled down her cheek, magnifying peachy freckles. 'But I don't know why you do it. What's it for?'

He looked at her for a long, silent moment, eyes filling with regret and disappointment and a flicker of dulled fear.

'Jenny. You need to get some help.'

There was a position you had to put people in when they had an accident, else they could choke to death. Jenny knew that from girl guides, with her well earned felt first aid badge.

She cushioned Roger's head on a pillow of soft rugs, placing him sideways with the pitchfork still intact. She touched his hands, he was becoming cold and clammy. She knew she had to get him warm.

Jenny was in Mister's stable retrieving her sleeping bag when a vehicle pulled into the yard. She swooned with relief, hoping the ambulance could race Roger away, and please stop him from bleeding. She did not want him to die. She'd hated seeing him sitting there in a stew of strawberry blood, looking at her like an abandoned puppy about to be put down.

There were no blue flashing lights when Jenny went outside, and no signs of an ambulance. But she had heard an engine, even the brakes when it had stopped.

Then she saw it, parked alongside the muck heap, headlights on. A familiar dark brown car.

As Jenny took a step forwards she was hit hard on the head. A shovel on her skull. She didn't see her assailant, just the gravel rushing up towards her as she fell.

The three biggest regrets in Jenny Barker's life:

1. Stabbing Roger with a pitchfork because she'd made a big mistake.

2. Killing her father, the youthful, smiling milkman.

3. Whatever was going to happen next.

Blackness, blueness, then the brown. Mud under her face, her mouth still gaping wide, grit grinding gruffly at her teeth. Her arms were tied behind her back, she could feel tight baling band cutting deep into her wrists. Long strings tying her feet together so she couldn't move her legs. Jenny twisted her neck to the side, inching to see who was wearing the black boots. Hunter wellies, but not the regular green. Jenny looked beyond them to a shallow, quick dug hole, waiting, ready to be filled.

It was only when Jenny was pushed into the trench that she caught a glimpse of her destroyer. Bitter eyes and fire red hair. A mouth set hard in hate. The Savager was here.

'What did you do with him! What did you do?' Rage bit deep into the hole, boots kicking sharp at Jenny's legs. 'He's my husband! Fucking bitch!'

Anne Mandrake shovelled on the dirt, each load reminding

her of every animal Roger went to treat instead of treating her to meals and presents. How he'd rush off to help sick horses instead of rushing home to her. How he'd leave her waiting alone in their cold bed while he wrapped himself round another woman, as suspected. She was better than a horse. Better than that slut's white animal he'd tried repeatedly to find. She hated the horses because he cared more for them than her.

And the object in the hole? It deserved to be destroyed. It was all its own doing.

Jenny shut her mouth, seeing soil falling towards it, gravy granules of thick brown that made her choke. Mud sticking to her clothes, pressing down her body as she blinked up at the far stars in the sky. Less stars and more soil.

She twisted round onto her front, pushing her back up in protection, feeling pressure against her as the shovel pumped her down. Anne wheezing, tossing mud into the hole, scrambling to fill the space round Jenny's body.

As mud rained down Jenny pushed her spine up further, creating a chasm of air beneath her as she held her stomach in. A human humpback bridge crusted with soil. If she pushed down on her head and shoulders and raised her back and bum, she could stop soil from filling the hole. She pushed elbows against the mud, keeping the gap beneath protected.

She closed her eyes and held her breath, her body prone and tense, stomach sucked in above the air filled gap. She felt the soil above her, in a bump.

She was the tortoise in the garden.

Jenny breathed in deeper, held on fast, her lungs a giant ball. She was glad of years of practice, savoured breaths. Jenny Barker the human armadillo, relishing saved oxygen underground. Armadillos could hold their breath for how many minutes? For as long as it would take a rescuer to arrive? Where were they? Why was it taking them so long?

Calm down.

Don't panic.

Don't.

Breathe.

Just breathe.

She could hear her lungs deflating, the beating of her heart, the pumping of shrill arteries, the groaning meat mechanics of her muscles. She could almost hear the tree roots sucking moisture from the earth. Deeper breaths, longer, softer. The hopeful sighs of approaching engines, getting louder as her eardrums listened hard for helpful sounds.

Nothing else, but night owls shrieking. A slamming metallic door. The stalled motor of a car. Engine flooded. Dead.

More sounds, roaring sirens. Jenny wanted to push herself upwards, force a way out of the ground, but each time a fraction of her moved mud trickled closer, stealing away her rationed air.

Feet stomping. Horses hooves, clatters on concrete. A muffled, excited yell. Jenny thought this was the point where life should flash before her eyes, but all she had were sounds. Her ears buzzed with the soft whirs of a long remembered milk float, the bottle clanks of crates. A screaming in her mind as she became more dizzy. A rhythmical, revolving screech, getting louder with every echo that she heard. Wailing sirens and eager tyre tracks.

You find everything in the end, she thought. You only have to look. She just had to keep breathing in until they found her now. She'd been practising for this her entire life.

As footsteps hit the gravel Jenny began a tight-lipped hum, a low, resonant sound, constant in its depths, an aural lighthouse beacon. Hard mud against her back, a topsoil coating. She twitched her fingers upwards, scratching muck, fingertips feeling for fresh air. Pushing her body upwards, straining hard against the weight.

Her mobile phone started to ring. Shrill, insistent. Jenny almost laughed, eyes stinging with salt tears. She heard the trailing off of voices into silence. All she could hear was her own phone.

Please don't let it stop ringing.

Please don't.

The call ended. Voicemail must have picked it up. Bloody useful.

Maybe Anne was still there and they had caught her? Would she tell them what she'd done? About the body in the hole? Maybe Roger could be of help. Please God, don't let him die.

Would the police spot an abandoned shovel, a fresh dug grave of mud? Was it her imagination or were the noises getting closer? Was that a scratching sound above? Constant, searching, like a small red seaside spade and a bucket full of shells. Like underneath the beach, the sand, the frantic digging, the sharp bite of Nina's eager hands, and then the golden glow of day.

Cold air against her fingertips, the mud pile caving in, tipping her over. Strong arms twisting around, pulling Jenny upwards from the earth. A beam of torch-light burned straight into her eyes, two shadow-shapes behind. Male voices, worried, waiting.

She was still holding her breath.